Jonah and the Pink Whale

JOSÉ WOLFANGO MONTES VANNUCI

TRANSLATED BY KAY PRITCHETT

Jonah and

the Pink Whale

THE UNIVERSITY OF ARKANSAS PRESS

FAYETTEVILLE   LONDON   1991

First published by Editorial Mercurio (Bolivia)
as *Jonás y la ballena rosada*
© José Wolfango Montes Vannuci, 1987
Translation © 1991 by the Board of Trustees
of the University of Arkansas
Manufactured in the United States of America
95 94 93 92 91   5 4 3 2 1

This book was designed by Chiquita Babb using the typeface New Baskerville.

The paper used in this publication meets the minimum
requirements of the American National Standard for
Permanence of paper for Printed Materials Z39. 48-1984.⊛

Library of Congress Cataloging-in-Publication Data

Montes, José Wolfango, 1951–
    [Jonás y la ballena rosada. English]
    Jonah and the pink whale / José Wolfango Montes Vannuci ;
translated by Kay Pritchett.
        p. cm.
    Translation of: Jonás y la ballena rosada.
    ISBN 1-55728-175-0 (alk. paper). — ISBN 1-55728-176-9
(pbk. : alk. paper)
    I. Title
PQ7820.M64J613 1991
863—dc20   90-11004
                                                                CIP

In memory of
Chichi Saucedo

FOREWORD

Don't you see the things that happen?
Best call them NOVELS.

Miguel Angel Asturias

German Vargas, a Colombian writer and critic who served on the jury of the 1987 "Casa de las Américas" Prize along with Arrufat, Daniel Chavarría, Fernando López, and Enmanuel Carballo, said in reference to the most important Latin American contest in recent times: "The task was arduous, difficult, and almost endless (one hundred and sixteen novels were presented from all the Spanish-speaking Latin American countries). But a unanimous decision from the five-member jury made our efforts seem worthwhile. The single candidate was *Jonah and the Pink Whale,* an excellent, humorous novel by the Bolivian writer José Wolfango Montes Vannuci."

The Colombian critic continued, "The humor in *Jonah and the Pink Whale* is grotesque, surprising, and unceasing. To avoid naturalism, the repugnance is introduced sparingly into the text. Montes Vannuci succeeded in writing a novel that truly is a novel, with abundant imagination and humor that make the sordid world described less painful. As we the jury noted during the proceedings, the author is especially skilled at synthesis: he handles description and narration masterfully, a rare ability in a young writer." When the narrators of the Latin American "boom" had accustomed us to the poetic novel in which words formed a symphony or an exquisite architecture, *Jonah and the Pink Whale* astonished us by ransoming the magical, dazzling power of the plain word, which speaks to us simply because it is real and because the narrator has breathed life into it.

Montes does not resort to linguistic sleights of hand or the fastidiously artful expression. Symbol and allegory are not a part of his discourse. Recreating reality, beautiful in itself, is enough. His language is simple, without concealed meanings, without fancy clothing, reminding us that art, in its truest sense, may come from those who are not artists by profession.

Though the novel is straightforward, its point of view contains multiple voices that, out of the nightmare of inspiration, rise like a phantom from the text and grab us. The omniscient narrator is weakened to open the way to an unforeseen, colloquial *you* that makes complicity contagious. The *I-we* that predominates creates a fusion of identity between the reader, author, narrator, and story. *Jonah and the Pink Whale* sets forth a thematic vision of the cosmos. An oppressive, stifling atmosphere surrounds the weary and empty characters. Disenchantment with the world and the hostility of the city, the growing rootlessness, loneliness, and dehumanization of individuals and families, and the extinction and decay of society turn the work spiritually into a confused, chaotic space where external reality is always poly-faceted and contradictory.

We find in Montes an existential, almost Kafkian, anguish. His search is ontological, axiological, and metaphysical. He is a cold, scientific observer (neither realistic nor naturalistic), burlesque, ironic, a philosopher who finds catharsis in writing. *Jonah and the Pink Whale* both denounces and installs a reality without the propagandistic eagerness of committed political definitions. Montes is interested in exploiting the social anecdote as present but questionable history, subject to the reader's transformation. The internal functioning of the narrative elements, the precision of the persuasive devices of the text, treated with rigor, move us away from that tendency, so Latin American and so Bolivian, of attempting through art a "liberating culture" or a "literature of liberation."

His characters, nearly always moved by an unrestrained passion to obtain the objects of their intentions—money, sex, status, and so forth—become compelling, universal proto-types. Thus, for example, Ira (mother-in-law), Talia (wife), and Julia (sister-in-law), form the Homeric triangle Calypso, Penelope, Circe, so feminine, so human, and, for these very reasons, so divine. Julia will likely live on to reach the pedestal that Cortázar and Sábato gave to the Magus and María Iribarne respectively, for their fascinating power, their ineffable mystery, transporting us to the depths of Freudian, oedipal realms.

As one of Borges's characters might say, "Life is a book that I read and that writes me"; likewise, in *Jonah and the Pink Whale,* many of us will encounter familiar places, South American ambiences, people we know, and perhaps our own selves.

As an enthusiastic reader of the works of José Wolfango Montes, author also of *El gorrión desplumado* (The Plucked Sparrow) and *Pateando la luna* (Kicking the Moon), I was invited to write these notions down by way of foreword. Making the most of the undeserved honor, I will predict greater triumphs for this young novelist from Santa Cruz who—together with Oscar Barbery and Enrique Kempff—is becoming a very important representative of the novel in this part of the world.

Edgar Lora Gumiel
Santa Cruz, March 1987

Jonah and the Pink Whale

ONE

One twisted day, I realized that my life was a joke, and it was my wife's damn fault! I was depressed all the time. My hair was falling out by the handfuls. My sex life was pathetic. My job was absurd. And, to top it all off, I had a chronic cough I'd been trying to get rid of for six months.

I knew what was wrong with me, and I knew why. But like a baby, I waited for someone to come along and stick a pacifier in my mouth. I kept telling myself something would turn up.

An accident! Talia might get into an accident! Every time she was late getting home from work, I'd get nervous. The phone would ring, and I'd start to panic. I was sure that someday I was going to pick up the receiver and a voice would say: "Talia's been killed in an accident." I imagined myself at the wake, receiving condolences from middle-aged women. Then I'd hear the door open, and Talia would come waltzing in, whole and smiling, like a punctual swallow. Talia was never going to get into a wreck. She was the most cautious driver I'd ever known—the only person who stopped at stoplights, slowed down in school zones, yielded the right of way, and signaled at all the right places. She drove forty kilometers an hour on the highway. Any insurance company in the country would consider itself lucky to write her a policy.

It was doubtful that Talia would die in any kind of accident. More likely, she'd get sick. I started reading about all sorts of ailments. I ran across something called an aneurysm. The wife of a friend of mine died of one. It's caused by a ballooning in the wall of a large blood vessel, and it usually strikes young women. They live for years not even knowing they've got weak arteries. And then boom!—the aneurysm bursts, and they die a gentle, painless death. It's not a bad way to go. My friend's wife was buried with a peaceful little smile on her lips, considerably more discreet than her husband's gaping grin. It's one death that preserves a woman's beauty and that's a consolation. If women could choose how to die, a lot would go for the aneurysm. I wonder if Snow White's dream might have been a benign, reversible aneurysm.

If it hadn't have been for Licurgo, this friend of mine who's a lawyer, like me, I would probably still be waiting for Talia to drop dead—hoping she would. Licurgo convinced me that I was wrong. She probably wasn't to blame.

"Can't you have a little originality? You're just like my clients. Every one of them blames his wife when something goes wrong. They come in here and say they want a divorce. In the worst cases, it's too late for that. They've already done her in and want me to defend them. Years later, their lives are just the same as they were. They go right on, bogged down in the same old shit."

The authority in his voice might have fooled a stranger. It didn't fool me. We'd been students together at the university, and Licurgo had been at the bottom of the class. When he took his orals, the room filled up with faculty and students waiting to hear his outrageous aberrations. No one went away disappointed. Licurgo never once gave the right answer. A fortune teller reading the Tarot uses less imagination than Licurgo did that day, reading legal codes. He used every trick in the book to keep from flunking out: copying off the student next to him, brown-nosing the teacher, and so on. Professional life required fewer wiles than school did. All it took was a little deceit and cleverness to cover up his broken-headed ignorance.

At any rate, I set his defects aside and took his criticism to heart. To blame my wife was egotistical and irrational. Still, my belligerent nature forced me to give it another shot:

"You'll admit that if I were married to Catherine Deneuve my life would be a hell of a lot better."

Licurgo let out a weary sigh, as if I were a retarded child. He avoided my glance and rested his chin on his hands, in a reflexive, stoic pose. Without managing it, he tried to add an expression of intelligence to his eyes. His eyes could show envy, distrust, servitude, perplexity, and panic; never intelligence. They had no spark. They were like burned-out coals.

"That wouldn't solve your problem. Marrying the best whore in Babylonia wouldn't solve it. The spells you're having aren't caused by women. Just by looking at you, I can tell what's wrong. You've reached the critical age. You're thirty. It's a classic case."

"I hate to disagree with you," I responded, "but I passed thirty years ago. I'm thirty-three."

"It doesn't matter. It hits some at twenty-eight; others, at thirty-five."

"And some at seven," I said. "Like me, for example. I was

precocious. A menopausal child. I got whooping cough and sciatica at the same time."

"It won't do you any good to make fun of what I'm trying to tell you."

"Pardon me, doc! But your diagnosis stinks."

"You don't understand," he said, shaking his head. "After you're thirty, you can't get soused with a clean conscience. The party's over. You're an adult, my friend, like the old pot-bellied reactionaries you can't stand."

He was condemning me to death, and he was right. I'd never again be the optimistic schoolkid that I was before. If a border exists between youth and adulthood, Licurgo had shoved me over it. I felt miserable on the other side. Thirty was something to be ashamed of. I was too old to be trusted—a *persona non grata* in the twenties' camp. I detested being grown-up. Yesterday no one demanded success of me or that I have a lot of money in the bank. I was a young man with a promising future. But today no one would think of saying: "He's a brilliant young man; let's be patient; he'll prove himself soon enough." The older guys who'd been counting on me would be expecting a return on their investment. If before I had been confused or had jumped from one job to another, my friends would have offered me advice, even staged campaigns to save me; my family would have paid for me to see a shrink. After thirty you're a lost cause; nobody'll bet a dime on your horse. When you look for a job, people want to see your resumé. Scary, when you haven't got anything to show. And there you are, with a bunch of twenty-two-year-olds who've been racking up points since the day they were born. The world is full of prodigies, geniuses that were Gerber babies, champions on the perfect use of the potty, kids who topped the highest IQ on record at any European university. What was I doing all those years?

I was embalmed, while others fattened up their service records. Anyone who thinks that love is a compensation is wrong. The not-quite-ripe chick who was thrilled to get Julio Iglesias's latest hit is now moderately grateful if diamond rings sprout from your hands. Zircons and costume jewelry won't do. She can spot an imitation with the speed and accuracy of a gemologist.

Believe it or not, in the midst of all this craziness, I fell in love. I completely lost my wits. I could feel the passion rising from my feet to my Adam's apple. I suffered silently. It came on slowly. I thought of those Oriental princes who would immunize themselves against poisons by taking them in little doses. That's the way it happened. She was a poisonous girl. In the beginning I savored her at a distance, in the smallest mouthfuls. I liked it. Then I swallowed her whole, and she lived inside of me like a romantic hermit. . . . I called her the Muse, maybe to make her less real. It didn't suit her. She didn't bring out the artist in me. The most she ever inspired was a good erection. I was desperate; I didn't care if I suffered. I went around in a daze, in ecstasy, as if I'd been kissed by a spider.

Licurgo saw all this.

"Are you smoking dope?" he asked me one day.

"Why do you ask?" I answered, playing innocent.

"Because you've got an idiotic look on your face."

I made up a story without blinking an eye.

"First, promise you won't tell anyone. If Talia ever found out, she'd tell me to go straight to hell. . . . Actually, I've got a lover."

I described a girl that a scoundrel like Licurgo would consider ideal. She was the kind who pays for her own drinks, picks you up, and carries you to the motel in daddy's car. She'd never take a chance on getting pregnant, but if she did—get pregnant, that is—she'd get an abortion without even telling you. A firm believer in family life, she'd never ask you to leave your wife. And lumped together with all these virtues, she had the sex drive of an alley cat. She wouldn't interfere in your life, but she'd be ready anytime you called.

Licurgo swallowed the story in one gulp. He was totally gullible. Didn't even ask me her name. He believed a gentleman ought to protect his lover's reputation. At the same time, he secretly hoped to figure it out for himself. The challenge was tempting, since I'd said she was someone we all knew, a member of our own social circle.

I got a kick out of making him jealous. One day I walked into his office, heaved a sigh, and said:

"I don't know how I stood it. We spent the entire afternoon in a motel; the temperature in the room must have been ninety-five. I got so hot I nearly passed out."

"I know a guy who got dehydrated that way. They had to carry him out on a stretcher. In the tropics, it's crazy to have sex in the daytime."

"But her parents watch her like a hawk. She can't stay out all night."

"Do you really expect me to believe that? She's not from a good family. You can't convince me."

"That depends on what you call a good family."

"You know very well what I mean."

And I did. Licurgo was a complete snob.

"You'd give her a ten," I mused.

"A ten? Shit . . . then she must be one of the really wild ones," he accused. He was beginning to look like a jealous dwarf in a fairy tale.

"You're mistaken," I corrected. "You'd marry her in an instant."

"Marry your leftovers? She's probably got a cunt like a canyon."

"You might be surprised."

"Don't give me that. Level with me. What's she like?"

"I'm not lying. She's as fresh as a daisy. But never mind, I'm not saying another word."

"Holding back on me, eh? I thought I was your friend."

"That's why I'm shutting up. Suppose I leave my wife tomorrow and marry the Muse. I wouldn't want to be married to a girl my friends knew inside and out."

I walked over to the window, glanced at the sky vacantly, and changed the subject.

8

Months later, I wished that I'd never made up that ridiculous story. The fantasy became real; the lies turned into truths. And if Licurgo figured out the Muse's true identity, I'd had it. Done in by my own stupid game.

❧

To MAKE matters worse, I had a birthday about then. It hit me over the head like a ton of bricks. I tried to ignore it, but Talia reminded me every ten minutes.

I entered into vague reflections on temporality. My mind was a muddle of Nietzsche and Einstein. Everything around me was falling apart. But so what? One day, on the way to class, my car stalled in the middle of Cañoto Avenue. I left it sitting there, in the middle of the intersection, and walked. I arrived late, went in, and taught the class. I was half-prepared. But I didn't really care. It was my birthday, and thank God nobody at school knew about it. "Happy Birthday" was the last thing I wanted to hear.

Licurgo came to pick me up that afternoon. I started snapping out of it. Who wouldn't? All those pretty, young girls pouring out, in their white smocks, like lotus blossoms stirring in the breeze.

Licurgo was sitting with his hands on the steering wheel. He hadn't started the car. He wasn't engaged in some poetic fantasy or thinking about the traffic jam; he was watching the girls—blatantly stabbing their breasts, pubes, and buttocks with his eyes.

A red-headed senior named Raquel came up to me.

"Can I talk to you before you leave?"

"Tomorrow."

"You may not have time tomorrow."

"I'll have time."

"Please, just five minutes."

"All right, but make it fast."

"I failed history, didn't I?"

"Yes, I'm afraid so."

"Is there any way you can change the grade?"

"No, I can't."

"The test was too hard," she complained.

"It was fair. And your *F* was well deserved. You don't know the first thing about history."

"I went blank during the exam. And besides, what difference does it make? Who cares what happened a hundred years ago?"

"That's what the State pays me to teach you."

"I *did* study, but I got everything mixed up."

"You mix things up too often."

"No, I'm usually sure of myself, except when I'm with a man who's charming, aggressive . . ."

She got me with that answer. Then Licurgo put his two cents' worth in, and I gave in. I said I'd give her another exam.

While the smell of Raquel's cheap cologne lingered, Licurgo began to speculate:

"That was the Muse."

"Don't be an idiot."

Licurgo didn't start the motor. A line of cars roared past us. The last stragglers from the school were waving good-bye.

"I'm not budging from this spot till you tell me who she is."

"You're looking in the wrong place. Let's get out of here!"

"I bet it's the one with the great ass—Irma."

"Wrong."

"Janine, the basketball player."

"Janine's a Lesbian," I said. "Anyway, you think I'd seduce my own student?"

"You never know."

TWO

On the way home, I prayed that some recalcitrant colonel would overthrow the government, impose a curfew, and ban public gatherings of more than three people. Anything to avoid another birthday celebration.

I warned my wife from the start: "I hate birthdays. I hate people slapping me on the back. It drives me crazy." I wasn't exaggerating. Birthdays depressed me, made me want to die.

It was like a wake, and I was the corpse. But my wife didn't understand. If I'd been in an asylum, she'd have dragged me in a straitjacket, kicking and screaming, to blow out my candles. Nothing I ever said did any good.

Her surprise parties were always a flop. A week before, I'd overhear her calling up my friends and relatives. Then I'd find my ice-cream cake melting in the closet. On the day of the party, I'd come home from work to find a houseful of guests drinking my whiskey, stinking up the house with their cigarettes, and telling jokes—about me.

My last birthday, I managed to get one concession out of Talia. She promised not to tell any of our friends that it was my birthday; she was counting on their good memories.

She greeted me at the front door.

"Hello, dear! Hi, Licurgo."

Impatient, fragile, melancholy, Talia had a certain elegance I was proud of at one time.

She whispered something I didn't understand.

"What did you say?"

"You're late. We've been waiting for hours," she repeated softly.

"We stopped by the park and drank a few beers. I didn't know you were waiting."

"Don't play dumb. You knew we were planning a surprise dinner."

"How was I supposed to know?"

"You had to know," she accused. "Otherwise you wouldn't have been late. You stayed away just to worry me. Don't say you didn't."

"I didn't know anything about it!"

"Never mind. I forgive you; just be nice to my parents."

"They're the only ones here?" I asked.

"Esteban and his wife—whatever her name is—are waiting, too."

Never, in five years of marriage, had so few people come to my party. I pictured Talia and me at future celebrations, standing alone in the shadows, staring, like two owls, at a frozen cake. That empty panorama frightened me.

The men hugged me. The women kissed me. I tolerated it.

My mother-in-law apologized for Pablo's and Julia's lateness. Pablo hardly ever showed up at family gatherings. He would disappear at New Year's Eve, Christmas, his father and Ira's anniversary, Labor Day, and the Day of the Holy Innocents. "At Mardi Gras two things are impossible to find: beer in the grocery stores and Pablito at home," commented Iracema, his stepmother. If his absences were predictable, his appearances were equally unpredictable. He'd suddenly show up on your sofa with a glass of Campari in his hand, making up lies about impossible business deals—or totally broke, pursued by a dozen collection agencies and dangling the family honor on a string. Julia never missed a party; but she always arrived late, flanked by a bunch of ravenous friends, who ate up all the food and left you feeling stingy for leaving off the roasted steer.

I was glad Esteban was there. We were in school together and founded the Club of Light and Knowledge. Esteban had been a tall boy, a sweaty, stiff perfectionist and very competitive. Fifteen years later, he'd turned into a trusted gynecologist. His sweat glands had tamed down. And all he really cared about was being a successful doctor, which meant keeping his patients happy and minding his manners. After a few drinks, he wasn't a bad sort.

My wife and in-laws adored him. I would have liked him a lot more, if he hadn't been so anxious to make Talia and me parents. He said it wasn't normal not to have kids, and, whenever I was off my guard, he'd start talking to Talia, telling her I was lazy. He thought it was my fault she wasn't pregnant. If we were out together, he'd point out kids on the street and ask us if we didn't want to have some of our own. He'd have done anything to see Talia pregnant. Even service her himself—except he was a fairly scrupulous guy.

"Happy birthday! A great year for the stork!"

"I'm not worried about the stork. It's the doctor's bill that scares me."

My jokes were never funny. No one laughed, not even me.

Besides, we were all starving to death. At Talia's subtle suggestion, everyone ran for the dining room. Chairs were turned over; glasses were broken. Emilia, our maid, was plastered against the wall behind the door.

The large display of trays suggested anything but improvisation. Roast beef, potato salad, palm salad, tomatoes, lettuce, beets, carrots, the works. Three varieties of rice. Chicken. Pork.

"This meat's delicious. I haven't had a piece of prime beef like this in weeks! Where did you get it?" Licurgo asked my wife.

Talia didn't answer. She hadn't set foot in a butcher shop in her life. At our house, grocery shopping meant picking up the phone and telling Daddy that the refrigerator was empty.

Patroclo satisfied Licurgo's curiosity.

"We went to La Guardia. Drove twenty kilometers to find a few kilos of loin. Can you imagine?"

Patroclo was lying. The meat we were eating came from his own refrigerator. Buying meat was his forte, but since it wasn't particularly chic, he never mentioned it. Jobs, for him, were either refined or plebeian. He'd spent his whole life growing sugar cane and importing electrical appliances. But the economic crisis bled those businesses dry. To make matters worse, farm hands were leaving the fields to press coca leaves for the drug dealers. Patroclo had to invest in the only business that was earning a profit: the produce market. Though making communion wafers would have suited him more, he'd been reduced to dealing in fruits and vegetables. He was no better than the *cholas* who ran the stands at the marketplace. "I wouldn't be surprised," he'd say sadly, "if I ended up selling hot dogs in front of the Victoria Theater." His daughters felt awful about it. "If it weren't for us," they'd say, "he could forget money and breed dogs for a living."

"Why did you go to La Guardia, when you could have gotten it out of your own meat freezer?" I asked cynically. I wasn't as kind as his daughters.

"I never go in there. It looks like a morgue, makes me nauseous. . . . But I did call the salesman, and he didn't even have a piece of tripe. Completely sold out. I had to drive all over town to find that meat. But that's all right. It didn't hurt me."

He raised his chin and assumed a dignified pose. With a staff and a camel-hair robe, he could have passed for a patriarch. No one believed a word he'd said, but, of course, he didn't notice.

No one tried to silence him. They allowed him to enjoy his favorite pastime—griping about the economic crisis. It didn't affect him, but he pretended that it did, to avoid being snobbishly indifferent, like the nouveaux riches. He was never ostentatious, always conservative; that was the only tasteful way to be. He was discreetly aristocratic to an extreme, which meant never wearing new clothes and going to cocktail parties in his work clothes, as if he'd just come in from the cane fields.

"If the government doesn't fix prices and get control of the black market, we're all going to end up on the street."

When Patroclo pronounced this final phrase of his harangue, I took out a coin and laid it in his hand: "This is one schoolteacher's contribution to hard-up businessmen."

Patroclo didn't know whether to laugh or get mad. Ira didn't give him time to react. She took the coin and proclaimed:

"I'll take this for the Poor House."

Ira never allowed anyone to hold the floor for more than five minutes. She loved being the center of attention. Like a juggler with a bag of tricks, she was always ready to take over. She was always ready with the latest gossip or some gruesome tale that would turn your stomach. Since she didn't have to work or keep house, she spent her time giving Patroclo's money to charity. Which provided her with a great source of tragedies to spice up her conversation.

Ira had fought in a record number of social-aid campaigns. Epidemics, floods, illiteracy, immorality, the plight of the homeless, juvenile delinquency. Wherever Death slung his scythe, Ira popped up to organize a crusade. She'd shaken hands with several presidents and had already received the Woman of the Year Award. Unfortunately, she had to share it with a dog-faced woman from La Paz she couldn't stand.

I like listening to her more than him. She was all right, unless she pulled out her raffle tickets or started recruiting workers for the Cancer Hospital Fair.

At dinner, she reenacted the odyssey of emigrants from the altiplano. She told us about their illness—many had tuberculosis or purulent hemoptysis—their promiscuity, their lice, dirty feet, and sweaty bodies.

After dinner, those who were able retired to the terrace for coffee.

Squeals and laughter announced the arrival of Julia and her friends. They didn't remember to wish me a happy birthday or to ask if this was a wedding, a wake, or a political conspiracy. They fell on the table like a flock of magpies on a cornfield.

They nosed through my record collection like bare-faced rioters. They weren't impressed. They ran Emilia out of the kitchen and launched their attack.

There were only four of them. A quartet of pampered fillies. Silvia, with her flame-colored hair, chubby, temperamental, and energetic. Olga, who resembled Julia, or maybe it was the other way around. They wore the same hairstyle, the same clothes. Marina, a haughty blonde, was the tallest. She was always grinning, and she always wiggled her butt when she walked. Then came Julia, the leader.

They broke up our conversation. Their vitality absorbed our attention. We went on chatting, but with one ear tuned to what they were saying.

We were making dumb remarks like:

"We're poor because our people don't like to work. If I were in the government . . ."

"What would you do if you were in the government?"

"Beat the bastards who wouldn't work!"

"I've got a better solution. Bolivia's got too many poor people. We could trade the surplus to the industrialized countries. Twenty genuine paupers for one rich man. Sweden would do it. If they don't find some people to help, their welfare program is going to go bankrupt."

Sitting comfortably on the sofa and slowly sipping a beer, I listened without partaking in their cretinous commentaries. I didn't drink much since the acid level of my stomach was already rising.

Suddenly I realized that Licurgo was gone. He'd made the leap the rest of us were dying to make. He'd left the adult circle and joined the girls—at a table piled up with dirty plates, spilled rice, and glasses of flat beer. Flies were buzzing all around them. Patroclo was jealous. His fatherly act had never fooled me. I'd caught the old rascal patting and squeezing his daughter's friends plenty of times.

I followed my friend's suit and sat down with the girls. Reluctantly, they allowed me to stay. Licurgo had already cornered Silvia, a law student, who was glad for a chance to chat with an experienced lawyer.

"Don't expect to learn anything at the university," Licurgo warned. "When you get your degree, you aren't going to know anything. In fact, you may think you know less than when you started."

"So why study?"

"To get a degree. When you start practicing, then you learn something." The sly fox was about to offer to be her mentor. I could see it coming.

"I love to teach. I don't know why I don't teach at the university. If you'd like, I could give you your first lesson on Monday."

"Oh really? What sort of lesson?"

"Hey, don't get me wrong."

"Just so you know that all you'll get is a swift kick in the shin," she assured him.

"I'm not like most men. You don't know me."

"You look the same to me."

"And you're right, I'm just like all the others," he confessed, "but I'm not like that at work. I never mix work and play."

Before giving in, she again threatened to break his shin at the slightest provocation.

"Leave my bones in peace. There's nothing to worry about," he promised, his voice slightly trembling.

Silvia was a saucy wench. She itched for Monday to come. She'd never asked me for help, and I knew a lot more law than Licurgo. I couldn't believe she'd let herself be taken in by the first lascivious old goat to give her a whiff of his masculinity.

The telephone rang, and Julia ran to answer it. The next room was dark. I could see her shadow leaning against the wall—the receiver balanced on her shoulder, her head bent, and her body swaying back and forth.

She returned blushing with excitement. "Guess who it was," she said to the group.

"Your anonymous half-wit," they responded in chorus.

"What did he say?" Olga asked.

"Nothing. Foolishness."

"I bet he said something obscene," Marina said.

"No. He never does."

The girls begged her to tell them what he'd said, word for word. She refused. She wanted to keep it to herself, savor every indecency later in the darkness, like stolen plums.

"If I got an anonymous phone call, I'd leave the receiver off the hook and report it to the telephone company. You never know, it could be some pervert." Silvia was wiser than the others.

Olga thought she understood her friend's curious nature:

"She encourages him. She likes mystery. He knows that and keeps calling."

Licurgo, in a serious baritone, issued a warning:

"Girls, don't encourage strangers. There's no guarantee they're harmless. I've heard too many stories about pranks that turned out badly."

They ignored him. I was glad. They were having a great time, calling out the names of suspects and laughing out loud.

"What's strange," Julia continued, "is that he always knows where to find me. Today, for example, how did he know I'd be here?"

"Seems like you could figure it out," someone said.

"Well," I said, "there's only one person who knows everything about us."

"And who's that?" asked Julia.

"God."

She smiled awkwardly—disappointed and excited at the same time. Could it be? She was too spoiled to rule it out completely. She began to imagine herself pursued by some handsome, dethroned deity.

THREE

Teaching history was a thankless job. My students were tired of the same old stuff. One tedious week followed another. I couldn't have stood the boredom if from time to time, poof! something unusual hadn't occurred. Like the afternoon I was lecturing on Hannibal's wars against Rome.

The classroom was in ruins—stains on the whitewashed walls swollen from the dampness, bricks made uneven by the sinking foundation, the perennial sound of termites gnawing beneath the surface. Imagine some ancient crypt, and you'll have a fairly accurate picture of what the room was like.

Hannibal's life amazed me. The valiant Carthaginian, who "accustomed his body to rigor, his appetite to moderation, his tongue to silence, and his thought to objectivity." Hannibal, the torch that carried the African fire to Europe. That crossed the Alps, leaving half of his troops frozen along the way. He won many battles against the Romans and, with one little push, could have knocked down Rome, which, by then, was scarcely more than a noisy henhouse. He could have installed a mysterious, sensual Semitic civilization on European soil. So why didn't he? What held him back? He made a stupid decision. He went back to Africa—his brother had asked him to—deserting the land he'd won in so many battles. Rotten luck!

I dictated the names of battles: Tesino, Trebia, Trasimenos, Cannas. Raquel wasn't listening. She was chewing on a lock of her hair and filing her nails. The other students fused together in a monotony of white smocks. I wished for something green to sprout or for something red to burst into flames.

No one was listening. Their inattentiveness, which had never bothered me before, was bothering me today. I'd poured my blood into that lesson. I was impassioned.

I looked for Hilda, my favorite student. She was sitting on the first row. She looked tired, but she was paying attention. After class, I'd give her a flower. A simple, frail flower for a delicate, young nun.

I reached the end of Hannibal's campaigns. I got to the part I hated, the part where I was supposed to tell them about his decision to return home. The words started piling up in my mouth like a hoard on the edge of a cliff. I suddenly got a wild idea.

I began to fantasize. I made up a battle, the battle of Cantrágina. Hannibal decimated the Roman army. Elephants trampled horses. A hundred and twenty-nine senators perished by the sword. Fifty thousand dead warriors lay rotting in the open field. Eight thousand patrician women married Carthaginian soldiers. Semitic and Latin bloods mixed. Hannibal, king of the Italic peninsula. African lustfulness and madness spurted life into the stoic Latium land.

Hilda was listening to me with her mouth open. She was the only one who'd figured out what was happening. I smiled, letting her know that I knew. She understood. Hilda was bright. She also had a fantastic ass. I couldn't deal with the two at once: sensuality and talent. If I thought about her mind, her body would disappear; I would see a lively, expressive face floating in a void. If I forgot about her mind, I'd want to ravage her on the spot.

The bell rang, and I left the room without finishing. I'd left out the part about a disillusioned child who went to see a movie called *Hannibal* some twenty years before. He hadn't liked the ending and left the theater in defeat. Today that snotty-nosed kid came to life in the classroom, climbed on an elephant, and led his hero to the heart of Rome. He fought in the great battle, the only battle he'd won in his whole life.

During recess, Hilda came up to me, licking an ice-cream cone, trying not to drip it on her smock.

"I liked that last part about Hannibal. Where did you find that?"

"Not in a book, as you may have guessed. It was an experiment. I wanted to see if you would swallow anything I fed you. And most of you did—everybody except you. Imagine the implications. . . ."

Why the hell did I say that? I wanted to bite off my tongue. I'd been victorious, riding through the Lyceum on a white Carthaginian elephant! Now I felt like a complete ass. If only I'd just told the truth. I'd made it up for fun—and to make up for other losses.

There'd be other times for spinning yarns. But none as pure as that one that afternoon at the Lyceum. I'd make up more lies for my students. Some would even like my distorted version the best. Imagine. There must have been millions of people in the nineteenth century who liked Bonaparte, enjoyed watching him humiliate the entire European nobility. He was the great hero of the nineteenth century, and his failure was the defeat of a certain rebellious humanity. So what if adversity spoiled his life? That doesn't give us the right to talk about his failure year after year, course after course, from one school to the next. Why not change him a little, turn him into a Superman?

Yes! That's what I would do. Turn history into fiction— another kind of literature. Many of us would gladly make a few changes in the annals of the modern world. If you were a neo-Nazi, in love with a defeated movement, wouldn't you like to have Hitler win the war? Scoundrels as well as saints have aroused pity in the twentieth century.

That day, I fell from ecstasy to the doldrums. Fragile joy crumbled. Solid, desperate boredom took over.

I was leaving the school. All the classrooms were full. Light and noise resounded through the halls.

I passed the secretary's office and saw Otto sitting at his desk, correcting papers. I ignored him, picked up my briefcase, and started to leave. Otto taught physics on Mondays, Wednesdays, and Fridays; the rest of the week he drank. He was all right sober. His sense of humor wasn't bad.

"Just in time to lend me a few dollars," he said. "Want a beer?"

"Not today, I'm busy," I answered, though I wouldn't have gone the next day or any other for that matter. I couldn't imagine myself drinking a round with Otto, any more than I could see myself flying a hot-air balloon. We were colleagues. We exchanged comments in the hall, slapped each other on the back, but that was it. Outside the Lyceum, we had nothing to say to each other.

I said good-bye.

"Tomorrow's payday," he reminded me. "Of course, our paychecks won't be worth as much tomorrow. A twenty percent drop is what they're saying. You could get twenty-two dollars for it today—on the black market."

I left the Lyceum with the number twenty-two ringing in my ears. It flashed on and off, like a neon sign. Twenty-two dollars, the rock-bottom cost of an education. A hooker in the Bronx earned more than that in half an hour. My entire salary—the price of a bottle of scotch whiskey. A month's labor for a liter of urine-colored spirits. I pitied Otto, if he ever developed a taste for imported liquor.

It was humiliating—making less money than the ice-cream vendor on the corner. The government didn't give a damn. They knew that a diploma was worthless, especially during a recession. Teachers didn't produce anything. Let them starve! Who cared? Who complained? Show them their pay-checks, and let them die laughing.

Of course, in my case, hunger was an empty word. Every-one knew that I was Patroclo del Paso y Troncoso's son-in-law, just as everyone knew that he paid my bills. My paycheck was neither here nor there, and everybody knew it. But that was all right. I wasn't about to give up my job. My wife thought I held onto it out of spite, to punish my in-laws. Maybe she was right.

That was a high price for solvency—becoming a pedant, cutting myself off from the real world.

I reached Libertad and drove toward the downtown area. The traffic began to get heavy. I was having to stop at every corner. Money-changers, selling dollars and cruzeiros, sur-rounded the car at each stop. They were scattered along a lengthy stretch of road. You could pick them out by their black briefcases, their nervous expectancy, and money-tainted sweat. They were buying and selling dollars on the street, unguardedly, unscrupulously, as if they'd been selling potatoes.

Where did their clients come from? Maybe they traded with each other, dollars for pesos, then pesos for dollars. They raised the price after every operation and devoured their own economy in the process—like the mythical serpent that swallowed its own tail.

I liked driving in the city, switching lanes, passing on the wrong side. No one obeyed the traffic laws. How could they? There weren't any lanes. None of the traffic lights worked. It was a no man's land, and the right of way belonged to the gutsiest or the one who got there first. Rows of vehicles moved along stuck to each other, like revelers at a carnival. And somewhere, an enormous steel uterus kept giving birth to more and more cars.

At the corner of the university, I came face to face with the Muse. The sun was shining directly in my eyes, leaving me a narrow field of vision. She appeared in that small clear spot. I parked the car abruptly. The owner of the Dodge behind me furiously honked his horn, shifted into reverse, and drove around me.

Just as the Muse leaned over and stuck her head in the window, a cloud swallowed up the sun. My sight returned, and I watched her descend slowly from the sky—an unnamed bird, the last female of a vanishing species. Her face opened up with a smile. Her hair was wet in a wild sort of way, as if she'd been diving in an underground stream. She came closer, quite casually, as if she'd been pushed by a sudden impulse. Her movements were unintentional, indifferent—like slipping on a ring, without thinking.

"Get in," I said. "I'll take you home."

She refused and mumbled some excuse. I think she said she was going shopping at Galería España. I didn't offer to go with her. There wouldn't have been any point. She didn't know she was the Muse. Didn't know I'd been carrying her around in my craw like an indigestible diamond. She couldn't see me responding to her every move. If she blinked her eyes, my eyes burned until I blinked, too. She could have buried me in the ground, and I would have sprouted roses to please her. She didn't know that.

She was completely indifferent. She didn't hang around. She left by Junín Street, swinging her hips and making her way through the money-changers. She walked along at an even pace, ignoring the men's remarks. She held the entire space on the sidewalk, like a large ship sailing through a canal.

Her oblivion drove me to distraction. A blind deaf-mute could have smelled the passion in my sweat, noticed the growling in my stomach, which churned violently to support or supplant my inept heart.

I started the car and quickly made a decision. I wasn't ever going to tell Licurgo who she was. I was pissed off, and for lack of a better scapegoat, I decided to take it out on him. Licurgo was a slob. One day, he'd been so close to her, he could have breathed the air she was breathing. And he never even suspected. He didn't deserve to know, and I wasn't going to tell him.

FOUR

"The yard smells awful! Somebody pissed on the grass last night," Talia told me as she led me by the hand to the spot. She wanted me to witness the crime. She pulled me along at full speed. I didn't have time to put down my briefcase or wipe my feet.

When it came to odors, my wife was more sensitive than a canary in a mine. I didn't smell anything or see any damp spots; the sun had done the job of a paper towel.

"You're right, someone watered your lawn," I agreed, to put an end to the matter.

"Slobs! Don't they know there's a bathroom inside?"

"Don't ask me."

"It was one of *your* guests," she insisted.

"I bet it was your mother."

"Don't be rude. Licurgo is the only one who would do such a thing."

Poor Licurgo. Always the accused. In school, every time somebody farted Licurgo was automatically thrown out of class. Marked from birth. But this time, I'd have sworn he was innocent. It had to be Julia del Paso y Troncoso. Whenever there was a party, she'd get a crazy urge to piss in a strange place—outside, in an empty room, next to an altar, or at the foot of some public monument. Both Talia and her parents were aware of Julia's mania. But since they pretended not to know, I decided to leave it alone.

I came home in a mood to play with my wife. She walked in front of me. I caught up with her, grabbed her around the waist, and pressed my pelvis against her bottom. I followed along, stuck to her body. Then I lifted her skirt and caressed her thighs.

"Let go of me, I'm tired," she cried.

I set her down in my lap. She closed her eyes. Stimulation put Talia to sleep. She curled up, closing herself off from my caresses. It was Thursday; she'd want me to wait till Saturday.

I didn't stop. I tried to unbutton her blouse.

"Please stop. Let's talk, like other people."

"I can talk and do this at the same time," I argued.

"Remember I'm getting over cystitis. The doctor said to wait a few days."

I let go of her. You'd think she'd been saved from a rapist.

Talia got weaker and weaker every year. Touching her was like balancing the entire Romanov crystal collection on the tip of your finger.

For some time Talia's body has been a veritable play-ground for vaginal infections: trichomonads during the warm months, *candida albicans* during the humid months, and bacteria of a more common type during the off-season. Her gynecologist, whom I'd considered asking for yearly rates, treated her vagina as if it were his private property. He always found a cure, but Talia would show up at his office two weeks later, not saying a word, just pointing at her pubis, like a bashful child. The test results were never positive—there were never any objective signs. No matter. The condition always worsened and eventually became Talia's favorite topic. Each time she described it, her terminology became more precise. But no one believed her. They all thought she was making it up. She'd get depressed. Then, eureka! Real symptoms would appear. Painful urination. Blood in the urine. She'd routed the skeptics. She had cystitis. Her reputation was saved.

I rested my head in her lap. Her words echoed back to me: no, no, no. Her half-closed eyes. Her body curled up, in awe of its own being. Her slow breathing. My thoughts were quietly poised, like guests awaiting the arrival of their host.

I entered the past. I remembered my first sexual encounter with Talia. We were in her living room. The image was transparent and fragile: Talia, glowing, tousled hair, vivacious, the way she was before we were married. I was next to her, terribly thin, my face feverish but pale. We stood up, and the sofa groaned as we rose. There was a clear, spring-like silence. She checked the other rooms; her parents were probably watching television. We felt free, excited. I wasn't sure what we were doing. Talia was. She'd done it the year before with Chris Molina. Jerk! He wouldn't let go of me—he was there in the middle of it, dressed like a gym instructor telling me what to do. Talia led me down the stairs. The upstairs door was barred; the one below was locked. We went down the steps till we reached a darker spot. She was standing two steps above me—tall, silent, and melancholy. She didn't seem excited. Had she been like that with Chris? She unbuttoned the back of her dress. There was a bustling of clothes, creaking of wood, and torpid heat in the darkness. My hands moved through her clean, neatly pressed clothes. I felt like a fat nurse getting a patient ready for surgery. I hardly looked at her, as if I were some professional used to dealing with undressed women. I carefully held the pile of clothes in my hands and raised my eyes. I saw her, immobile, happy, and perplexed, above her red, high-heeled shoes. I'd never seen her naked before. She didn't look the way I thought she would, as if she'd put on a more eloquent, aggressive body. She smoothed her hair and smiled at me. I drank her nakedness straight and dry. The triangle of her pubis was like a center of gravity, the axis from which her thighs and torso were born, like the points of a star.

I'd made love to other women; but no one had ever undressed for me out of sheer exhibitionism. They'd strip to go to bed with me. But Talia had offered me her nudity as a pure act, as appetizer, main dish, and dessert. I must have been an immense, bodiless eye.

Talia became an expert in that art. The year before, poor, unhappy Chris couldn't stand the excitement and masturbated in front of her. There was something of a lament in that masturbation. And I, holding her clothes in my hand and remembering Chris, tried to find a better ending, but couldn't. I adopted the expression of a penitent, and Talia, showing mercy, called me to her side. Her hands paused lightly on my zipper. She pulled my penis out roughly, causing pain I pretended not to feel. She began to rub it without skill or rhythm, with variable pressure, but learning a better way to caress me with every movement. Until I ejaculated, and she cleaned me with a handkerchief.

You could see my in-laws' house from our window. Fifty meters separated me from the staircase where Talia undressed for me that first time. But a million light years separated me from the young lawyer who had let himself be devoured by that explosive star of flesh. I recognized myself in that young man. An identical genetic match, the same physical traits and the same identification card. But if both of us were put to some test, were asked our opinion of a landscape, for example, or a woman, the results would be very different. His view would show sensitivity, fiber, and madness. Mine would be overly technical. It was painful to admit it. They were the same machine, except one was rusted out.

Talia called me out of my reflections. She was sorry for not going along.

"I'll do everything you want on Saturday. I've even decided to have a child next year. You wouldn't say no, would you?"

Since the day we married, Talia had been devising a plan. We'd go to Rio, get a suite at the Copacabana, and one night, she—the queen bee—would take her mate, receive the seminal sting, and return home with her uterus pleasantly invigorated.

Delaying the trip had become a habit.

She was tired of people asking when she was going to get pregnant. Their curiosity had begun to sound like an accusation. She felt condemned, a traitor to her kind, an unnatural female. But it wasn't entirely her fault, she said. I was to blame, too.

More than once, she'd gone to great lengths to convince me that we should have a child. Finally, I'd surrender. Tell her mating season was open. Tell her to go ahead and pick the sex and the color of the eyes and hair. I'd give her the baby she wanted.

"Really?" she'd say. "You wouldn't mind having a child?"

"I'm not thrilled to death about it, but if that's what you want . . ."

"You have to be happy, too. I want to plan and dream like everyone else."

"I'm sorry, this is the best I can do. And you'd better take advantage of it, before I change my mind."

"I won't take advantage of a decision you've made in a moment of weakness. It's right only if both of us want it. Your hostile feelings would be bad for the child."

"He'll never know."

"Of course he will. Children are very sensitive."

Psychology had spoiled Talia. Her desire to do everything

perfectly had paralyzed her. She wouldn't get pregnant unless I and her parents approved; she wanted to deliver while we were on vacation; the weather had to be just right, not too cold or too hot; and the child's sign had to be compatible with hers—preferably Aquarius or Taurus.

Also, it couldn't be born when her doctor was away on vacation or at a conference.

Carnival, Christmas, and New Year's were out: the hospitals would be understaffed.

The moon should be right, as well as the political situation—preferably conservative. A civilian government, right of center, and supported by the Church would be ideal.

Being Ira's daughter had been Talia's greatest disadvantage. The mother's exuberance had disturbed the daughter's growth. She was born, not to be the center of attention, but to gravitate around the matrix, to be an exotic jewel for her mother to show off. My wife was a mere tubercle that showed up on the sly. She succumbed to her mother from the beginning, from her first cry. She could never be exactly like her mother, but imitated her actions in miniature. While the daughter worked for a handful of charities, the mother organized national campaigns. Just hearing them laugh showed how different they were. Ira's laugh was intense, extravagant, and undulating, like the final movement of a waltz; Talia's was like a murmur, a distant brook. Talia turned off the small lights inside of her when she was a child, since her mother's enormous beam made them unnecessary. If she'd left them on, she'd have been a lot happier. But out of loyalty, she smothered her own fire. Even so, she wasn't jealous of her mother. She received energy from Ira by osmosis. She would still draw near her, like a small calf. It was a tender sight.

❧

LATER THAT EVENING, Emilia served us her best dish: steak, rice, eggs, and fried bananas. After cooking for fifteen years at an excellent restaurant, she still couldn't cook anything except the most common dishes. But if she started bragging about the exotic dishes she used to cook, it was safer not to challenge her. Lunch had gone into the garbage a few times.

I chewed my food slowly, as I cut up a tomato. My appetite was healthy. Talia was a light eater but obstinately forced down more than she wanted. She was afraid of what might happen if she didn't clean her plate.

"Did you go to your studio?" she asked, referring to the place her father had rented for me the year before, when my whim for photography had become public knowledge. I'd thought I had a hidden talent for portraits, and Patroclo set me up in business. My enthusiasm vanished two days after the open house. I turned the studio over to some crazy Japanese, who kept the books perfectly balanced. No profit, no loss.

"No, I'll stop by tomorrow."

"Daddy says a business never shows a profit if the proprietor doesn't keep an eye on his employees."

"I have better things to do than baby-sit Tanazaki."

"You used to like photography, Jonah," Talia reminded me. She still believed that some day I'd get a hankering for hard work and take off running like a mule.

"I like photography, but I don't feel like ruining my eyes in a darkroom," I argued.

"You're lucky to have a vocation. Plenty of people would trade places with you."

"That's a lie! Most people don't give a damn about a vocation. All they care about is money. They'd rather scrub toilets and be rich than be a Michelangelo and stay poor. Didn't you learn anything about people at your university?"

"I'm not interested in people; I'm interested in you, Jonah."

The dessert dishes contained a black concoction.

"It's pudding," Emilia explained.

Talia examined the dark, gelatinous substance with disgust. But, having been an ascetic since childhood, she forced herself to eat everything.

"Black pudding?" she asked.

"You can't find refined sugar at the market; I had to buy dark. And even that wasn't easy. There was a line going all the way around the corner."

"Close your eyes and dig in," I suggested.

Talia, armed with a spirit of mystic mortification, dug in with her spoon and devoured a mouthful of pudding. I couldn't do it, not even if I'd been hypnotized. It looked like clotted blood.

"Mother came by today," Talia commented. "We talked for two hours."

I knew it; I could tell by looking at her.

"When you're sad and out of sorts, I know your mother's been here. You don't settle down till you've done something to change your life—joined a dance class, sold your car, quit your job, or worse, tried to rehabilitate me."

She'd stopped listening. She had a talent for totally disconnecting herself from conversations. It was hard to detect the exact moment when she dropped out. I could talk for an hour and suddenly find her faraway, like a bird floating in the sky, wings spread, brain asleep, totally ignoring me and my nonsense. Those furtive raptures infuriated whoever was speaking. She did it when she didn't like what was being said. It was easy to see why she was treated for a rare form of epilepsy when she was a child. Her health was fine, but blaming her distractions on an illness was more comfortable for her parents.

Talia finished the pudding.

"Aren't you going to have any?" she asked.

"No. You may have it," I responded, pushing the bowl toward her.

"It's delicious," she commented. She took another bite. Her eyes lit up.

"It's funny," she said, scooting her chair nearer the table, "what you said about Mother's visits. I was never aware of it before. But here I am, thinking of dying my hair—maybe red."

"Wouldn't suit you."

"I'm tired of the way I look; I need a change. . . . I know I'd like it red. I also know I won't dye it. I'd be afraid I'd be ugly and never look like myself again."

Her spoon circled elegantly in the air. She was a classy eater. She chewed tiny mouthfuls, just like a canary.

"There's a job that's right for you. Mother could find it."

"I'm sure she could. She's already found several thousand."

"Would you like to work at a bank? Legal counsel. Reasonable salary."

"I hate banks. Handling other people's money depresses me. It's like guarding a harem and not being a eunuch."

"They'd pay you a lot better than the school."

"Don't even think about me becoming a banker. I'd rather dig ditches than put on a tie every day. And besides, I'll never saddle myself with a nine-to-five job."

"Everybody works at least eight hours a day. Some of the happiest people I know work twelve. You have to do it if you want to be successful."

"Who wants to be successful?"

"Why not?"

"Because I'm happy as a failure. My classmates elected me Most Likely Not to Succeed, and I held the title for several years. It was what I was best at, and I won't give it up without a really good reason."

Emilia brought in coffee. I sweetened mine, and the dark sugar made it look like real coffee, which Emilia had never been able to make.

Talia didn't buy my argument. "Be honest, Jonah. Your problem's not a lack of ambition but the reverse. You stay on at the Lyceum because you think there isn't a job anywhere that's good enough for you."

She was wrong, but I liked her interpretation. There weren't any hidden motives. I just wanted to vegetate where I was.

Unfortunately, no one believed me. Since the day I was

born, somebody had pushed me to excel. They took me out of the cradle and taught me to crawl. And don't say it was for my own good; as an adult I've never once found a need for it. My first da-da wasn't good enough. They made me say ma and then ma-ma, until they'd filled my brain with spelling, grammar, and syntax. Then they taught me the virtue of remaining silent. Nothing satisfied them. There was always something else for me to learn. I wasted twenty years in school. Couldn't they come up with a more pleasant way for us to occupy our time on this planet? Of course they could. If they could dream up the Greek gods, whose principle goal seemed to have been seducing women on earth, surely they could have figured out something simpler for men to do.

So, Licurgo said my problem was turning thirty. Wrong. I'd been like that from birth, maybe before, prenatal, intrauterine. It had taken a long time to surface. It had waited patiently for me to ripen, like cheese. As soon as I had my degree in hand and a nuptial carnation on my lapel, it surged. I was a young, middle-class adult, the ideal consumer—the one they had in mind when they opened nightclubs, boutiques, and luxury motels; when they imported whiskies and perfumes illegally. They fought terrorism for my sake. When doctors spoke of building a "clientele," they weren't looking for cane cutters from the north. Citizens like myself kept a whole army of workers on the job: doctors, dentists, hairstylists, nannies, cooks, appliance salesmen, appliance repairmen, women for an afternoon's pleasure, Scheherazades for a thousand and one nights, and lawyers to arrange the divorce the following day. The airplanes that took off daily for Miami carried passengers like me. The North American consulate gladly handed out visas to my kind—we wouldn't stay behind to increase the population of some Latin ghetto.

What but sickly pride scorned that kind of privilege? Before I'd even gotten comfortable in my lawyer's robe, magnificent offers poured in from all sides. And the most spectacular of them all, shining like a diamond in space, the ambition of every young man: the North American Oil Company. An easy job and easy dollars. My reaction? I stood frozen at the open door of Eden. I was terrified. It looked to me like Jonah's whale; it would swallow me up to vomit me out forty years later, senile, toothless, bald, and mediocre. I said no, a demented, incomprehensible no—so my family thought.

Success was stubborn. It kept right on courting me. Job proposals lined up in my path; I knocked them down like bowling pins. It did no good. My wife's family, my mother in La Paz, and well-intentioned friends tempted me daily with new opportunities; I ran away, like a skittish, young bull.

"Too bad wigs went out of style," said Talia. "I'd like to go out and buy a dozen or more, all different colors and textures, some ridiculous, others sexy. I'd love it; today blond curls, tomorrow a kinky afro."

She was thrilled at the thought of changing into another woman. She had an erotic dream about a woman who turned into a monkey, the sexiest cheetah that ever lived, and made love to Tarzan and all the chimpanzees, orangutans, and gorillas in the jungle. She never knew if she was the protagonist or just a spectator. But her confusion didn't stop her from enjoying the orgy.

"I like you the way you are, with your own hair," I said, obviously trying to cheer her up.

I stirred the coffee left in my cup. White filaments floated to the surface, some stretched out, others rolled up, some immobile, others seized by strange convulsions.

I called the maid.

"Emilia, what's in my coffee? Look at it."

"They're worms," she answered, innocently.

"Worms? How the hell did they get into the coffee?"

"Mine is full of them, too," Talia exclaimed in horror.

"They aren't in the coffee. Maybe they're in the sugar," Emilia suggested, and to verify her theory, she emptied the sugar into a plate. It looked like damp garden soil that could hold hundreds of worms, wiggling promiscuously.

"Good God. I ate two bowls of pudding," Talia cried, turning pale.

"Don't worry, ma'am, they're worms from the cane, clean and sweet."

"Lots of protein," I added.

Trembling, my wife rose from the table and asked for a bottle of oil to help her vomit the rotten pudding.

FIVE

Routine at the Lyceum was becoming irksome again. I had to do something, anything to relieve the tedium. I came up with some unusual methods I'd never used before. The first day, I taught for a whole hour without mentioning a single proper name. Every time a city, country, or natural disaster came up, I'd call it by its initials.

I first tried it out in a lecture on Julius Caesar. "J. C. crossed the R. and took on P. in the battle of F." It took the concentration of a Tibetan lama to get through the whole period without mentioning a single name. The students were stupefied. They took down every sentence, like UN stenographers copying a speech by the Pakistani ambassador. They thought it was part of some conspiracy, instigated by the Department of Education to put an end to subversive activities. They were so scared, they didn't stop to think about the advantages. My new technique cut out the bull, reduced each subject to its essence: war and treason, death and plagues, in their true impersonal and omnipresent state.

When I got bored with that, I came up with something else—a sort of time machine that allowed me to move people around, from one century to another.

Hilda understood. She listened enthusiastically, with a tender look in her eyes.

We used the machine to find a candidate for Secretary General of the UN, someone who'd really know how to solve today's problems. Raquel suggested King Solomon—the wisest, best ruler of the ancient world. As soon as we got him here, he was rejected. Somebody remembered he'd been charged with a terrible crime—infanticide—for threatening to split a child down the middle.

Hilda proposed Diogenes the Cynic. But before he could reach UN headquarters, he was arrested for indecent exposure.

Francis of Assisi seemed a likely candidate. We managed to get him as far as the airport. Then someone mentioned to the sanitation authorities that he'd been living with wild animals. He was quarantined. With no proof of vaccination, he could have been carrying anything.

Then I got a call and had to stop. I walked down the hall to the phone. It was my father-in-law's secretary.

"Señor Del Paso y Troncoso would like to speak to you immediately."

"Is it urgent?" I asked.

"Yes."

"He always says it's urgent."

"That's the way he operates. If it were really important, he wouldn't call, he'd send the chauffeur to find you."

"Yes, I see."

I went to the Director's office to ask permission.

"I'm sick. Is it all right if I leave?"

"Is it contagious?" she asked, disgruntled by the interruption. She'd been reading *Amalia* since I started to work at the Lyceum.

"I've got diarrhea," I lied. I knew she wouldn't ask me any more questions.

I arrived at Patroclo's house, half a block from mine, in the residential part of town. It was a classic, two-story house, severe, and with a barbed fence around it. The fence had been charged at one time—until some poor kid got electrocuted. I heard somebody say he was in love with the maid; somebody else said he was in love with Julia. The house was imposing. It made the houses around it look small and ugly, including mine. My house . . . I use the term loosely. Patroclo gave it to Talia and me. But every time he walked into it, he'd stroll around, like Sancho Panza inspecting his private island.

Fifteen years before, he purchased the property—the entire barrio—at rock-bottom price. The whole area had dropped in value, when the predictions of a Belgian engineer became public knowledge. He said the river had once run through that part of the city and, sooner or later, would return to the same spot. Patroclo bought the land and hired the Belgian—Druout, he was called. He retracted his earlier statement, then drew up the plans for the barrio. In twelve months, every house had been sold.

The river flowed silently four hundred meters away. Some of the people who lived there didn't even know it existed. Some knew about it but rarely went there—they preferred swimming in a pool. The people who lived in the neighborhood next to ours spent a good part of the summer dabbling in the current.

When I walked into my in-laws' house, I suddenly crossed paths with my brother-in-law, Pablo. He smiled and shook my hand. I could tell from his sluggishness that he'd just declared bankruptcy. He usually calmed down when he was broke.

He had his father's face—it's common for an illegitimate child to look just like his father. He and Patroclo were so much alike, they looked more like brothers than father and son, especially since Pablo looked old for his age. He was almost bald. And what hair he had left was gray. Not even his own father could remember how old he was. But they all knew he wasn't as old as his bald head suggested. Nor as young as he acted.

"Did Dad call you? I wouldn't go in there if I were you," Pablo warned. "Stay as far away from him as you can. He's getting senile."

"He's been senile for years. I'm used to it. What's he done now?"

"He's just told me about his new project. Go in and find out for yourself." With that, he returned to his natural agitated state—Pablo the nervous rabbit, constantly chasing the deal of the century.

"You look great, Pablo," I commented. "I don't suppose you're bankrupt."

"Hey, I'm doing fine—better than you might think. I've got a deal that's a gold mine."

It was the same old Pablo, never living in the present, always living on the eve of the big day—the day when his money would come in. Then fortune would shift into reverse and dump a bundle of returned checks in his lap. That didn't discourage him. His future, like a lizard's tail, always grew back from the stump.

He couldn't keep a secret. He immediately started telling me about his new scheme.

"The deal is, we're going to sell Haitian blood to the Yankees! Blood's earning more than oil, more than gold! It's the only thing better than cocaine."

"You can't get permission to sell Haitian blood!"

"Of course I can. Easy. Nobody else is interested. It's cheaper than manure—it's been linked with the AIDS virus."

"So you'd be selling contaminated blood?"

"Of course not. There's no such thing as AIDS. The C.I.A. made it up, so they'd have an excuse to arrest fags."

"I don't believe that."

"AIDS doesn't exist!" Pablo insisted. "I'll give you a million pesos if you can show me one single person with AIDS."

"I don't know anybody with AIDS. But I've seen pictures."

"That doesn't prove anything. I've seen pictures of King Kong."

I stopped arguing. It wouldn't have done any good. He was lying and he knew it. When he wasn't running after a real business deal, he made one up. They all sounded phony, the real ones and the fake alike. Which made his reaction to his father's plan seem even stranger. The father was a lot saner than the son.

Patroclo welcomed me into his office—a big, empty room with an enormous desk. There was an adjoining library with leather-bound books, all just alike.

"Do you know Druout, my engineer? He's Belgian."

I shook the man's hand. He was smoking a pipe and was red in the face. He was dressed like an engineer, with mud-caked boots and khaki clothes. He slouched in his chair. I could imagine him lying on a pile of bricks in front of an unfinished project. The double-axle truck parked in the drive must have been his. As soon as he realized I was Patroclo's son-in-law, he became friendlier.

"My dear Jonah," Patroclo said. "I've known for some time that you haven't been happy with your job. That's what I want to talk to you about."

"I appreciate your concern," I replied, "but I'm happy at the Lyceum."

Patroclo got up and rang the bell. A woman entered the room.

"Bring some whiskey for the gentlemen."

"Whiskey?" she asked, looking at the floor. "My lord has absolutely forbidden me to serve whiskey in the morning."

"I revoke that prohibition," said Patroclo.

"My lord has ordered me to turn a deaf ear to revocations of prohibitions," she reminded him.

"The prohibition against revoking prohibitions is revoked," he announced with the solemnity of a dictator convoking free elections.

She left the room.

He shook his head. "It's hard to communicate with these people."

I gathered from the way he'd treated her that she was either a poor relation or the bastard child of a friend—somebody he'd run across, hired for slave wages, and made an enemy of for life.

The woman brought a tray with whiskey, ice, and glasses. No one took a drink. She looked at us disapprovingly.

"Jonah, I know you hate your job," said Patroclo.

"It's the best job I ever had," I protested.

"We all want you to quit. The students, the other teachers, Talia . . ."

"Everyone except me," I said.

"But it would help you more than anyone. Druout, don't you agree? Wouldn't he be better off somewhere else?"

"I think you're right. He'd be happier somewhere else."

"This is crazy! I know if I'm happy or not."

"Poor man. He needs help. He can't admit that he isn't happy," Patroclo lamented. "You remind me of the king in the fairy tale, the good persuader. One day, he left the palace naked, but he managed to convince everyone that he was wearing clothes. You're the unsuccessful version of that king. You haven't fooled anyone but yourself. You're transparent to your fellow men, opaque to yourself!"

The maid brought in another tray to replace the one no one had touched.

"Dolores, doesn't this young man look sad to you?"

"Why, yes. He's the spitting image of Jesus on the cross," she answered, without looking up.

"Didn't I tell you? It's obvious to everyone. Give it some thought. And think about Talia, too. I'll do what I can, even give you a job."

"Thanks, but I don't want to change jobs."

Patroclo opened a box of Havanas that had been sitting on his desk for years. He placed a cigar in his mouth and picked up the lighter. It didn't work, so he returned the cigar to the container.

"Young people today want to work in a large office, with air conditioning, a whole harem of secretaries and a private receptionist to arrange everything, even their dates with call girls. If you think I'm prepared to make that sort of offer, you're mistaken. I want to make that clear from the start."

"So your offer's completely worthless after all!" I joked.

"I want you to take charge of a one-of-a-kind operation. It's a project anyone would be proud to be involved in."

"And exactly what is this one-of-a-kind operation?"

"I won't tell you until I've convinced you that it is important."

Patroclo liked to create an aura of mystery. The Belgian engineer was bored, yet stretched his lips into a frozen smile. Meanwhile, Dolores kept replacing the untouched buckets of ice.

"My greatest enemy—who is it?" Patroclo asked.

"The devil, I guess. You're Catholic."

"Don't be silly."

"Relatives, who try to borrow money."

"No."

"Income taxes."

"I don't pay taxes."

"Communists."

"No."

"Drunks, brown-nosers, your wife . . ."

"Stop guessing, dammit. It's the damned *pichicateros!* Drug lords!"

"Drug lords? What have they ever done to you?"

"Stripped me of my glory, that's what!"

And to hear him tell it, they were, indeed, the source of

his misfortune. When he was poor, it was hard to become wealthy. By the time he'd made his fortune, the rules of the game had changed; any young adventurer could outdo him in a few months. He felt like a mountain climber who'd reached the summit just as a new funicular rushed by. The tree that bore the golden apples was cocaine. When cocaine exports became really large, the bottom fell out of the stock market, making getting rich the honorable way obsolete. Nobody played it straight anymore, like Patiño. Patiño had followed the rules of capitalism—quartered the hills of tin, bled them dry, squeezed every ounce of work out of the Indians. A great instrument of labor, the Indians! No one saw that anymore, he reflected. Men like him were a dying breed, the ones who'd gone to war to protect the rubber plantations. The patriotic spirit was lost. . . . No one courted the consumer anymore. With the right tactics, you could make him crave a product, pay a thousand pesos for what cost ten. Getting rich demanded craftiness, perseverance, skill. Young folks didn't want to work. The old way of doing things was dead.

After he'd finished his harangue, he stood quietly in the middle of the room, like a kid with a Monopoly game and nobody to play it with.

The cocaine producers—the press called them "drug traffickers," Patroclo called them by their Creole name, *pichicateros*—had taken the city by storm. Every time he stuck his nose out the door, he risked being run down by a Mercedes with tinted-glass windows. He couldn't understand it. The girls who won the beauty pageants used to come from good families. Now daughters of *pichicateros* were taking home the trophies. Government officials—who once protected the interests of the upper class—were sitting back, fanning themselves with cocaine dollars. And, to top it all off, the *pichicateros* weren't even interesting. They were tactless and tasteless. They had gold fillings in their teeth. Hired mariachis to serenade their mistresses. And bought expensive airplanes—to wreck them in the jungle the next day.

"Why do you think I let my daughter stay married to a lazy bum like yourself? At least as long as she's married, no *pichi-catero* is going to bother her. I'm more worried about Julia. If one of those thieves even looks at her, I'll grind him up for hamburger."

He squeezed his fists and clinched his teeth until his face turned red. Then he took a deep breath and said, in a pitiful voice:

"The truth is, we're done for. They've beat us down." He told us how hard he'd fought—in clubs, commerce guilds, churches, political parties—to try to keep them out of places decent people liked to go. He'd failed. They'd invaded Bolivian society, like vines around a pre-Columbian ruin.

"With all that money, they do whatever they please. Bolivia's a chaos. It's the perfect place for them. I couldn't muster the strength to take them on in a hundred years. I can't do anything—politically or legally. But," he said with determination, "there is one way I can outdo them. I can die better. They know how to live—better than a czar. Any animal can eat and have sex. Dying's harder. That takes a man with spiritual knowledge. I am that man. I'll show them how a decent man dies."

"What are you going to do, commit hara-kiri?"

"Don't be stupid. I'm not talking about suicide. I'm talking about a mausoleum, the most beautiful mausoleum in the whole hemisphere! . . . So, do you want to earn some money, easy money?"

"Of course," I replied, without hesitation.

"Then manage it for me."

"Me, build a tomb? Forget it. Hire somebody who does it for a living."

He rolled his eyes with a look of divine weariness, as if he were Buddha, listening to the conversation of an ape. He answered patiently:

"Rise above this mundane world. Come up to a higher level. Manage the project for me. It's not just a tomb. It's the first pyramid in Christendom."

"A real pyramid, like Khufu's?"

"Like Khofu's, you mean."

"Khufu," I insisted, with a history teacher's certainty.

"Khofu," he said again.

"Khufu."

"If I feel like saying Khofu, I'll say Khofu! Or maybe you've studied ancient Egyptian. Druout, have you ever heard anyone speak ancient Egyptian?"

"Can't say I have." He wouldn't have contradicted Patroclo if he'd pronounced it in baboon language.

He continued his speech. He was transformed; he thought he was Isaiah, Zarathustra, or Rasputin. His words flowed from his mouth like doves. But they weren't his words. It was as if he'd lent his throat to some anonymous being. His message was so urgent, he would have kicked anyone's teeth in who tried to stop him. I might have done it myself. I'd never seen him in such a passionate state.

He spread a dozen blueprints out on the table and explained each one. I didn't understand a thing. I was in awe of the man, of his ecstasy. He was the architect who designed the Great Wall, and I was the Emperor of Cathay.

He pointed out perspectives, passages, chambers, and points of support. He went on to discuss the form, height, and appropriate astrological positioning; he wanted his pyramid to be in harmony with the stars.

Patroclo had seen the burning bush, and I was caught up in his fervor. I always fell for fanatics, anybody obsessed with a wild fantasy. Any born leader, who could lead me to the Promised Land—since I was never sure where I was heading. I was entranced, hypnotized by his dazzling faith.

Seconds later, Patroclo wasn't just *telling* us about the mausoleum. It was as if every word set a stone in place. A giant cone gradually rose up in my imagination.

I poured myself a glass of whiskey. I needed it to burn my throat, to open my mind, like a hallucinogenic drug. I had to loosen up. I didn't want reason to get in the way and make it all seem ridiculous.

Egypt. A trapdoor opened up at my feet, and I fell through, into that mysterious kingdom. Egypt. No people had ever had a faith stronger than theirs. Faith in an afterlife. Faith in the preservation of the body, of its double ka, and of the soul (which, according to their creed, posed above the body like a small bird in a tree). To keep death from destroying everything—flesh, ka, and the soul—they developed excellent embalming techniques. They also placed food, water, and jewels in the tomb. Some pyramids even had bathrooms. Some of the earlier pharaohs were buried with all their belongings—wealth, wives, and servants.

Their main concern—death—gave meaning to life.

The Egyptians hadn't known about the eight-hour day. They worked as hard as corporation executives to save enough money to build their own private mausoleums. Vacations on the beach at Thebes? Not interested. All they cared about was that last journey to the great beyond. Pantheon builders were their best-paid professionals. A woman would sell her body for a sarcophagus. Instead of a ring, you gave your lover a death mask.

Ironically, that entire world, created for the spirit, ended up under a heap of sand. But Patroclo wasn't content to leave it there.

His ecstasy had charmed me. But it hadn't convinced me to take the job. I could see myself. Dripping with sweat. Walking around on a lot covered with bricks and cement. Trying to keep an eye on the workers, who'd be trying to carry off everything they could get their hands on. And, of course, the Belgian engineer, sitting under a parasol, would be watching from a distance. And everyone would be looking at me and laughing behind my back.

My refusal didn't move Patroclo.

"I knew you wouldn't accept. I just wanted to prove a point. To prove how little you care about getting ahead," he explained.

"So who's really going to do the job?" I asked out of curiosity.

"No one. It was just something I came up with to keep you busy. No contract. No nothing. An easy job. And you turned it down."

"So, I guess his duties will fall to me," the Belgian complained, justly annoyed. It was beginning to look like Patroclo wasn't going to hire anyone but Druout. And he was going to have to build the whole thing himself. Given Patroclo's stinginess, it was a real possibility.

I left feeling a little drunk and decided to walk around for a while. When my shoes hit sand, I realized I'd walked toward the river. The Piray ran silent and slow. The white herons fishing in the distance made me want to stick my feet in the water. Every time I went to the river, I got strange desires, but I always repressed them.

I sat down on the bank with the sun burning my face. I kept thinking about Egypt and the religion of the pharaohs. A prayer from the Book of the Dead rattled around in my brain. I could see a whole gallery of gods with animal-like faces: crocodiles, jackals, falcons, geese, goats, sheep, serpents. I thought I'd forgotten their names—learned from the inflamed readings of my adolescence—but one by one they surfaced like words in a secret message: Osiria, Amon, Ra, Horus, Hator, Toth, Anubis, Shu, Tefnut, Ket, Nut. Then one particular name blazed forth and brought the scrutiny to a halt. Nephetys, the name of a goddess. Immediately I thought of the Muse and called her by that name. I had no idea what it meant. But I knew that four thousand years ago, she'd been a minor deity, worshipped by only a small group of followers. I imagined her loved by some splendid, spiritual youth, who'd been forgotten over time but was revealed to me now, in a painting—a triple-phallused falcon. Yes, Nephetys . . .

SIX

Julia del Paso y Troncoso got us out of bed on Sunday to tell us she'd been raped.

Talia grew paler than the victim herself and hurriedly buttoned up her robe, as if the rapist had been lurking outside. I was horrified but at the same time couldn't wait to hear the gruesome details.

Julia stood there staring at us innocently, like a messenger boy waiting for a tip.

I didn't know what to do. I wanted her to burst into tears, so I could at least give her a hug, comfort her somehow. She didn't move. Pathetic and childlike in her pale yellow jumpsuit—if you could ignore her voluptuous hips—she looked like a banana waiting to be eaten.

Julia didn't know what to do. "I'm confused," she said, "but promise me one thing, that you won't say anything to Mother and Daddy."

"Who was it?" asked Talia.

"Alex Tambas."

Three years before, Julia had been in love with Alejandro Tambas. He was a friend of ours. A sensitive, talented, charismatic man with more good qualities than the average mortal could tolerate. He would have made an excellent artist, scientist, or politician, except for one thing. He was a little crazy. For a few years, he'd been in and out of mental institutions. He'd seen so many doctors, had so many tests, that eventually no one really knew if he was sane, crazy, a genius, or just an asshole. If you asked him, he'd tell you; in fact, he was more likely to speak honestly about his lunacy than his sanity. But all that aside, I couldn't believe he'd hurt a fly, much less rape someone.

"Alex Tambas, the Alex we know?" I asked.

"Alex, the man you were in love with? Mother paid his hospital bill once."

Julia nodded; her lips were tightly closed. She liked pantomime, but this time, I figured it was the shock that made her speechless. I waited anxiously for her to speak; my curiosity was killing me. Finally she began to speak and told us the whole story.

The night before—actually it was about three o'clock in the morning—Paco García dropped her off in front of her house and immediately drove away. He hadn't escorted her to the door, because he knew she didn't like that sort of thing. She didn't like for men to open the door for her or even to accompany her through a dark alley. After he'd left, Julia saw a figure in the shadows some twenty meters from the house. She remembered the kid who got electrocuted on the barbed fence. The figure came nearer, and, as soon as it reached the street light, turned into Alex Tambas.

"Well, look who's on the prowl," she said, smiling.

At first she thought he was drunk, but she couldn't smell any alcohol. She wasn't afraid. She'd never been afraid of Alex. Actually, he was the one who'd always drawn up like an oyster when she'd come into a room. What was he doing there? He said he wanted to use the telephone. She couldn't say no, and, together, they tiptoed into the house. The light was still on in Patroclo's office. He was looking over the plans for the pyramid. They climbed the stairs silently and went into the library to use the phone. Alex dialed the number and waited. No one answered. "Shit!" he exclaimed and slammed the receiver down. Then he turned his angry stare on Julia. She felt engulfed, squeezed. His movements became brusque. His eyes looked wild. He looked like a different person. Julia was frightened. Suddenly, the moon, which had lit their way up the stairs, went behind a cloud. The room was dark.

"Let's go out on the terrace," he whispered, grabbing her by the arm.

Her body was trembling. Her face was wet with perspiration. "Why do you want to go out there?" she stammered. She felt weak all over.

She thought she heard him say, "Let's lie down together and watch the stars."

He dragged her toward the terrace, holding her roughly, then gently, like a policeman hauling a prostitute off to jail.

The night, in pools of darkness, was perfect for a swim. Julia could hear two drunk men laughing in the distance. He told her to take off her clothes, and she did as he said.

She summed up the rest of her story in one sentence: "Then he did everything to me."

"Standing up?" I asked.

"No, lying on the hard tiles. There was a lounge chair nearby, but I wasn't about to suggest we use it."

Talia was angry. "Why did you take him into the house at three o'clock in the morning?"

"I didn't see any harm in it. Mother was there asleep, and Daddy was working in the study. I could have screamed, and they would have heard me."

Talia retorted like a prosecuting attorney. "So why didn't you?"

"He hadn't done anything—not in the house. I didn't want him to think I was crazy."

"But when he got you out on the terrace, you could have run or called for help," Talia argued.

"I was afraid. They say you shouldn't try to fight off a rapist. It's a good way to get yourself killed."

"You certainly made his job easy for him. He was probably trying to seduce you, and you played right along," Talia said maliciously.

"Leave her alone," I interrupted. "Have a little compassion. You might try calling a doctor, instead of giving her the third degree. She may be hurt."

"A doctor? You think she's been stabbed or something? He made love to her, for Pete's sake! Which doesn't require medical attention!"

Julia burst into tears.

"If I'd come here bleeding to death, you wouldn't be treating me this way. You'd be happy if he had stuck a knife in me." She fell to her knees and started beating the floor with her fists. I tried to control her. She screamed with rage and struggled to get free. I held her wrists so tightly that her hands turned blue.

She stopped crying and sat quietly on the floor. Talia squatted down beside her, without touching her. Talia had never learned to express her feelings physically.

"I'm sorry," she said. "I didn't mean to be so hard on you. I've seen a lot of rape victims. It makes me angry. I don't stop asking questions until I find something, anything, to convict the attacker. I know it's hard to say exactly what happened.

These stories never make any sense. That's what frustrates me. Do you understand?"

"I understand. But I'm not going to have Alex arrested. I'd be embarrassed to death to have to testify in court." Her nose was red, and tears were running down her face.

"You don't need to decide that now," I intervened. "Let's get you taken care of first. Did he hit you or hurt you in any way?"

"No, he wasn't violent. He kept saying over and over, 'I love you, I love you,' till I practically fainted from hearing it. Then he took my necklace, bracelet, and rings."

"He ripped them off of you?" Talia asked, still looking for evidence.

"Not exactly. He asked me for them, and I handed them over. He said, 'Lend me your trinkets, my queen,' and I took them off and gave them to him. I was afraid not to."

Julia's description of the robbery sent Talia completely out of control. She started lambasting rapists, murderers, male chauvinists, and men in general. She wanted to strangle Alex, stick needles in his eyes, castrate him with a dull knife. Talia seldom flew off the handle, but when she did, she would shake all over, like a broken-down motor. That day, the whole room seemed to shake.

No one could have said a word till she finished, but when she did, we all remained silent. We sank down in the shadows of the room. The curtains held in its cool seclusion. One ray of light came in and fell on Julia's red sandals.

Our silence was pointless. It couldn't conceal the question which stood out like a Christmas tree: What were we supposed to do? There wasn't any clear answer. Talia and I could have simply slipped away. But to do so meant turning away from the girl in the pale yellow jumpsuit sitting in the middle of the floor, like a question mark. Ignore the black circles under her eyes, her pale cheeks, her sadness. At any rate, she didn't let us ignore her. Her mind was clear on one point:

"There's one thing I'm sure about. I'm not going to let

anyone examine me. Having a pelvic would be almost as bad as being raped."

Our hands were tied. She wouldn't allow us to tell the authorities or her parents. I'm not sure why she behaved that way, but I suspect she was afraid of her father, of what he might do. She knew he'd have Alex eliminated, and she didn't want a man killed on her account. We listened, halfway expecting her to ask us to forgive him. That was out of the question. He might try it again—there was no way of knowing.

"I don't give a damn what happens to Alex," Julia said. "What worries me now is the chance that I might be pregnant."

"Is that possible?" Talia asked.

"Yes, it's possible. He wet inside of me."

I smiled. Julia had just given a new meaning to the word "wet."

I sneaked a look at her waistline. Believe it or not, it looked bigger. I knew that a one-day-old fetus couldn't possibly make her stomach swell. But still, I was sure she was pregnant. I would have bet money on it.

❧

I CALLED Esteban, the gynecologist, and got him out of bed. On Sundays, he slept the sleep of the dead—if he didn't get dragged out of bed to deliver a baby. Otherwise, his children intercepted his nonprofessional calls. When he woke up, they'd have breakfast and spend the rest of the day looking at bad videos—the worst he could find. That way, if he got a call, he wouldn't mind so much leaving in the middle.

"Sorry to wake you, but I've got a problem. I need some sort of morning-after remedy, something to prevent pregnancy after the fact. It's been less than twelve hours."

"You've gotten yourself into a mess, and now you want me to straighten it out," he said, yawning between words.

"I'll be there in five minutes to pick up the prescription."

"Wait a minute. I'm not going to give you any such thing. Talia has every right to get pregnant, if she wants to. Go ahead and become a father, before you're old enough to be a grandfather."

"You don't understand. It's not for Talia. It's for a close friend."

"You've got a mistress?"

"Yes."

"I don't believe it. Put Talia on the phone."

"Why, so you can destroy what's left of our marriage? She doesn't know, so keep your mouth shut."

I begged and flattered, flattered and begged, until finally he agreed to give me a prescription.

"You handsome rascal," Talia said, pinching me on the cheek. "You're an incorrigible liar." She paused for a minute and, realizing the implications of what I'd told him, asked, "Why did you make up such a story?"

"What else could I say? You know how obsessed he is with your getting pregnant," I explained.

"But now I look like a fool, the cuckold wife. Couldn't you have thought of something else to say? He'll probably tell his wife, and then I'll be the laughingstock of the town."

"He's not going to tell Rosa. Doctors don't talk about their patients to their wives."

"You mark my word. At this very moment, he's waking her up and telling her the whole lurid story. He doesn't fool me. He's completely henpecked, and she probably knows every file in his office by heart. That's why I wouldn't set foot in that office. I'm not about to give her anything to talk about."

"That's not true," I hastily denied. "You don't go to him, because I won't let you. He's in love with you, and I've known it for a long time. But he'll never get his hands on you, not if I can help it. I'm not that stupid."

"Shut up!" Julia cried. "You sound like a couple of

magpies. Besides, what does any of this have to do with you? I'm the one with the problem, not you. Just tell me what Esteban said. Is he going to give me the medicine or not?"

A short time later, I gave Julia the morning-after shot, not in the bottom, as I had hoped, but in the arm. She instinctively rolled up her sleeve. I was afraid I might break the needle off in her muscle, but, fortunately, it met with little resistance, and, with a squeal from Julia, penetrated the skin. I thought I might have scrapped a nerve and paralyzed her whole arm. But it was all right. One drop of blood oozed out, and I wiped it away with a cotton ball.

I saved the cotton and, later, looked at it, smelled it, might have even tasted it, if the blood hadn't been mixed with medicine and alcohol. But sadly, I hadn't been able to capture the essence of the Muse.

You see, Julia was the Muse. And when she knocked on my door that morning, she broke down the wall between us. The distance between us snapped like a piece of elastic. Before then, she'd been untouchable, abstract, the protagonist of a false drama I acted out day after day, to an audience of one— Licurgo. But that Sunday, she surfaced, took on real dimensions, became tangible. It was as if I'd gone to a séance, laughing my head off at the absurdity of it all, and poof! my long-deceased lover had suddenly materialized before my eyes. That Sunday, when I opened the door and Julia walked in, she wasn't smiling, wasn't her usual optimistic self. She was destroyed. A cloud hung over her.

I'd known Julia for years, watched her grow, seen her jump from her mother's lap into the arms of her first boyfriend. But when she came into the house that morning, her pained expression revealed a new side of her, a side that reminded me of myself. Discovering that common trait forced me to remake my image of her, and to create a new image, one that I could accept completely.

Julia was her parents' favorite. Paradoxically, she thought they didn't love her. In place of love, she demanded clothes, money, and freedom. But whatever they offered, she was

58

never satisfied. If they paid too much attention to her, she accused them of smothering her. If they let her go her merry way, they were indifferent.

Many men fell in love with Julia, but most of them were too delicate for her taste. She liked the hairy he-man type, though I believe they actually frightened her. That was the only type who could control her. Around more passive men, she became a she-devil. With aggressive men, she became totally docile.

Julia came and went as she pleased. Her parents never knew where she was or when to expect her. When she had a date, she never showed up on time, if at all. She seemed to enjoy standing men up. It would have taken someone with little pride and a great deal of patience to get along with her. Actually, she didn't seem very fond of men. She spent most of her time with her girlfriends, who, according to Patroclo, spent her money, borrowed her clothes, used up her cosmetics, wrecked her car, and, once in a while, even stole her boyfriends. None of which seemed to bother her one bit.

Julia was attending classes at the university. She was a great coed. She could copy several pages of exam material on one thigh. She was studying to be a veterinarian, but not because she liked dogs and cats. She hated pets but loved horses, especially the noises they made and their big erections. Also, she thought being a vet would be safer than being a doctor. At least if one of her patients died, she wouldn't feel like a murderer.

When she was eight, she fell off a pony and had to have stitches over one eyebrow. Of course, Patroclo had the horse killed at once, without even asking what had happened. The cut left a small scar that always bothered her, but the plastic surgeon refused to operate. He told her to see a psychiatrist. But she refused and never fully recovered from the damage it had done to her ego. She often felt ugly, inferior, or depressed—feelings that got in the way of everything she tried to do. She gave up tennis, because she knew she'd never be a champion, and being mediocre wasn't enough. Her dancing career went a similar route. Her father thought she might become a real swan, but, by puberty, she'd begun to look more like a cancan girl than a sylph. It's unfortunate that she didn't continue. Dancing would have been good for her. An orthopedist had recommended it. She'd been born with one leg longer than the other one and, for a long time, had to wear a built-up shoe. I'm not sure that she ever got all right.

Julia's sex life was a mystery. Sometimes I imagined her with secret lovers—servants, bums. Sometimes I suspected her of sleeping with her sissy boyfriends or with some hairy, macho type. Other times I trusted her completely. Her parents had doubts, too. They wondered about her relationships with women. None of us could find out anything. Her sex life remained as mysterious as a Tibetan mandala.

Talia was affectionately hostile toward her sister. She treated her with a sort of gentle toughness. That morning, she'd gone overboard. She had been entirely too hard on Julia.

"You didn't have to be so tough on Julia," I said.

"I didn't have any choice," she replied. "What happened was partly her own fault, for being out till three o'clock in the morning. She forgets that she's a woman. She thinks she can go out gallivanting, like a man. I ought to tell Mother and Daddy so they can see what she's gotten herself into. It's their fault, too, for being so lenient. They never let me get away with half the things she does."

SEVEN

Alex's barrio was very different from mine. Going from one to the other was like entering another dimension. The houses were simple and old-fashioned. A squadron of sleepy chickens perched in a burned tree guarded the entrance to the barrio. On every side, I could see barefooted children, patches of vegetables, and poorly kept grass. The sidewalks had gradually been worn away by the cold.

I walked up to the front of Alex's house. The door had two parts, and the upper part was open. I looked in at the freshly scrubbed brick floor. A manger scene sat on the table year round.

Alex's mother was standing in the living room. She was a sad-looking woman, whose only object in life had been to take care of her son. Her dress was faded and worn. She never talked to visitors but appeared at the right moment carrying a tray of drinks. Some of Alex's friends thought she was the maid.

When I walked into Alex's room, I nearly choked on the tobacco smoke. Ashes covered every available surface. There was hardly a molecule of oxygen in the air.

Alex was lying in bed, nude from the waist up. A slow jazz piece was playing on the stereo. The record was scratched and the same part kept playing over and over. Alex wasn't paying any attention. He was just lying there, pale and unshaven, a sickly, romantic version of Hamlet.

He got up, said hello, and felt my coat pocket. "Got a cigarette?" he asked.

His calmness totally disarmed me. I'd gone there, like Ivanhoe, to defend a woman's honor. I was ready to slap him across the face with my glove. Instead, I encountered an old schoolmate, who was ill, almost delirious. Our history together pleaded his case. I was calm, hoping he might be innocent. He wasn't retarded or insane, not the kind of lunatic who went around raping women.

I was so angry I was shaking. I could feel the blood throbbing in my temples. I couldn't help myself. It had come over me as easily and indifferently as putting on a hat. I grabbed him by the collar and pushed him up against the wall, while I screamed in his face:

"You low-down bastard! I didn't come here so you could bum cigarettes off me. I came to settle a score. You were man enough to rape my sister-in-law. Now let's see if you're man enough to take a beating."

"I didn't do anything to Julia. I swear I didn't touch her. Let go of me. I can explain everything," he said. My nose was an inch from his. The tobacco on his breath was making me sick. His cheeks were trembling. His lips turned blue every time I knocked him against the wall.

"You dirty son of a bitch. If I ever see you near Julia again, I'll hang you up by the balls and cut you up into little pieces."

Then, suddenly, I deflated, like a balloon. All of the anger went out of me. I let him go and sat down, wounded by my own fury. He ran out of the room, and I was relieved. I hoped he'd keep on running and never come back. If he did, I would have to keep my promise, and I was in no shape to carry out such a threat.

I opened the drawer to his night stand. A pair of round stones, like sad cow eyes, looked up at me. They were Julia's. The idiot hadn't even bothered to hide them. A clear sign of mental unbalance, I thought.

His poor distraught mother came into the room. She didn't try to scold me. Like the good thief's mother, she pleaded her son's case with her eyes. But the index finger of one hand seemed to accuse me. I'd have to explain what had happened.

I sat down in a worn-out chair. Everything in the room seemed worn-out, except for a cool, damp breeze that was blowing in through the open door. I looked at her and couldn't think of a way to explain my presence in her house. She looked like an offended madonna, with her old-fashioned bun and somber expression. She wasn't going to hear me out.

As briefly as possible, I told her what had happened. She remained motionless. Flies were swarming around my head, but not even one moved in her direction. I said that we wouldn't go to the police, but that Alex would have to stay away from Julia. If he didn't, he'd live to regret it. She didn't seem to understand. I told her that Alex ought to be in a mental hospital, and she nodded.

"I knew something wasn't right. Alex has changed. My poor boy . . . He used to be so gentle. That was his best quality. I don't know what's happened to him. He's bad, then good, then bad again."

She made Alex sound like some mischievous prince. Fate had turned her noble son into a sad buffoon. It broke my heart to hear her speak. I turned down the drink she offered me and left the house, feeling really lousy.

When I got outside, I started feeling nostalgic. I could have repressed it, but, instead, I gave free rein to my memories of high school. I couldn't wait to get home and look at my graduation picture. Study the faces of happy adolescents now changed into sad adults. I forced myself to remember every detail of the photograph. The members of the Light and Knowledge Club. A chorus of civilized grins, perfect teeth, shining faces, and strong bones. There wasn't a single vitamin deficiency among them. All physically and spiritually healthy. All Roman Catholic, except for the occasional atheist, to be expected in a group of eighteen-year-olds.

They all had ordinary names and each one meant something, like the names of characters in an absurdist play. Teófilo Fernández, who'd never managed to get past the Age of Pericles; when he spoke, he transported his audience to a theater in the round. Antonio Extremadura, a born leader, an ambitious social climber; I'd have never guessed he'd end up dealing drugs. Licurgo and Esteban, who always sat at the back. Raúl Miller, the weird one in the group; he'd spent half his life in foreign mental hospitals but eventually came home sane and a little shy. Lucas Ruíz, with his mouth between a smile and a complaint, a mouth that would survive an overdose and a leap from the highest building in the city.

I couldn't remember the girls' names. They all had saints' names, like Teresita, Martha, and María del Rosario. Their interest in the club was just a pretense; once in a while, one of the bolder girls would get up the nerve to ask a question. It was always something stupid. But we'd act like it wasn't stupid and try to come up with an answer. Every Saturday, one of us would give a little talk on something, anything that came to mind. Pre-Socratic philosophy. The Kabala. Karl Marx or Groucho—we liked Groucho best. Papal encyclicals. The dark side of the Marquis de Sade. Nobody ever listened. Then we'd have a debate. The girls didn't give a damn about any of it. But they sat through it, so they could go with us later to a club. Then, on the dance floor of some discotheque, they'd get in a little dialectics of their own. Just about all of them fell in love with Alejandro Tambas. He never gave any of them a second look. So they'd move on to another guy, anybody they could get to sit with them in a dark corner of the room.

Alex was the bright star of the club, and the other members revolved around him. We all thought he was smart, and nobody ever suggested otherwise, especially Alex. But he never really did anything to prove it. He just gave speeches, like the rest of us, and I know for a fact he copied at least one of them out of a book.

Alex was born to succeed. That's probably why he never tried very hard. No matter what he did, he was going to do well, so why try? We just knew that he'd make it to the top, and some of his influence was bound to rub off on his friends.

His future was as clear as his past was murky. I'm not really sure if he knew who his father was or not. For years, he bemoaned the fact that his father, a pilot, had been killed in a plane crash. Later, he said his father was a Spanish noble and had gone back to Madrid where he could live the easy life. Some people said his father was a general and had been killed in an uprising in La Paz. And then there was this really crazy rumor that Alex had developed spontaneously from an egg that hated men. Supposedly, that's what his mother told him when he was a kid.

In spite of so many fictitious fathers, Alex didn't have a single real one. So he adopted a Spanish priest called León to be his spiritual father. León was a member of Opus Dei and thought Alex had the potential to become a great Christian politician. Alex spent his childhood preparing for that eventuality. While we were playing hide-and-seek, Alex was memorizing the speeches of obscure Spanish leaders. About the time we were paying our first visit to a whorehouse, Alex was stewing over the abstract theories of Ortega y Gasset.

When León was finished with him, he sent him off to a university in the States, one of those places where half the students are geniuses. Alex had a scholarship. Five years later, he came back with some sort of degree no one had ever heard of—a Ph.D. in political analysis, I think I heard somebody say. Somebody else said medieval art. I also heard that he'd been working for the C.I.A. I don't think it really mattered, because the fact was, Alex never got a job doing what he was trained for. He did, though, manage to get a couple of cushy government jobs. And having a strange American degree probably helped.

Then, one day that fall, he claimed that León was his father. He told him he wanted some of his inheritance in advance; half the parish house would do. He threatened to take over a radio station and demand his inheritance publicly.

People thought he was crazy, though no one seemed to know exactly what his problem was. Each one of the psychiatrists who saw him gave a different diagnosis. So he was sent to a specialist who'd never had any doubts about anything. Everybody he'd ever examined left knowing exactly what was wrong and what to do about it. In Alex's case, he immediately scribbled down, "Thirty rounds of electric shock." By the time he'd finished the treatment, Alex had totally forgotten about his birthright.

Alex's protector was terribly upset and asked to be sent to Africa. After he got there, he left the priesthood and married a widow with six kids. Maybe he needed all those children to make up for the loss of his most promising disciple.

From that time on, Alex had bouts of insanity in fairly predictable cycles. After each bout, he'd go back to living a normal life. If he could, he'd return to his old job. And if not, his friends would help him find another one. His friends wanted him to have a girlfriend, so he'd find one, usually a nice girl from a respectable middle-class family. Then everyone would shake his hand and welcome him back to reality. Just as everything seemed to be going along quite smoothly, he'd say something outrageous, like he was engaged to Caroline of Monaco. Since nobody ever knew what to make of it—was he acting silly or was he going berserk again?—they'd call up the shrink who never had any doubts about anything, and he'd give the verdict: home or the asylum. Whatever he said, the family always accepted the sentence.

EIGHT

Julia stopped by the school to see me. She was wearing an orange, loose-fitting dress made out of thin material. She wanted to talk to me about something that was bothering her, but there were other teachers in the recreation room. We'd talk later. I wanted to draw her into the light, see her body through the transparent cloth. She must have read my mind, for, without a word from me, she walked over to the window and stood leaning against the sill. Perfect. Now, I only had to position myself. I walked over and stood directly in front of her. The sun was shining all around her. Dammit! I couldn't see a thing. The material was as coarse as a gunnysack.

I had a class in five minutes, and I asked Julia if she wanted to come with me. She didn't know she was about to attend my last class at the Lyceum. I hadn't known it either, half an hour before. The principal had called me to her office. I found her reading *Amalia,* as usual. She was worried about something but managed a smile. She usually treated me as if I were one of her ex-husbands. I wondered if I was like them.

"I've received a letter from La Paz telling me you've been fired."

I didn't know whether to laugh or to cry.

"God . . . Why? What have I done now?"

"Jonah, it's not like that. You haven't been accused of *doing* anything. They're so bogged down in paperwork they hardly have time to keep an eye on a minor leaguer like you. If you really want to know why, I can try to find out. But they aren't going to tell me the truth. They never do. But if it'll make you feel better . . ."

"I don't want to talk to anybody in La Paz. I'm asking *you.* If anyone knows, you do. The teachers who like me say I'm a neurotic, irresponsible snob. I can imagine what the ones who don't like me say."

"They don't fire anybody for being irresponsible or neurotic. The reason is always political."

"Political? That's impossible. I've never joined a party. It doesn't matter to me if the Left wins or the Right."

"Everybody is on one side or the other, and if you aren't, you're the very one they're going to watch. You'd be surprised. Their spies can uncover tendencies that not even you know you have."

"But surely there aren't any spies around here," I said.

"Probably not, but it pays to be careful."

"Spies or no spies, they've messed up this time. I have friends in high places."

"You're right," she said. "You have more influence than anyone else who works here. And particularly with this government. They care more about connections than any we've had in a while."

She thought for a minute and then continued. "I wonder if this could be some kind of trick. Maybe they think that by firing someone like you, they can convince the people that they aren't playing favorites. Could that be it? Anyway, it doesn't matter what their reasons are, I say you can stay here if you want. They probably won't remember to take your name off the payroll."

I couldn't believe how kind she was being. At that moment I would have done anything to show my gratitude, read *Amalia* from cover to cover and tell her the whole story. But I didn't say that. I didn't want to offend her. I didn't accept her offer, either.

Julia and I walked down the hall. A puff of wind blew her dress up over her head. She pulled her skirt tight around her knees. I just watched. The sight of her pink panties drove me wild. Then I felt depressed.

I had just lost a job that was perfect. Perfect because it had kept me safe. Safe from the envy of my friends—who would want a job with such a miserable salary? Safe from vice of any kind. No shady dealings, no money to embezzle. The Lyceum was good for my health. I was protected against heart attacks, arterial sclerosis, sexually transmitted diseases—my students were all virgins.

Mental virgins, as well. The less you knew, the happier they were. You didn't have to worry about getting sick and missing class. They loved it when I wasn't there. Even lit candles for me to get sick or, better still, have an operation. They rejoiced at any opportunity to miss class—a strike, a death in my family, my own laziness, whatever. And I must admit, I felt the same way. We had that in common. It took so little to keep them happy. Putting off an exam. Good grades. Forgetting to take roll. Letting them cheat a little. That's all it took to keep a smile on their faces.

We went into the classroom. I was a little late, but not the last one to get there. A few girls followed me in, at the slow, steady pace of a bodyguard. Julia sat down on the back row. The girls smiled and whispered among themselves.

"Listen, please. I have an announcement to make." I rapped on the desk with my knuckles. "According to the schedule, your mid-term exam is on Tuesday the fifteenth. Don't bother to show up. You're all going to get a *B*. For sixteen weeks, you've managed to dodge every attempt I've made to teach you anything. Socrates said that ignorance was a virtue. For your ignorance—and virtue—you'll receive a *B*. In return, I have a favor to ask. It bothers me when you don't pay attention to what I'm saying. I would like for all those who are not interested to sit outside on the patio. It's a great day for a sunbath. If you want to leave, leave. That goes for everybody who's sleepy, in love, has got cramps, can't stand me, et cetera. And for those of you in Mr. Otto's fan club, you'll be able to see in his office window from the patio."

They knocked each other down trying to get out of the room. It was as if someone had let loose a man-eating rat. A handful stayed behind, which was disappointing. I'd won a few over in spite of myself. I tried not to count. There were fewer than ten. I suggested we form a circle. As they dragged their desks into position, I stepped down from the podium and joined the group, next to Julia.

"There's something I want to say," I began, "and for once, I'm not going to beat around the bush. There've been times when I hated to teach this class. Do you know what it's like when you're trying to explain something and everybody just stares at you, like you were an idiot, or looks at their watches every five minutes? O.K. So, today it's your turn. One of you is going to teach. On any topic you want: love, gossip, your favorite recipe, anything. If no one volunteers, you'll have to choose someone."

I turned away from the group, and my eyes strayed to

Julia's beautiful thighs. Meanwhile, the students shouted back and forth, trying to reach a consensus. They put it to a vote and I won.

"That won't work. I'm not a candidate. Vote again."

I was proud. I was Julio Iglesias, and they were calling me back for an encore.

"You act like teachers are the only people who can teach," I said. "How do you think anyone gets good at anything? You learn by making mistakes. A degree doesn't make you a teacher. You know who taught me more than anyone I've ever known? A kid I knew when I was little. My father told me to stay away from him, but I ignored him. If I'd paid attention to my parents, I'd still be sucking my thumb. That bad kid taught me more than I ever learned at home."

I told them about all the things Felipe had taught me. How to steal chickens, and how to steal a ride on the back of a cane truck. How to make cigarettes out of cornhusks, newspaper, and all sorts of stuff, including tobacco. How to cheat at cards and drink a whole bottle of whiskey without getting drunk.

My mistake was throwing it all out the window. See, Felipe knew you had to take risks to get where you wanted to go. Sometimes you had to jump the fence and pick the apple you wanted from somebody else's tree. I didn't do it that way. I could be far away from here, eating stolen mangoes and bathing in some lagoon. I got a degree instead.

NINE

When we left the school, I asked Julia if she wanted to have a cup of coffee. A cool breeze was blowing, and the sun had gone behind a cloud.

"I've changed my mind about you," said Julia, with a grin. "I used to think you were an intolerable idiot. Now I think you're a charming idiot." My class had rattled her brain. Her silly mood was contagious.

"Now that I know it's not all useless theory, I'd like to sit in on your class. I didn't know you taught your students to steal apples. From now on, I'm not going to miss a day."

"Sorry I can't oblige you, but I'm not going to be teaching anymore. They fired me."

"That's ridiculous. Why would they do a thing like that?"

"A telegram came from La Paz. It didn't say why."

"That's awful. You must feel awful."

"No, not really. I guess I never was a real teacher. That's why you liked the class. I didn't teach anything."

Her hand was on the table next to her coffee cup. I wanted to hold it. I thought if I picked it up carelessly, the way you pick up a bowl of sugar, she wouldn't stop me. But I lost my nerve halfway across the table.

"Why did you come by the Lyceum?"

"I'm worried about Olga. She's been getting phone calls from some crank, just like I was, and I'm afraid he's going to do something."

"Why, did he say he was?"

"No. He says nice things, even tells her he loves her, just like the one who called me. I know it's Alex."

"Did you hear him?"

"Yes, but he disguised his voice."

"But how can you be sure it's him, if it doesn't sound like him?"

"Because he did the same thing to me—pretended he was somebody else. He wouldn't think it was fun to rape someone outright, without making a game out of it."

Just then, my knee rubbed against her leg. I pressed it into her soft thigh and held my breath. She pulled back.

She went on talking. Her concern for Olga had changed the expression on her face. It looked like a big zero. I tried to comfort her. I told her she didn't have to worry about Alex, that he was in a mental hospital in Sucre, hundreds of kilometers away. If he didn't stay there, I'd put him on a plane myself.

"They probably had to put him in a straitjacket," she said. "I hate to think of him tied up like that."

74

"They wouldn't have to restrain him. They could give him a shot."

"I don't want them to do anything bad to him, not on my account."

"Do you have to feel guilty all the time?"

"No, it's something I do in my spare time," she said coldly.

"Well, I used to be that way. When I was a kid, I was really bad. I felt responsible for everything. I wouldn't even let my father trim the rose bushes."

"They have feelings. I read somewhere . . ."

"Please. Spare me the details. Every time I send a woman a bouquet, I'll think about the pain I'm inflicting on the flowers."

She reached over and pinched the tip of my nose. Her hand smelled like lavender.

"Jonah," she kidded, "you'd better not mention flowers or women, or I'll have to tell Talia. Forget about women and start looking for a job. Remember, you're unemployed."

"Not really. I still have the studio."

"That's right. You're a camera nut. I'd forgotten."

"It's my secret hobby. But I don't want to do it for a living. So I don't talk about it."

I'd never seen Julia so attentive, unless it was listening to Mercedes Sosa. The wind was blowing through her hair.

"I like photography, too. Ever since I saw a movie about a woman who got raped by some rich guy. She followed him around for days, with a small, hidden camera, till, one day, she caught him doing something bad."

I'd seen the same movie on television but hadn't been impressed.

"It was O.K., but the director didn't know much about photography as an art. Can you imagine Van Gogh running around with a pallet in his hand, trying to paint some criminal's portrait. Photography hasn't got anything to do with police work."

I'd offended her. Apparently, she was interested in the movie, because she'd been raped.

"I didn't know you had such high standards. Exactly what sort of pictures do you want to take?"

"Nudes. I like erotic art. Didn't you know?"

"No, but I'm not surprised." She looked like Little Red Riding Hood smiling at her grandmother.

"So . . . you think I'm depraved. For your information, nude portraits are very important to contemporary art. Some of us aren't content to let beauty just roam around freely in the world. We have to capture it, package it, so the public can see it, enjoy it."

My words were getting warm and moist, like Julia's lips.

"Have you been successful as a 'package maker'?" she asked.

"I don't care about that. All I really care about is making people feel something."

"The reason I ask is—well, I wonder if you might be able to help me with my photography. Teach me how to develop and everything else. School bores me, and I need to find something to do."

"Sure. I'll teach you everything you want to know. We can get started right away. We can use the studio."

I answered too soon, and I knew it. You have to string women along, act indifferent, like you'd rather be some-where else, watching football or picking your teeth.

"Great!" she exclaimed. "But get one thing straight. I'm not going to pose nude."

"I never thought about asking you to be my model," I answered.

"Well, if you should ever get the idea, now you know. I'm not interested."

"Save your breath, it'll never happen."

"And why not? Don't you think I'd be good enough, or pretty enough?"

"That's the problem. You're too pretty for what I want. I need somebody who's thin, pale, sickly, consumed with pain. It's got to be dramatic. You aren't right for it. You'd look great on the front of a fashion magazine, but I don't do that sort of thing."

My explanation wiped the smile right off her face. She had a baffled look, as if we'd been playing tennis and she'd lost.

"Suppose," she suggested, "I get amoebic dysentery and get skinny as a rail. Would you change your mind?"

I perked up. "Sure, if you lost twenty pounds."

"Well, forget it. Because I wouldn't pose nude for you, or anybody else—especially if I looked like a sack of bones."

The blood drained out of my face, but I acted like I didn't care.

❦

TALIA WAS sick with a headache. She'd been popping pills every couple of hours for two days. Then she got a cold, which made her get another headache, and so on, until it would have taken a witch doctor to drive off all her ailments.

That morning, when I left for school, the house was dark. When I got home it was lit up like a circus. Talia was well.

She greeted me happily. "Anything new happen today, dear?"

"Nothing important," I answered. "I got fired."

She was thrilled. At last her campaign to make me over had scored a victory. She could hardly keep from expressing her excitement. Her small mouth couldn't manage so much joy. Such overflowing joy that I wondered if I could have been its sole cause. She was wearing her Kelly-green dress. She always smiled when she wore it. Either the dress exuded enthusiasm all by itself, or Talia forced herself into a mood as bright as the dress.

She gave me such a smack on the lips, it deafened me. She ran off to make a call and then went to the kitchen. She came back carrying a tray of martinis—a cherry in each glass. I wondered if she was going to ask me to make love to her.

"Don't worry," she said. "There's a good side to everything. Just wait, tomorrow I bet you get a much better job."

She flopped down in my lap. I shifted quickly to protect myself against a sharp hip bone. Talia was an inept lover. She came at me like a fox set loose in a henhouse.

She spilled her martini on my shirt. Her hips mashed my crotch and cut off the circulation. I shifted again, before gangrene set in. And in that moment of relief, she plastered me with a kiss that tasted like candy and booze.

What a wife! The martini had turned her into a slut. Yes, a slut with doubtful lovemaking abilities, I thought, as she popped a button off my shirt.

Just then, the doorbell rang. I buttoned the two remaining buttons on my shirt and answered the door. It was my in-laws.

"Don't worry. There's a good side to everything," said Ira del Paso y Troncoso, after hearing the news of the day.

They watched over our finances like a couple of mother hens. We were their favorite lost cause, and to keep them happy, we always had a few problems on hand. It would have been cruel for us to deprive them of a chance to worry.

The red alert had sounded, and they were grabbing every weapon they could get their hands on. There was no stopping them. When it got to be too much for me, I curled up on the sofa with the hostile indifference of an unfriendly dog. Talia was practically kissing their feet.

Talia brought in another round of martinis. She forgot to pass them around but grabbed one for herself and slammed it down.

"I bet you're going to offer me that pyramid job again," I said to Patroclo.

"And I'll bet you wouldn't take it if I did," he replied.

"We're even then. Except you're really ahead, because you didn't need me anyway. Why did you offer me the job? You've already got that Belgian engineer."

"French engineer," he corrected me. "Don't you think

French sounds better than Belgian? The only Belgian I ever heard of was Hercule Poirot, and he wasn't real anyway—or if he was, he's dead now. And besides, this job doesn't have anything to do with detectives. Eiffel was French. So were Brigitte Bardot and Doris Day."

"Doris Day is American."

"Until some producer decides to make her French," he answered angrily.

Patroclo liked it when I made him mad. That was his favorite mood. He liked to get mad and yell at people. He managed to amass an entire fortune that way—getting pissed off and screaming at people. His ranting and raving didn't affect Ira or his daughters in the least. Which didn't say much for his temper.

"I brought you a little gift," he said, taking out a gold, metallic pyramid that fit in the palm of his hand. He said it had over four hundred powers. It could make a barren woman have triplets. It could cure all sorts of ailments—sinus trouble, hemorrhoids, colic, blood impurities. It could turn an impotent man into a raging bull and make a virile man sprout hooves, like a satyr. It could drive off bastard children, godchildren, Jehovah witnesses, and even encyclopedia salesmen.

That night Talia read the instructions and put the pyramid under our bed. She lined it up along the north-south axis, in harmony with the Big Dipper and Venus. She was trying to invoke its sexual powers, but, from the sound of her voice, she didn't need any cosmic aphrodisiac. I knew what she was up to and picked a fight. I accused her of being in cahoots with her parents.

"Your whole family has been conspiring to get me thrown out of the Lyceum. You can't fool me. And I'm not going to let you get by with it, either. If you think I'm going to take a job at a bank, forget it."

The next morning I felt like the damn thing had been shooting me with its rays all night. I had a terrible taste in my mouth. Talia had the look of a murderess. She was about to get her period. I picked up the pyramid and threw it in the trash.

I'd set the first photography class for four, so I got there at six. I figured Julia would forget our appointment. And since I didn't want to be stood up, I got there late on purpose. I can't stand people who forget to show up. So I don't show up either. That way I don't get mad.

When I got there, Andrés Tanazaki, the guy who ran the studio, was apologizing to a customer for an order that wouldn't be ready on time.

"Your sister-in-law was here. She got mad when you didn't come. That woman has a temper like a hornet. She left a message, something about cramming your lessons. I didn't understand."

I understood perfectly. I went into the office and picked up the phone. While I was calling, another customer was complaining to Andrés. He said he'd turned in a roll of film from his son's birthday party and gotten back some real porno shots. The mix-up was resolved, and the man left. Andrés was angrily muttering something about the girl in the photographs being the guy's lover.

Julia answered and bit my head off.

"I hate apologies," she said.

"Fine, then I won't expect you to apologize for being so impatient. It wouldn't have hurt you to wait fifteen minutes."

"I sat there for an hour, listening to that Chinese man's silly compliments."

"Japanese."

"I don't care what he is. His humor was about as dry as a fortune cookie."

"I'll tell him to straighten up his act."

"Well . . . what happened to you?" she asked.

"I didn't think you'd be there at four. And I don't like to be stood up. I was wrong. It'll never happen again."

"Do you know what it's called when you're afraid to trust people?"

"Being realistic? Proud? What?"

"It's called paranoia. Paranoids are always covering their asses. Trying to keep someone from doing them in."

"I thought you studied veterinary medicine, not psychology."

"I do, and that's where I've learned about men like you."

We started classes the next day. It was a beautiful, sunny afternoon, but she insisted we stay at the studio. Her burning enthusiasm made up for the loss of sunshine. I took a camera apart and explained how it worked. It's like an artificial eye that captures images, I told her. Andrés came in and smiled a knowing smile. He kept interrupting us, every two seconds, until I told him to get out and stay out.

"Don't be so rude to the man, you remind me of Daddy," said Julia.

"He's jealous. Can't you tell?"

"Jealous of whom?"

"You, me, what difference does it make? I'm going to give him his own office, so he'll stay out of mine."

I sat looking at Julia's legs and drooling. I couldn't keep my eyes off them, not even for a minute. My blood was about to reach the boiling point. If only I had X-ray vision. I wanted to see all the way to the top. The spot where her legs came together, a slit, like a big, moist smile.

Julia let me look at her legs—she didn't mind wasting them on me—, but when Andrés came in, she covered them with her skirt. She listened to my explanation without really concentrating, and every once in a while, interrupted to tell me about something that happened at the university or about some veterinary procedure, like castrating dogs. Or she'd talk about her friends. She spoke kindly of them, but it didn't make me forget how they used her.

I lost count of the afternoons we spent at the studio. She became more comfortable around me. More relaxed in the way she sat. I continued to stare at her beautiful, shining thighs. From time to time I could even see her panties. Panties of all colors. I kept up with the color she wore every day. I counted more than twelve. Some days she wore pants and messed up my calculations. Sometimes she talked to me in confidence, about herself.

"If I tell you, you won't believe me," she said. "But ever since Alex took advantage of me, I haven't been able to kiss anyone. It's like my lips are paralyzed."

"Don't worry about it. Those jerks don't deserve to be kissed, anyway. Give them a peck on the cheek."

"There's this one guy I really like who's been calling me. We go out every weekend. But it's like a weird cat-and-mouse game. I'm dying for him to get close to me and then, when he does, I pull back."

"And you're really worried about that? Maybe it's because he looks like the hunchback of Notre Dame."

"Very funny. He's great-looking. Intelligent. Nicer than you."

"Well, it's obvious. Alex has turned you against men. But let me give you a little advice. When this gorgeous man of yours starts to kiss you, bite him. I guarantee you'll get over your fear."

Going to the studio every day, I realized what a terrible mess my business was in. My Japanese employee had turned the place into his own private domain. He didn't like me being around. In fact, if he'd had the nerve, he'd have sweetened my coffee with cyanide. Instead, he tried to cover up his anger by flattering me and being overly nice. Every time I turned around, he was there offering to help me. He was driving me to distraction, and to get back at him, I started asking him for an account of the earnings.

"Tanazaki, how much have we made this month?"

"We haven't made or lost anything. Always the same."

"In other words, stagnant," I exclaimed. "Do you have any idea why?"

"Yes. It's my business sense," Andrés explained. "Now businesses fall apart, go broke, factories close, rich men lose their fortunes, commit suicide. Thanks to me, this business survives."

"I can't really agree with you. We aren't getting anywhere—you're a fake Japanese, a bluff. You don't act like a Japanese. You don't even talk like a Japanese. It disappoints the customers. Don't you see? They'd feel better about themselves if you didn't speak their language so well."

"I'm not Japanese, I'm nisei," he corrected.

"These people around here don't know the difference. And another thing. You don't know karate. Any skinny guy on the street could flatten you. You're supposed to be able to punch a guy out without his even noticing."

"To prease the señol, I join in kalate academy," he answered, and instead of saying good-bye, he executed a bow that would have put the Emperor of the Sun to shame.

After the discussion, Andrés didn't mind so much my being around. At any rate, there was plenty of room for both of us. The studio was much too large, but since Patroclo paid the rent, I hadn't bothered to find a smaller place. We attended the public in the front rooms. The darkroom was in the back. I had an office. Andrés had two rooms, one where he made coffee and another, with a bed in it, where he entertained his geishas. That left space for a junk room, which eventually became a breeding site for a new kind of light-colored cockroach.

During the first winter, the roof leaked in a dozen places. That summer, we nearly burned up. We got someone to fix the roof and put in air conditioning. After that, the roof leaked year round, and it was hotter than hell.

About the time I was teaching Julia how to develop film, she came in one day and told me that Olga had been raped. Olga, standing at her friend's side, looking stiff and pale, corrected her:

"I don't really know if I was raped or not."

"What do you mean, you don't know?" I asked.

"She doesn't know," said Julia.

"Well, what did he do, have sex with her or take her out for coffee?"

They looked at me with alarm, so I changed my tone.

"Don't get upset. Let's just try to understand what happened. Where did this savage act take place?"

"In her own home. In the entrance hall. It's closed off between two doors. She ran into Alex on the street, and he offered to walk her home. She didn't suspect a thing. Her parents were in the next room, watching *Isuara, the Slave*."

"Olga, this is really awful. I'm so sorry," I said.

"Don't say you're sorry yet. We don't even know if I've been raped or not."

What I should have said was "I'm sorry you missed the best episode of the story," and that would have ended the whole business. Instead, I kept on playing the same tune:

"Really awful! He must have drugged you."

"No, he didn't give me anything. He just stared at me and stripped me from the waist down. That's all I remember."

"You're in shock. That's why you can't remember," I suggested.

"Maybe. Maybe not. There're all these images in my head, but they don't seem real. I guess I went blank, and then I panicked and the images were created by the panic. To fill my mind with something."

"So concentrate on the images. Can you see yourself being raped?"

"I don't know. I've never been raped before."

Olga wanted to find out if she was still a virgin. An intact hymen was absolutely necessary if she were to continue leading the same life. So far, she'd played the role of maiden to a T. Always sat with her knees pressed tightly together. Didn't trust tampons, no matter what the advertisements said. Always spoke properly. Never used harsh, masculine tones. When she stuck her finger in a glass of milk, nothing happened. If she hadn't been a virgin, it would have turned sour. And even if her boyfriend sprouted horns and she was in his arms, all puckered up like a fish, he wouldn't have done a thing. He respected her too much.

Olga was a lot like Julia, but she wouldn't agree, unless you said it the other way around: Julia was a lot like her. It was a case of which came first, the chicken or the egg. And nobody could say which, so they both claimed to be the first. Olga liked it when boys flocked around Julia, and she'd flirt back, with her hair falling over one eye. For Olga, it was like looking at herself in the mirror. But she wasn't totally satisfied. When she looked at Julia, she saw her own shortcomings, too. So she fussed at Julia for copying her. Dressing the way she dressed. Trying to make her body look like her body. She thought Julia was trying to steal her soul. So Julia would go out and buy new clothes. Then Olga would get over it and start copying Julia. She had the right, she thought. Julia had copied her.

Olga's father owned a dress shop and catered only to the most elegantly dressed women in town. He was married to a dyed blonde, who helped him in the shop and never made but one mistake in her life—which was thinking her husband was more of a man than he was. About the time she started having hot flashes, she sought consolation with a sales representative from the shop. That was the first and only time she cheated on her husband. She wondered why she'd never done it before. And that same night, she sat down on the foot of her fifteen-year-old daughter's bed and warned her:

"Don't wait till you're married. That's the best advice I can give you."

"Why, Mother?"

"Because I waited, and till this day I regret it. Do you want to spend your whole life eating chicken soup without even getting a little taste of anything else?"

Olga ignored her mother's advice. While her friends were off keeping some back-alley abortionist in business, she watched over her virginity like a mother hen. "I'm not going to go to bed with anybody before I get married—I don't care who it is." And between strikes and military takeovers, she wasn't going to get through school before doomsday.

Strangely enough, there were men willing to put up with her high morals. Willing to keep their hands to themselves, while they raided her father's liquor cabinet. Sometimes Olga regretted taking such a hard line against her mother's advice, especially when her boyfriend zipped up his fly. She was tired of being pure and frustrated. But how could she tell *him* that? What could she do? She couldn't go out and do it with somebody else. Fat chance of finding somebody else. What guy would be fool enough to try anything with her? Her virginity was a *fait accompli*. Only a crazy man, like Alex, would have tried to mess around with her.

Even so, she wasn't exactly sure what had happened. Did he rape me . . . or didn't he, she wondered. The thing she remembered most clearly was what really baffled her. He kept saying over and over, "I love you, Julia. I love you, Julia."

Olga, without realizing it, was making both of us feel guilty as hell. Julia could have kicked herself for not telling Olga that Alex had raped her. Her friend would have known better than to let Alex into her house. I felt badly, because I hadn't forced Alex's family to put him away for good. And there sat Olga, between the two of us, trembling and smiling, like a child who'd just had her first tooth yanked out.

I decided to take the initiative. "I have a friend who's a gynecologist. Esteban is his name. If you'll let him examine you, he can tell you if you've been raped."

"I've already been examined by a nun who's a nurse. She said about sixty percent of my virginity was intact."

"This may not be exactly her line," I said. "Either you are a virgin or you aren't. There's no in between."

"You're right," Olga said. "Before I get upset, I ought to know if I've been raped or not. I'd like to see your friend."

Esteban's office was empty. It was one of those days when he actually wished one of his patients would come down with some awful disease. He reminded the Almighty not to go overboard curing the sick. He'd put doctors on the earth for a reason.

We explained the problem to him and then left him alone with Olga. Olga looked a little frightened at the prospect of crawling up on the examination table, with its foot supports so far apart.

We sat in the waiting room and looked at disgusting pictures in a medical journal till we were sick to our stomachs.

Olga came out with a smile on her face. She was so happy she'd forgotten to zip up her pants.

"I'm fine. I'm still a virgin."

I went into Esteban's office. I wanted them to think I was paying the bill. I knew he wouldn't take the money.

"You've taken a load off her mind," I told him.

"I imagine so. If I'd told her the truth, she'd have flipped her lid."

"What do you mean?"

"Her hymen's a goner. It's been torn—recently I'd say. No sign of a scar yet. He finished her off, all right."

"Why did you lie to her? Don't you think she should know the truth?"

"We don't just cure our patients, we also try to keep them from getting sick. Olga's so innocent, and her virginity is so important—if I tell her the truth she might kill herself. It's better this way." He was straight and solemn, as if Galen himself had just patted him on the back.

TEN

I used to hate cats until one of them led me to Julia. It was an alley cat, a pesky little thing. I knew there was a cat around, as soon as I smelled his shit in the garage.

That Tuesday, Julia dropped by the house to give Talia a talking-to. It was a family custom—berating the weaker members of the clan. Every time Talia had one of her sick spells, someone would come over and give her a tongue-lashing.

It never did any good. If anything, it made her worse. But

they had to do it. No matter what. They thought it was good for her.

"You're a pitiful excuse for a social worker," Julia said. "What would your clients think if they could see you now? How can you do anything for them, if you can't even help yourself?"

A cat was meowing somewhere in the room. I was reading Cortázar. Talia was sitting next to me, brushing her hair with rough strokes. The face in the mirror was cruelly indifferent. If she'd realized how angry she was, she'd have walked out in the middle of her sister's sermon. She decided to sit it out, until she could finish putting on her make-up. Lately she'd started painting her face before she left for work. I thought she might be trying to look sexy. It didn't matter to me if she looked like a streetwalker. But she couldn't pull it off. The best she could do was a dolled-up usherette.

Talia gave me a kiss. She was wearing fruit-flavored lipstick—apple, or maybe grape. I could hear her heels still clicking after she'd closed the front door. I wasn't sure if she'd left for work or gone shopping. She'd left me alone in the house with Julia! I kept wracking my brain for something to say to her. My tongue wouldn't budge. She was in a bad mood, and I decided not to bother her.

"Can you hear a kitten?" she asked. "Where is it? It sounds like it's hungry. Do you feed it?"

Julia didn't like pets—or so I thought—but that little kitten could have softened the heart of a storm trooper. Its voice echoed in all directions, like a ghost.

We searched under the bed, in the dressing room, and in the bathroom. Not a sign. The sound, which seemed to be coming from the main patio, got louder and louder. We walked toward it. The cat had to be inside the pipes. I could guess what had happened. The water pipes from that part of the house emptied out into the main patio. One end was open, and the other was covered with a grate. The kitten must have crawled into the open end and gotten trapped. I could see its head near the end of the pipe.

"Let's go to the other patio. He got in that way, so he

should be able to get out," Julia suggested. "What's the cat's name?"

"Petunia."

"Petunia? I thought it was a male."

"It is, but he looks like a Petunia when he walks."

"Here kitty, kitty," Julia called. The cat meowed louder. I don't know if he was pissed off for what I'd said or if he couldn't walk backwards.

Julia got so hoarse she had to stop. She looked kind, but it wasn't an unselfish kindness. She thought she was better than most people. She loved herself in a childish, blind sort of way. Maybe she thought the cat was a little like her. They shared a childlike fear, a kind of timidity that sometimes got them into trouble. I wasn't like that at all—there wasn't anything child-like about me anymore. When I was sad, I was sad like a grown-up—feebly and dispassionately sad.

I could see what was going to happen. The cat wasn't going to come out. It was going to stay in there and starve to death. I'd have to put it out of its misery, and the body would probably start to reek before the day was out.

"Can't we call the fire department?" she asked.

I wasn't about to call the fire department. I could just hear it on the evening news: "Firemen Save Cat for Pretty Coed."

Ridiculous, middle-class gossip.

Her anguish was beginning to get on my nerves, when, suddenly, I got an idea. I could take the grate off the pipe and pull the cat out.

I hit the grate three times, and it came loose. But the cat started to back off. I had to stick my arm in up to the elbow. I pulled him out and handed him to Julia.

She cried for joy. She was about to give her kitty up for lost, but there he was, safe and sound.

I stood next to them, idly scratching Petunia's head. I was a terrible hypocrite.

The direct approach wasn't my style, so I began to move in circles. I let my hand float from the cat to Julia's left hand. I sort of let it fall on top of hers and then grabbed hold of her hand, like a kitten taking hold of its mother's nipple. I looked at Petunia, and he looked back at me.

I wasn't getting anything out of holding Julia's hand. I felt like a dog with a plastic bone. Besides that, I was beginning to sweat; she didn't seem to be offended. She was sweating, too. I put my arm around her shoulders and led her into the house.

I'd forgotten that Emilia was in the house, but, fortunately, she was struggling with a mountain of dirty dishes. She never suspected that we were sitting on the sofa or that I had my arm around Julia. Julia was holding the cat in her lap. We must have looked as chaste as Mary, Joseph, and the Baby. I didn't feel much like Joseph. A voice inside my head kept saying, "Don't just sit there. Do something, stupid!"

I was torn between continuing the innocent embrace or going ahead with it. It was an all or nothing situation. I might as well risk it. But what if she bit me? I suddenly remembered her fear of kissing. "If you'll let me, I could cure your phobia." That's what I wanted to say. But she didn't give me a chance. She stuck her nose in Petunia's face and said, "He smells like milk."

Milk? How could he smell like milk, if he hadn't nursed in two months?

❧

I WALKED around smiling the rest of the day. I felt like a schoolkid. I was as high as a kite. Talia's family could sense that something was wrong. I was vulnerable—they knew it—and they flocked around me like buzzards. "Here's our chance to get him settled into a new job," they said to themselves. "But if we blow it, he may never work another day in his life." Before I knew what had hit me, they'd arranged an interview down at the Bank of Commerce.

My interview was at noon. When I got there the bank was empty. Either business was bad, or everyone had gone to lunch. I crossed the clean waxed floor. I liked it. I seldom got a chance to walk on a mirror. The employees—who were wearing white shirts and blue ties, like airline pilots—didn't look up from their work.

A severe-looking secretary was guarding the entrance to the administrative offices on the second floor.

"I'd like to see the manager," I said.

"Señor Canez is in Panama. May I ask why you need to see him?"

"I'm Jonah Larriva. I have an interview."

"Oh, you must be the new legal advisor."

I hoped not, but I smiled and said I was.

"You need to see the assistant manager. He'll be with you in a moment."

The office was immaculately clean. For a quarter of an hour, I sat there as stiff as a statue; the secretary never opened her mouth.

"Is the assistant manager here or not?" I asked.

"He must be a little late getting back. He went to lunch with his secretary. Sometimes they take a little longer. They get to talking, and, well . . . But he left the head of foreign exchange in charge. You may speak with him."

She called a Señor Martínez. He wasn't there, either.

"He's not here today. He's trying to find a dog that bit him. They think it has rabies. The credit manager is taking his place."

She made another call.

"His secretary says he's not in, but I think she may be covering for him. He gets so many calls, sometimes he holes up in his office."

"And there isn't anyone who takes his place?"

"Yes, of course. If someone's out, the person directly below always takes over. It's like the army. Let's see, I could call . . ."

"Don't bother. I have to be going, but my yard man will be over in a few minutes. Perhaps he could speak to your doorman. Maybe they could work something out."

I turned and left the office. The floor was so slick, I couldn't resist taking a few running steps and sliding the length of the hall. No one seemed to notice.

❧

I'VE TRIED over and over to piece together what happened that afternoon. I've ordered, inserted, mutilated, and repaired my thoughts. But I haven't been able to come up with a clear picture. I've gone over it so many times, it's beginning to look like a worn-out fingernail file. Even so, I can't leave it out.

After the episode with the cat, I didn't feel comfortable around Julia. I kept trying to impress her. I gave her a photograph album with pictures from the movie *Bilitis*, and we looked through it together. I told her the story as we went. I felt encouraged, looking at those poetic, nude images. I described them as if I'd taken them myself, as if the author had entered my body and was speaking through my mouth.

"Know the secret to photographing a nude woman?" I asked. "You have to pretend that the camera is a penis. Look at this picture. He's been bold here. In this one, he's been more gentle."

She didn't care for the pictures of Lesbians. She liked what I had to say about them even less.

"This is all just a lot of talk," she complained. "You're all right with words, but what about the camera? I'm beginning to wonder if you're serious about this. I thought you really wanted to be a photographer. By the way, where are your models?"

"Don't you worry. When I need them, I have plenty."

"I'd like to see them for myself. I want to see these pale, thin models of yours."

"Fine. I'd be happy to introduce you."

"They must look like real, romantic heroines. Tuberculosis is such a romantic disease."

"That's right."

"Of course, if it would help, I could lose weight. But I guess I'm just too sexy," she said. She was wearing skin-tight jeans and a pale blue shirt. "But you can't fool me," she added. "You're dying to photograph me nude."

"Me? Photograph you nude? I've never thought about it. You don't know anything about modeling."

"I certainly do," she insisted.

"Walking around the Country Club in a bikini isn't exactly modeling."

"Well, I've never taken off my clothes in front of an audience, if that's what you mean."

"No, that's not what I mean. I just wish you'd stop acting like you know everything about everything. It takes more than a couple of Francoise Sagan novels to know something about life."

"I may not know much, but at least I'm not a hypocrite, like you! You want me to pose, and I know it."

"O.K., I admit it."

"See! I knew you'd drag me into this."

"But I knew you wouldn't want to. So just say no and forget about it."

"No, I'm going to do it. Under one condition."

"What's that?"

"I'll take off my blouse, and that's all."

"Fine."

"And one more thing. You have to use a Polaroid. I don't want any negatives floating around."

"Fine."

"You can take one picture, and you can't show it to anyone."

"You have my word of honor."

"And the room has to be dark."

"That's impossible," I protested. "I can't take a picture without any light."

"What's wrong with using a flash?"

"You want to look like the bride of Frankenstein?"

She didn't answer. She was already unbuttoning her blouse. She didn't have on a bra. Her breasts were white and smooth, like two ice-cream cones. Her nipples were pink, without a single hair, mole, or even a passion mark. They were as soft and smooth as a child's lips.

Those breasts could have carried me through a hard winter. I could have clung to them for years, like a suckling pig. If Julia had been those breasts and nothing more, it would have been enough. They drove me to distraction. They had a personality all their own. I could have talked to them, and they would have answered back. I could have married those breasts!

The photograph didn't do them justice. I couldn't do a thing with a Polaroid. I couldn't adjust it the way I adjusted my Nikon. Trying to capture Julia's beauty with that camera was like trying to catch a bird with your bare hands.

I nearly missed my chance completely. When she took off her blouse and smiled at me, my whole body started to shake. I took so many deep breaths trying to calm down, I nearly sucked up all the oxygen in the room.

When I stopped shaking, I reached over and touched her left breast. Her heart was beating under my fingertips. Her lips were dry and docile. When I kissed them, my mouth felt small. I rubbed my tongue against hers; it began to move and play with mine.

She kept saying no, over and over, but I wouldn't stop. I caressed her shoulder. She said no. I unzipped her pants. "Please, no," she moaned. She kept saying no while I was struggling to get them off. "We shouldn't do this!" she insisted, as I rubbed my hands over her body. Her face widened, her lips opened and turned red. She looked like she was getting bigger and bigger. It was like I was seeing her through an enormous magnifying glass.

Suddenly she realized she was naked.

"Let go of me," she said, pulling away.

"Don't be like that," I pleaded. "Let me get on top of you, just for a minute."

I could barely get inside of her. Some invisible doorman seemed to be blocking my entrance. I pressed, gently but firmly. She moaned and uttered the last joyful no.

By the time we finished, the whole room smelled like sex. There was a damp spot on the rug. The smell was strongest on Julia's stomach where I came. I hadn't stopped to ask if she was on the pill. But I hadn't taken any chances.

We got dressed and went out for a hamburger. Neither of us said a word about what we'd done.

ELEVEN

My mother-in-law called me up to find out about the interview.

"How did it go at the bank?"

"Awful," I said.

"Did you talk to the manager?"

"No, I didn't talk to the manager. I didn't even talk to the shoeshine boy."

"Well, don't worry. I'll handle it."

They hadn't given me the time of day at the bank, but that kind of indifference stimulated Ira. She was very sympathetic toward people who couldn't tell their heads from a hole in the ground—Woody Allen, for example. If only she could have set him straight, started him off in the right direction . . . Helping people made Ira feel needed.

When I first met Ira, she called herself Iracy. Neither name appeared on her I.D. Her real name was Iracema López de del Paso y Troncoso. She shortened it. She didn't like words of more than five letters.

"I used to fall asleep listening to my own name," she explained.

Ira was a decidedly handsome woman. She didn't have to dress up to be beautiful, but she liked to wear pretty clothes. What did a middle-aged woman have to spend her money on anyway, besides clothes and wrinkle cream? Her skin was very fair against her dark hair, cut short in a bob. When she smiled, she got little wrinkles around her eyes. She looked ten years older when she smiled, so she tried to keep a straight face. Smiling wasn't worth the price in years. According to her, her eyes were her best feature. They were dark green. She hadn't seen fit to pass them on to her daughters, but she was dying for Talia to have a child with sparkling, devilish green eyes.

She considered herself superior to her daughters. More of a woman, more mature, more imposing than they were. She liked to feel superior. That way she didn't have to envy them. At the same time, it worried her a little—being better than her own daughters. Frightened her to think *they* might envy *her*. They might not even know they were envious. Maybe their affection was envy in disguise.

Her friends knew she wasn't happy being a mother, so they told her she could pass for her daughters' sister. She hated it. It galled Patroclo even more. Made him feel like Methuselah's grandfather.

Ira would have preferred to be a stepmother. That way she and her daughters could have hated each other, pure and simple. She could have given them poison in a glass of warm milk. Fed them the tarantulas they put in her boots. It would have made life easier for her daughters, too. If Talia could have hated her mother, her psychosomatic illnesses would have disappeared. Julia could have cut out the self-abuse and told her scrounging friends to go to hell.

Of course, nothing could change the situation. The girls would go on keeping their mother in suspense, out of sorts, defensive, and fearful. Ira would go on protecting them and making sure they didn't get hurt. After all, she loved them. Like a she-wolf, but she did love them. By some prank of nature, she'd gotten a Midas touch in reverse. Everyone she touched became worthless. I can hear her now: "What's going to happen when *I* need somebody? Who's going to help *me*?"

Somebody was always giving her a hard time, first Talia, then Julia.

"Julia, your car wasn't in the garage last night."

"I lent it to Silvia."

"Yes . . . and your blue dress and the earrings your grandmother gave you."

"That's right," Julia replied, pleased to score another victory against her mother.

"Can you please tell me why Silvia needed your car all night?"

"To go to the Airport."

"The airport? To pick someone up?"

"Mother, you don't need to pretend. You know very well that the Airport is a motel."

"If people saw your Datsun there, they'd probably think it was you and not her spending the night."

"Not necessarily. Everybody knows I let Silvia use my car."

"Julia, when are you going to stop fooling yourself? Do you really think Silvia would let *you* borrow *her* car?" Ira asked.

"She doesn't have a car. And if she bought one, I wouldn't borrow it. I like to use my own," Julia argued.

"Very smart. But remember one thing: she not only

borrows your things, she tears them up. Not long ago she wrecked your car and didn't even pay to have it fixed."

"That was Sonia. She insisted on paying, but I wouldn't let her."

"Are you out of your mind? Why didn't you take the money?"

"Because I can't stand her. I didn't take her money so I would look rich, and then she would be humiliated. It worked. She's still mad."

"You have no right to use our money to show off. Instead of refusing your friend's money, why don't you refuse *our* money, for a change?"

"I could never refuse anything from you and Daddy. I love you too much."

"Try hating us a little. We could use the extra cash."

"Mother! That's a stingy attitude to take. Guess I shouldn't be surprised, coming from a rich yokel. But that's all right. I'll get you back. I'll join the jet set, and then we'll be arguing over yachts instead of cars. Can you imagine me going out with Sylvester Stallone?"

"No. Because he wouldn't like your sense of humor anymore than I do. And . . . since you're not an Onassis, you're not using the car for a week. Maybe you'll learn to take care of your things."

But Julia wouldn't learn. Patroclo would give her keys back to her by the next day. He was a tyrant with everyone except his daughters. Ira was just the opposite.

Patroclo worried about his wife being so altruistic with people outside the family, especially young men. He was suspicious of her interest in Ciro, one of his workers. He never knew if it was charity or physical attraction that Ira felt for him. I don't think he wanted to know, since he left the situation alone. Somebody told him to fire Ciro. But he didn't have to. Ciro quit. Some said he was too proud to let his boss's wife boost him up the corporate ladder. Some said he was angry about the rumors. And others said he'd run off with some roughneck chauffeur. Ira was the only one who really knew what happened.

❧

JULIA AND I were lovers. But we never said a word about it. For exactly twenty-three hours and fifty minutes, we would act like distant friends. Then for ten minutes, we'd crawl all over each other.

We went right on with the lessons. Julia was beginning to get the hang of it, more or less. I behaved like a serious teacher. But right in the middle of the lesson, I'd take her down on the carpet. With clothes piled all around us, I'd finish the lesson first, then make love to her. The carpet was covered with stains. But that was the only sign of our lovemaking.

I bought her a big cushion to lie down on, covered in a flowered print. She'd lie down quietly, chewing on a piece of gum, her eyes looking up at me obediently, and her skirt pulled up. She'd spread her legs, as if some terrible heat made her do it. I'd bend down between the arch of her legs. It didn't seem to matter that it was I and not some animal or a big puff of wind. She'd have an orgasm, get up, pull down her dress, and go right on chewing her gum, without saying a word. Just as if she'd masturbated and gone back to reading her book.

Sex for Julia was like a dream, a break from reality. If her mother had walked in without a warning, their conversation would have run like this:

"Julia, what are you doing on the floor, naked, with your brother-in-law?"

"Me, naked?"

"Yes, you. Haven't you noticed?"

"Oh . . . you're right. You'll never believe this, but I thought I was dreaming that I was taking my clothes off."

Jonah and the Pink Whale 101

"But Jonah is naked, too."

"Yes, he is. In my dream both of us were taking our clothes off."

"This is scandalous."

"Then . . . you came in and got mad at me. I felt naughty. I wanted to wake up."

"That's funny. What did you want to wake up from?"

"Mother, help me to remember. Pinch me," she would say, starting to cry.

Of course, such a silly dialogue couldn't have taken place. I always locked the door. Ira would have had to break it down with a battering ram to get in. For the time being, no one was even suspicious. Our lives hadn't seemed to change. Julia went right on going out with nice young men whom she couldn't stand. I was still my grumpy self. I was like the cat that swallowed the canary. And I was very good at covering up.

Lying to everyone else made sense to me. What I couldn't understand was hiding the truth from ourselves. It was O.K. to have sex, but talking about it was taboo! The following cryptic conversation between Julia and me was typical:

"Jonah, I need to tell you something."

"What is it?"

"Nothing has happened this month."

"When was it supposed to happen?"

"Three days ago."

"Take it easy. Even paychecks come late sometimes."

"I've always been on time."

"What do you think's wrong?"

"Maybe it's the heat."

"Maybe so. It's been really hot."

"Yeah. Particularly last month."

"We have to be more careful from now on."

"Why?"

"So you don't get so hot."

"And what if it doesn't ever happen again?"

"It'll happen, even if it takes nine months. It's like a bad check. Sooner or later it catches up with you. . . . You seem a little anxious."

"It's my nerves."

"Probably. I want you to start taking the pill."

"No. I don't want to."

"Don't be childish. If you want it to happen on time, take the pill."

"I'm not being childish. I can't swallow pills. If you could get me something that was easier to swallow . . ."

"I don't think they make a children's formula. But I'll check. In case they do, which flavor do you want?"

"Strawberry."

I was at my wit's end. Finally, I sat Julia down on my knee and explained a few things.

"Julia, my child, you are a woman and I am a man. Both of us are sexual beings. We are not neutered angels, as our behavior suggests. You must have noticed that for the last month I have been putting my penis inside of you. You must have noticed also that a white liquid comes out. Unfortunately, that liquid can make you have a baby. So, you either take the pill or buy a cradle. And another thing. I'm tired of this silence. Lovers talk about what they do, which isn't as nice as the act itself, but it's important."

"I'm sorry, but I feel ashamed," she answered.

"It upsets you, because I'm your brother-in-law."

"No. I know no one will ever find out. It's my navel. It sticks out. You must think it's ugly and deformed."

"I like your navel. Don't worry, please. It's your silence that's driving me crazy. You don't say anything, you don't do anything. You make me feel like I'm raping you."

"Funny you said that," she said, with a surprised look on her face. "The other night I dreamed an orangutan was putting his big, thick dick inside of me. Then he ran up a tree. I could see him swinging in the tree, and it was you."

Cockeyed, I thought to myself. "Julia, you haven't forgotten that it was Alex who raped you. You made love to me of your own free will."

She smiled, a little embarrassed.

"I didn't mean it as an accusation. My feelings aren't always logical. Alex made me feel like a prostitute. I felt like it was my fault, even though I knew I didn't do anything to provoke him. When I'm with you, I feel like an innocent victim. Every time we make love, it's like you're ravishing me. I don't do anything. I like it, but I don't take part in it. Rationally, I know you aren't taking advantage of me, but on the inside, I feel like you are. Do you understand?"

"No, I don't."

"I didn't explain it right. It's complicated. I don't know what to do."

"Forget about all these weird feelings."

"I can't. I can't control my feelings. But I want you to know something. I really like you . . . a lot."

"Thanks. That's the first complimentary thing you've said to me. If a judge got a hold of your diary, he'd have me locked up."

"I'd go to see you every weekend," she said, kindly.

"I'd prefer you burned your diary and kept your fantasies to yourself."

TWELVE

The man I replaced at the bank, Dr. Gumucio, was very absent-minded. When he moved out of the office, he left behind many personal belongings, including three monogrammed towels, a cigarette lighter with the inscription "For A . . . passionately, from A," a box of condoms—one removed from the container—a stale cup of coffee, and a secretary, four months pregnant.

"What happened to your boss?" I asked the young woman. "Did someone throw him out the window?"

"Abel was a bit impulsive. His horoscope said he needed a change, so he turned in his resignation and left."

"Did he get a job at another bank?"

"No. He's selling counterfeit money over on Libertad. And doing quite well."

When she smiled, she revealed her white teeth that would surely say yes to any petition or promise. Arminda had dark almond eyes—that feigned nearsightedness—and black, silky tresses. The kind of girl a guy could easily fall for.

I felt mildly uncomfortable in her presence. I moved about the office clumsily, cleaning up after Gumucio. In the file cabinet, I found a pair of stockings, a pair of pink panties, and a matching bra.

"Was Gumucio a transvestite?" I asked.

"No," she replied. "Those are my things. A few months ago I had so much work to do that I had to change here, to save time."

"Of course," I said. "I understand."

The other members of the staff received me as kindly as Arminda had. Everyone knew I'd gotten the job because of my father-in-law. That was all right with them. They preferred me to some know-it-all, who'd try to make changes in the existing order. I wasn't a threat to anyone in that little love nest.

The Bank of Commerce treated its employees fairly. They protected the higher-ups and pummeled the ones below. The harder you worked, the less you earned, and vice versa. Cashiers, secretaries, receptionists, and errand boys were up to their eyeballs in work. Their supervisors criticized them, hovered over them, and, in general, made their lives miserable. The supervisors of the lower echelon had to answer to another group of supervisors, who, in turn, answered to the assistant managers, a sappy bunch of executives who spent their time entertaining large investors and chasing secretaries. The more important the executive, the better-looking his secretary.

The man who ran the bank was called the General Manager. Since his authority was unquestioned, he never had to prove himself. He played golf five days a week. Exercise prepared his mind for the serious decisions he might have to make. His serenity was so profound, in fact, that nary a thought entered his brain. If something needed doing, it was passed on to the first person who stuck his head in the door.

Stacks of perfectly written documents, lacking only a stamp and a signature, spilled out of his drawers. They all referred to current cases involving the bank. I read over them, wondering why they had been put away in that state. I signed several of them and passed them on to Arminda to be dispatched.

"My, how efficient!" she said, intending praise.

"Wait till I get cranked up," I replied, enthusiastically.

She paid me for my effort by serving me coffee at all hours of the day. My stomach was on fire. I wouldn't be able to close my eyes for two days.

About then, Julia and Olga walked in. Viewed from behind my desk, they seemed more childish than ever. They acted just like a couple of schoolgirls, tapping on the typewriter, as if it were a piano, drawing horns on some bigwig's portrait. Julia put Arminda's pink bra on her head, and Olga tied the stockings around her neck like a tie.

"Unbelievable," Julia said. "You look just like a lawyer. Like you could be trusted—trusted not to be honest." She giggled.

"I've never thought of you as being the serious, professional type," Olga confessed. "I'm glad you've changed."

"Olga didn't believe me when I told her you'd decided to practice law."

"It just so happens I need a lawyer," said Olga.

"And you're in luck," Julia said, gaily. "You can be Jonah's first client. Go ahead, tell him."

The light that filtered through the window fell on the left

side of the girls' faces. The other sides were shadowed in pink. Olga's face looked like a reflection of Julia's. The air conditioning was groaning in the background.

"I want you to put that friend of yours, Esteban, in jail," Olga demanded.

"What are you accusing him of?"

"He deflowered me with his instruments, when he examined me. I should have known better than to put myself into the hands of a doctor. And to think, he told me I was still a virgin. I wondered why he was so eager to convince me. I've seen another doctor, and he's positive the hymen is broken."

"Esteban didn't break it," I explained. "He lied to you so you wouldn't worry."

"I knew you'd defend him. If you won't help me, I'll find someone else to put that quack behind bars."

"The judge is going to laugh in your face. Nobody, nowadays, cares whether or not a hymen is intact."

"Well, I do," Olga replied. "And I don't want my mother to know about this. She'll be thrilled that I decided to follow her good advice. I won't listen to it."

"I suggest you see my colleague Licurgo. He specializes in the problems of maidens. I'm sure he can tell you what to do. According to my contract, I can't take on any private cases," I said, crossing my fingers behind my back.

"That's not the cad who was helping Silvia, is it? The one she kicked in the shin when he put his hand down her blouse?"

"That's the one," Julia confirmed.

"Then forget it," Olga replied.

"Why don't you see a plastic surgeon?" I ventured. "He could fix you up."

"I want that gynecologist shot."

"Then see Licurgo. If he can't find a way to handle it legally—and he won't, since the doctor is innocent—he'll be glad to get rid of Esteban. He'd give an enema to the devil, for a price."

"Unfortunately, I don't like white knights with roving hands," Olga explained.

"If he misbehaves, kick him, but not in the shin, unless you want a lame lawyer," I suggested.

"He'd better be able to run like a rabbit, if he loses the case."

They left, happily, and headed for Licurgo's office.

THIRTEEN

Before dinner, at my in-laws' house, I relaxed with a glass of whiskey in my hand, enjoying the tantalizing aromas coming from the kitchen. Talia was lying on the floor, absorbed in the music coming through her earphones. Patroclo tossed me a magazine and asked me to look at the cover. I didn't see anything out of the ordinary. A girl in a bikini, with a ribbon that said Miss Something-or-Other across her chest. She had a crown on her head and was holding a scepter in her hand.

"Haven't you seen the new Miss Bolivia?" he asked.

"I don't know her," I answered, "but she's gorgeous. I've seen prettier brunettes, but she certainly won't go unnoticed." I lowered my voice. "Is she one of your girlfriends?"

"I don't have any girlfriends. She's the daughter of the country's biggest drug lord! Those gangsters have taken over. They run everything. The next thing you know, they'll be appointing judges, putting up statues of themselves, having the bishop preside at their daughters' weddings. They've got to be stopped."

"Money runs the country," I reminded him. "That's what you've always said."

He looked sad. For several weeks, ill humor had darkened his face. The reason: no one had recognized the social import of his Great Mausoleum. Articles about its construction had appeared on the inside pages of two newspapers. Apart from a few favorable lines, the comments were largely negative. Some prankster complained to the mayor, and the following Sunday's headline read: "Mayor's Office Investigates Construction of Clandestine Cemetery."

One journalist wrote:

"Rumor has it that a private cemetery is under construction. In times of economic crisis, it isn't surprising that capitalists have resorted to an untapped resource: death. They noticed, before public officials, that the public cemeteries were overstocked. Within a few years, many of us will have to resort to private burial grounds. And if private firms charge their customary high prices, the situation will be desperate. The grave will no longer be a place of rest for the poor. Death will not put an end to their mortification. They will be forced to sign IOUs that will keep their families in debt *in saecula saeculorum.*"

"This is the work of some jealous person," Patroclo explained at city hall. "It's a well-known fact that I'm building a mausoleum and not a private cemetery. It's for my family."

The bureaucrat puffed steadily on his cigarette and contemplated possible solutions to Patroclo's problem. He looked through his book of statutes but found not a single line that mentioned pyramids. How, he thought, could he issue a building permit? What sort of fee would he charge? To begin with, the building would have to be classified. A difficult procedure. The pyramid would be a private construction . . . of interest to the public . . . available to only a few select people . . . built on the outskirts of the city . . . off-limits to foreigners or undesirables. An extraordinary sort of place, he thought, . . . something like a private brothel.

The follow-up was assigned to a disoriented inspector, who, in his confusion, took Patroclo for the owner of a house of ill repute.

"I've come here," he told Patroclo, "to inspect the safety and sanitary conditions of the locale."

"Go right ahead," Patroclo answered.

"The building has a somewhat unusual form," said the inspector, a bald, nervous little man.

"It's an Egyptian pyramid, a giant tomb," Patroclo explained.

"That's very original," he said. "I've never seen one in the shape of a pyramid." And thought to himself: "It used to be enough, just putting a red light next to the door. The extremes they go to nowadays to attract clients . . ."

"If you wouldn't mind showing me the room where the girls will be . . ." the inspector said, glancing around, nervously.

"If you mean my daughters, God forbid they should ever come here. But then, some things in life cannot be avoided. I only hope their time will not come soon. At any rate, the room for the dead will be in this spot."

"Dead?" he exclaimed.

"Of course. I am planning a magnificent room for the dead. No pharaoh ever had such an elegant bedroom as the one I'm building for my deceased relatives," Patroclo said with pride.

"My," the little man exclaimed, wiping his brow, "how the city has grown. I've read about such diversions in large, foreign cities, but I never suspected there'd be a market for it here."

"Diversion!" Patroclo snapped. "It's no diversion, but it's time we paid some respect to the dead. Show them the same affection we show to the living. You, sir, who seem to have some sensitivity for this sort of thing . . . I'll see you're invited to the opening."

"Thank you," he muttered, "but I can't accept. I'm just your average man in that regard. Necrophilia is a little beyond me. I prefer making love to the living. But don't misunderstand. I'm not criticizing. Nowadays I'm sure a brothel of cadavers must be quite the thing."

"Druout," Patroclo shouted, "this inspector is accusing me of being a pervert. What shall I do with him?"

"I give up," replied Druout. "Why don't you talk to the building supervisor."

"I'd cut off his balls," the building supervisor said. "But maybe that would be a little violent. I think I'd ask the mason. Flores, what would you do to this guy?"

"I'd spit in his face," Flores answered.

"Spit in his face, Druout," Patroclo demanded.

"Spit in his face," said the engineer to the supervisor.

"Spit in this asshole's face," said the supervisor to the mason, who did as he was told and spit three times in the inspector's face.

Patroclo shook his head in disgust. "There was a time when a guy like that wouldn't have dared to look me in the eye."

The punishment didn't soothe Patroclo's wounded pride. He was the lord of the manor, and he wanted blood revenge. So he decided to lead his forces against the drug lords. He carried his grievance to his club's annual meeting and won a victory. The club agreed to strike every cocaine dealer from its roll and to bar them from membership in the future.

Since prospective members never listed "drug lord" as their occupation, the club came up with a profile to facilitate their detection.

"Drug lords" might include all those who became wealthy quickly and effortlessly, politicians excepted. Other suspicious signs might be: the use of large gold rings and chains by individuals who were never accosted on the street; the use of tinted glass in vehicles (unless the dark appearance should prove to be mere dirt); frequent trips—first class, all expenses paid—to Colombia, Mexico, or Miami, except in the case of government officials or executives of the World Bank.

Restaurant customers who demanded extra attention in a loud voice were also brought under suspicion. As well as anyone entering a restaurant flanked by a large group of friends who laughed at his jokes, no matter how insipid, while he paid the entire bill. And those who were never pursued by bill collectors. Or, in other words, anyone who was especially happy.

With that resolution out of the way, Patroclo carried his campaign to other clubs, brotherhoods, and associations. His motto: "Let us spray the air that decent people breathe with the DDT of virtue."

❧

YOU MAY have gathered from what I have just said that Patroclo wasn't a complete pig. Really, he was not materialistic all the time. He weakened his enterprising spirit with an ounce of religion. Even the boatman on the Lethe, he read in a book, charged his passengers a fare. He supposed that Saint Peter might also receive something for his trouble.

His belief in supernatural powers was confirmed when he told Talia to seek the help of a group of spiritualists. The doctors weren't doing her any good. And he knew of a certain society that, for a nominal fee, would take a delicate soul under its protection.

The sessions took place Wednesdays and Fridays at seven o'clock in the evening. The carpeted room contained heavy furnishings and several Goya reproductions. In the middle of the room stood a table and six chairs. The rays of the setting sun entered through the curtains and cast fading, rectangular shadows, speckled with light, on the floor.

The table provided a sort of landing strip for spirits. The invokers sat around it. The onlookers watched at a distance, in absolute silence.

I can remember Talia, the only time I attended a session. She was trembling and seemed deep in concentration. Actually she was dying to go to the bathroom, which happened often, particularly in frightening situations. She gripped the hand of a young, dark-complexioned man on her left and, on her right, that of a heavyset matron. The six participants formed a macabre-looking crew, worthy of a cabalistic painting.

Their object was to establish contact with the lost souls that were haunting Talia. To attract them, they had created a comfortable setting that wouldn't intimidate even the shyest ghost.

Three sessions passed and it was clear that Talia wasn't cooperating. The medium's suggestions—that she concentrate and open herself up to astral influences—didn't suffice. Talia simply could not fit in. While the others swooned in various states of rapture, Talia peeped out of the corner of her eye at the dark shadows in the room. She couldn't let go and give herself up to the darkness. She thought that all that hocus-pocus might be real, and her dead enemies, at any moment, might appear.

Meanwhile, the arrivals and departures of spirits made the table in the middle of the room bustle like a metropolitan airport. But the ghost that haunted Talia didn't come down, even by parachute. Likely a case of extreme introversion.

At the fourteenth session, the young, dark-complexioned man that sat on Talia's left fell into a trance and began to mumble in Latin. His monologue was rich in "kiries" and "dominus," as if he were celebrating mass. Was it the soul of a lost Roman? Maybe Virgil? They coaxed the visitor to identify himself. Suddenly, he switched to a good, vulgar tongue and said he was a Portuguese monk. Two hundred years before, he had fallen in love with Talia. They had met on the Mediterranean coast. He had sworn allegiance to God; she, to a perpetually absent husband. For a time, they indulged themselves in an adulterous affair. Then she realized that she loved her husband after all. She asked the monk to set her free; he refused and threatened to tell her husband if she left him. The distraught wife arranged to meet her lover at a house in the forest. After they had made love and he was soundly sleeping, she set fire to the house. Nothing was left of the monk but a handful of ashes.

But his passion was so intense as to defy death itself. His soul refused to take its place in the cycle of incarnations and set out—ungentlemanly as it might seem—to pay Talia back. As I've always said, Talia has no taste when it comes to picking friends.

Talia, to my surprise, instead of putting the past behind her, decided to make friends with the young medium. A dangerous game, since one day he'd claim to be the earthly representative of a lovesick soul, and the next, a fresh embodiment of the monk himself. What were Talia's intentions, I wondered. Maybe she wanted him to forgive her for burning him to a crisp. Or maybe—esoteric notions aside—she just wanted someone to talk to.

Lucio, the medium, had thick eyebrows, dark circles under his eyes, and a face marked by deep shadows. He looked like he'd been burned—but by flames of passion? His features were delicate, almost graceful. He could have easily been some sensitive poet from the past.

One night, Talia invited him to dinner. He arrived, with his girlfriend, a pale, gazelle-like creature, with the look of a frustrated pianist. She blended nicely with Lucio. We chatted for a while, and then he told me, quite frankly:

"I'm glad my friendship with your wife isn't a problem. Most husbands wouldn't understand. At first, I was hesitant to come here."

"I'm not so relaxed as you may think," I replied. "Remember, you got a two-hundred-year head start. Or maybe you think I've forgotten about your torrid little affair with my wife."

Lucio blushed. His girlfriend laughed. She was not so melancholy as he.

"I must say," he said, hoping to please me, "your wife is really marvelous."

"You can't trust appearances," I warned. "After hearing about her past, I hide all the matches before I go to bed at night. You'd better watch out."

We drank a couple of rounds of whiskey and finished off a roasted duck. We spent the rest of the evening talking about haunted houses, my guests' favorite topic of conversation.

FOURTEEN

Once a year, the alumni of the Light and Knowledge Club had a little get-together. We were just a bunch of frustrated men, and every reunion confirmed it. There wasn't a group in town with more cases of attempted suicide, insanity, or general ineptness. We held the national record for Lives Gone Awry.

When I was eighteen, I thought that by the age of thirty we'd own half the country. Instead, Lucas Ruíz had dived out of a building and landed on the pavement, becoming the most popular, unsuccessful suicide that year. Supposedly, Alex had gone mad, but it was the most unconvincing case I'd ever seen. That year our gathering was really pathetic. We didn't have enough cash among us to cover the coffee and doughnuts.

We were all anxious to leave as soon as possible, before some fiasco occurred. There had certainly been enough disasters in past years to justify our apprehension. By leaving early, one might hope to escape the theatrical demonstrations of success staged by some members of the club.

Esteban had already received a dozen calls. There must have been a full moon that night, or nine months had lapsed since the last carnival. Actually, he'd left instructions for his wife to call him every fifteen minutes, to prove to everyone what a successful doctor he was.

Raúl Miller was sipping a glass of mineral water. He was taking tranquilizers and couldn't drink alcohol. He was tediously calm. We sometimes forgot that he'd spent half his youth in an insane asylum.

Licurgo was filling the empty glasses. His friends hated it when he acted like a servant. As they scowled in silence, he got in a few plugs:

"If anybody has any legal problems, come see me. I require payment in dollars, but I guarantee my services."

"What do you guarantee?"

"He can't promise he'll win your case," I said, "but if he loses, he'll send you a box of candy in jail."

Luis Paredes, a blond, untrusting type, who blamed the world for his troubles, stared at Licurgo in disgust and raised his nose about an inch higher in the air.

Antonio Extremadura was the only happy one in the group. He'd never become an economist, as he'd wanted to be. If he'd acted on his youthful whims, he'd probably have been as bitter as we were. By divine grace, his attempts failed, and he became the U.S. representative for Chico Lindo, the famous drug lord. Antonio lived in Miami and came back to

Bolivia every two months. I often saw his wife riding around in her red convertible, wearing sunglasses and a long scarf that rippled in the wind. She had a look of infidelity about her. But whether she was really unfaithful or not, no one knew. Antonio told the same jokes year after year, and we laughed louder and louder, hoping he'd pick up the tab.

Nobody thought Lucas would come. He hadn't been there for three years. But suddenly he appeared, dragging his crutches and greeting everyone politely. He looked euphoric. His joy, I thought, stemmed from a new suicide plan—a successful one—and he'd come to celebrate before pulling it off.

After dinner, Esteban started reminiscing about the pranks we played in school. The time we stole the wine from the chapel. The time we split the cost of a prostitute. I promised to hand out photocopies at the next reunion, so we wouldn't have to listen to the same old stuff again.

"A telephone call for Mr. Jonah Larriva," the waiter announced, and I got up and left the table.

"I didn't know," Antonio said, "we had two gynecologists in the group."

I walked over to the counter, picked up the receiver, and heard Julia's voice.

"Jonah, I want you to call Licurgo to the phone for me. Will you, please?"

I shouted for Licurgo and walked into the restroom near the telephone, where I could listen to their conversation.

"What a pleasant surprise . . . Where are you calling from? . . . Of course, I want to see you . . . No, my wife isn't jealous. . . . Have you run out of change? . . . O.K., quickly. Let's meet tonight . . . Tomorrow? . . . At two o'clock . . . What's the name of the hotel? . . . I know where it is, but don't you think it's a little too public? . . . I'll wait for you by the pool. . . . I'll get there before you do."

There was no doubt about it. Julia was a whore. The biggest whore in town. The biggest whore in the whole country. She ought to call herself Madame Fifi. The name fit her well, was made for her.

I wanted to smash Licurgo's face in. I didn't do it, though. It seemed foolish to hit a friend on account of a whore. Thinking it through rationally, maybe he was doing me a favor, by showing me the kind of woman she was. But I wasn't about to thank him. After all, Licurgo didn't know that Julia was the Muse. I pretended like I had diarrhea and stayed in the bathroom. After a few minutes, I really did have it, with chills and sweats. I was humiliated. I sat on the toilet, wishing I could get rid of her as quickly as I was getting rid of my supper. I pulled up my pants and went home, without saying good-bye or paying my bill.

❧

I STUCK to my decision to stay away from Julia. I spent the whole morning trying to forget about her. But I couldn't get her off my mind. I decided to force myself to see her and Licurgo together. The shock would make me forget her for good. They were supposed to meet at two o'clock. That was five hours away. Too long to wait. A quicker remedy would be to fall in love with somebody else, some nice, easy, affectionate type. While I was turning the idea over in my mind, Arminda came into my office. Fate was handing her to me on a platter. I tried telling myself I was wild about her. I forced myself to fall madly, inexplicably in love with her on the spot. To give my name to her bastard child, even if he turned out to be an ingrate and murdered me in my sleep.

She was wearing a parrot-green maternity dress.

"Arminda, I have a confession to make. I'm in love with you."

She laughed, then asked, pointing at her belly, "Belly and all?"

"Belly, appendix, gall bladder, everything."

"I don't have an appendix, but I do have gall stones."

"Emeralds to me."

"I'm afraid they're more like pebbles."

"It doesn't matter."

"You're lying."

"Think about it," I suggested. "You can tell me how you feel tomorrow."

"Sure . . . I'll think about it. But before I forget, the General Manager wants to see you."

His office smelled like damp coal tar. Like old furniture. It suited Víctor Canez's old-fashioned demeanor: his Charlie Chaplin mustache, narrow lapel coat, and wide tie. He bore the weary look of a defeated politician.

He offered me a Havana. I accepted and opened the cigar box. It was empty.

"Sorry. Most folks turn me down. No one ever sticks around here long enough to smoke a cigar."

"I wasn't planning on camping out," I explained with a smile.

He took some documents out of a drawer. I recognized them. They were the ones prepared by my predecessor. The ones I'd signed, as if I'd written them myself.

"These are excellent," he said. "If you continue to work this hard, you won't lose a single case."

"Thank you," I answered.

"To the contrary. I don't want you to win any cases. So put your efficiency in your pocket and forget about it."

"I don't understand . . ."

"Larriva, I'm disappointed in you. I hired you, thinking you'd make a mess of things. I won't put up with this perfectionistic attitude of yours."

He explained that the bank was involved in a dozen cases against delinquent clients. All the cases were two, three, even five years old, from the days before the economic crisis. The 20 to 70 percent daily inflation rate had caused the loans to be worth less than the paper they were printed on. It was ridiculous to try to collect—the amount you'd collect wouldn't cover the court costs. Debtors were looking for a reason to declare bankruptcy, in case the economy stabilized and the peso returned to its original value.

"Wouldn't it make more sense," I suggested, "to close our doors and reopen sometime in the future? What's the use of a bank now when nobody deposits any money? The peso's worthless. The only thing in circulation is the dollar."

"It's our patriotic duty to stay open. Our citizens shouldn't know that their country is bankrupt."

"But how can you keep it a secret?"

"Easy. They go to work, and they get paid. We keep things running smoothly. Take our employees, for example. They're all working on old accounts. It's useless, but it keeps them busy. I suggest you follow our example. Look busy, spin your wheels, but don't go anywhere. It's crazy to try to get anything done in a time of crisis."

The General Manager set me straight, with myself and the rest of the world. That idiotic job—which I was starting to detest—was the ideal job for that time. Spin like a spinning wheel. A great motto! A motto to be followed, dutifully, wholeheartedly, by us all!

FIFTEEN

The beginning of a warm, drowsy afternoon . . . Martinis at the edge of the pool, a cherry in each glass . . . as sweet as a maiden's breast. The pool . . . secluded and cool. The cherries . . . like Julia's nipples. Maiden—strike that part.

Useless whims.

I swore I'd get her out of my life. It was two o'clock, and I went into the hotel, thinking I'd find them writhing around like two oversexed lizards.

I was worried about one thing and almost turned around. I'd forgotten to put on the emergency brake, and the car was parked on a hill. Oh, to hell with it! I didn't care if it rolled down the hill and smashed into a million pieces.

I nearly ran over a group of men. I lowered my head and opened a path between them.

"Hey!" said one of them, grabbing me by the arm. "Aren't you going to speak or what?"

It was Antonio Extremadura. He introduced me to his friends, a man in his forties and another in his twenties. The older man, wearing a short coat and red pants, was Chico Lindo, the drug lord. He was dark and had a thin mustache and mestizo features. With a hat and guitar in his hand, he could have passed for a mariachi. He never stopped grinning or laughing, even for a minute. And each time his lips parted, it was like peering into the window of the most expensive jewelry shop in town. His teeth, top and bottom, glittered as if he'd bitten into a golden watermelon.

"You didn't recognize me, did you, Jonah?" Chico Lindo asked.

"No, actually I didn't," I replied, looking at my watch. "I know we've met somewhere . . ."

"I used to work for your father."

"He died eight years ago."

"It was when your folks owned 'La Senda.'"

"'La Senda' . . . right. That was twenty years ago."

"Do you remember his dog, Mandrake?"

"Yes, I remember him."

"I was the one who fixed him up when he got run over."

He smiled, overlooking my amnesia. His joy was starting to depress me. I wished a messenger boy would show up with some telegram that would wipe that big, sparkling grin off his face.

"I was a great admirer of your father," he confessed. "He was a very important man, a good, liberal politician. He fought hard—and clean—for what he believed in. The poor will always be with us, he said, but let them accept their fate and leave the rich alone; after all, *they* would have to suffer for all eternity. Good, Christian ideas. But I decided—no disrespect intended—to give up the reward of the poor in exchange for a little enjoyment here on earth. And things have gone pretty well. I can't complain."

"Congratulations. I can see you've done well for yourself."

"Fairly well, but nothing out of this world. It puts bread on the table. Isn't that right?" he asked Antonio, slapping him on the back. Then he took the younger man by the arm and brought him closer to me.

"This is my son Grigotá."

I looked at him for the first time. He was about twenty-two, had high cheekbones, olive skin, straight hair, and almond eyes. He was sort of swank, to compensate for his shyness. He was quiet, but there was something explosive underneath.

"A fine young buck," his father observed, "and with what I give him, he could have any girl in town."

Grigotá didn't appreciate his father's compliment. He looked away and didn't smile. He wanted to get away from there as much as I did.

I said I was late for an appointment and started to leave.

"How's your mother?" Chico asked.

"She's in La Paz. She likes it there. They moved there when my father was in politics."

"Tell her I said hello, when you write."

I rushed off like a delivery boy.

When I reached the swimming pool, I was shaking. I looked at all the tables. Not a sign of them.

"Excuse me," I said to one of the waiters, "but have you seen a man and a pretty young woman?"

"They're in the pool."

I looked at the water. "The couple I'm looking for aren't swimmers. They might be interested in something a little more intimate, if you know what I mean." And I handed him a folded ten-dollar bill.

"They've taken a room," he said, "over there. If you run, you can catch them."

I shot off like a bullet, stumbling over two tourists and colliding with a potted plant. I turned around and kicked a dog that was trying to follow me. I got there late, just as the bellboy unlocked their door and let them in. The last thing I saw was Julia's round, smiling hips disappearing into the room like a pair of balloons carried off by the wind.

❧

I GOT into my car. The emergency brake wasn't on, just as I had remembered, but some unknown force had kept it from rolling down the hill. Energy that would have been better spent intercepting bombs in Beirut.

I was mad hot. I pressed down on the accelerator. The wind wiped the sweat off my face. I didn't feel sad. I was getting cravings, as if I'd been expecting a baby. What if Julia had seduced me and left me pregnant. But it wasn't Julia I was thinking of. I was craving something sweet. I raced along the street, with visions of raspberry tarts, chocolate candy, pudding, and meringue dancing in my head.

I stopped at a cold-drink stand and ordered a cherry soda. "Sweet, sweet drink," I muttered, "take the bitter taste out of my mouth." I lifted the glass of icy, red liquid to my mouth and took a swallow. Three of my teeth started to ache, two molars and an eyetooth. They'd been all right half an hour before. I took another drink. Another tooth started to ache. I paid and got back in my car.

I headed for home. The bright afternoon sun faded the color of the pavement. Gray trees. Silver tiles on the rooftops. The brightness of a thousand lights erased the normal color of things. I put on sunglasses to protect my eyes from the burning light.

I turned the corner near my house. You can guess who was there—Julia. One red spot on a sheet of bright light.

I stepped on the brake. I thought it might be a hallucination. But she didn't disappear. She must have changed her mind at the last minute, gotten up, and left the hotel. She was coming toward me. Her eyes, set; her lips, surrendered. Her thighs, rising and falling beneath her skirt, like waves rushing to sweep me up.

"Hi, sweetie," she said. "You're so pale! Are you sick at your stomach?"

I tried not to look so pleased, since the garage door was open and Patroclo was backing out. I lost my erection. We looked tenderly at one another.

You might conclude that Julia, like some medieval saint, could be in two places at once. For a time, I entertained that thought myself. But later, Julia explained what had happened—a plot worthy of a Mexican melodrama.

The woman at the hotel with Licurgo was Olga, and Julia had been acting as their go-between. The conversation I overheard at the restaurant was between him and Olga.

"Well," I said, "did your friend decide to have another examination?"

"No," answered Julia, "she and Licurgo fell in love, on the spot. They just wanted to talk about the way they felt. It wasn't like you think."

"I believe you. Licurgo loves to talk."

And, as far as I was concerned, that was the end of it.

I took her by the hand. Just being close to her was magic. Even at arm's length, I was inside the magic circle of her aura. It was hot and sultry, but Julia smelled like she'd just stepped out of a bubble bath.

SIXTEEN

Remember the proposition I made Arminda? Well, I completely forgot about it until the next day. That morning she came into my office and gave me her answer in body language. She swung her hips back and forth in a sensual, delicious yes. She was wearing a red dress. Even her belly swayed gently. The child she carried inside was already taking part in its mother's flirtations.

She'd come to tell me what was on the agenda for that day. She walked over to where I was standing and handed me the open appointment book.

"You aren't going to drop it, are you?" she asked.

"Why would I drop it?"

"Most of my bosses have been prone to drop things. Then, when we were squatting next to one another on the floor, their hands would suddenly recover their strength," she said, flirtatiously.

"So you wasted a lot of time picking up papers, eh?"

"That depended," she said, smiling, "on whether I wanted to or not. You don't try any tricks. You just come right out and ask me. I like that."

"I'm not so much of a gentleman as you may think."

"I thought about your proposal. . . . At first I thought I'd say yes. But then I thought about it some more, and I couldn't decide whether to get angry or to feel flattered."

"Get angry! Act offended! I was stupid. My intentions weren't good. . . . Slap me if you'd like."

I suppose Arminda thought I'd lost my mind. But, all in all, she was relieved. She wasn't in love with me. She just felt obligated to comply with my request. She'd been in that position before. Her former bosses were a bunch of assholes.

"I'm going to the courthouse," I said. "I need to see if any of the bank's cases are on the docket. I'm going to settle every last one of them."

The morning was clear and bright, like a glass of white vermouth. The rays of the sun sifted through the tree branches into a gentle, pure light. I felt strangely proud, walking along under the trees. I felt like I was somehow involved in the spectacle. I was the manufacturer of mornings out inspecting his work. Being loved by Julia had turned me into a megalomaniac. She stirred me up, roused me to acts of kindness, to leave my secretary alone, and to love the whole human race, my wife and Margaret Thatcher included.

I stopped by a pharmacy on the way to the courthouse.

"Give me a box of condoms, the colored kind, the prettiest ones you've got."

I didn't care what they looked like, but Julia did. I bought them to please her. The first time we ever made love, I used a colored one. Julia was fascinated with it. After we'd used it, she carefully rinsed it off and took it home with her. The second time, she went through the same ritual. I found out later that she was putting them in her scrapbook, with the date and circumstances of each encounter printed beneath. When she showed me the collection, I started to tremble. It was like looking at a photograph of my own penis. A cult to my virility. It turned me on so much I made love to her four times that day. Later on, when I browsed through the album more slowly, they looked small, like they'd shrunk up. Anyone would have thought that Julia had taken a circus midget for a lover. I suggested she stretch them out a little before sticking them to the page. To do justice to my actual size, of course.

❧

I WENT to the studio and impatiently waited for Julia. My Japanese employee had finished and gone home for the day. To avoid interruptions later on, I slipped a red condom over my penis. We hadn't made love for six days, and I was as ripe as an ear of corn, ready to burst. She came in. Tight bluejeans, a red-checkered shirt. We rushed toward each other. I told her not to take off her blouse. I wanted to make love to her half dressed. She pulled down her jeans. Her panties were damp. I was thrilled. It meant she'd been thinking about me on her way there. That tiny, damp spot in her panties was worth more to me than a Chagall, more than a Picasso. I wished I could keep them that way forever. It didn't matter, though. There'd be wet ones again the next day, and the next.

At first, uncertainty. I didn't forget that I was older than she. I wanted to be perfect, which was absurd. I pressed my penis inside of her. Divine tightness. Her vagina closed around my penis like a coffin. I thrust it in and out with cat-like frenzy. In and out. In and out. Julia's delicious scent filled the room. I adored her fragrance. On gloomy days, just a sniff of it would have made me happy. But today I didn't need fragrances of any kind. She was enough. Her pelvis. Her pelvis and her throat—she was particularly noisy that day. She moaned artfully, and I accompanied her with my swift in's and out's. I got faster. If she'd stopped screaming, I would have dropped to the ground, as limp as a dishrag. Her ardent lament was holding me up. It grew louder and louder. Then her vagina started to make a squishing sound, like someone wading in water. I kept going. Squish, squish, squish. She detested the sound—it embarrassed her. She admitted it to me once. It made her feel obscene and vulgar. But today she wasn't listening. A bomb could have exploded and she wouldn't have noticed. Blind and deaf, she slid toward the end. Her body contracted. She squeezed me tight. Her vagina trembled. For a while I felt like I was trying to balance myself over a puddle of quicksand. Then I threw myself headlong into my own pleasure. She agonized from the sidelines.

The calm returned. We were lying on the cushion. I couldn't believe we'd made love there. It seemed as though we'd been transported to another place and had just returned. My senses adjusted to the surroundings. An everyday place. One aggressive beam of light pierced the window. The sky was divided between fluctuating regions of blue and white. There were birds in the distance.

"Why," she asked, "did you fall in love with me? I'm curious. I'd like to know."

If the other women I'd fallen in love with had asked me that, I wouldn't have known how to answer. With Julia, it was different. I knew perfectly well when and how I had begun to love her.

"And I'd really like to tell you. But it wasn't you I fell in love with. It was your smell. You were playing tennis one day. You came home from the Club and found your house locked. There wasn't anyone at home, and you'd forgotten your keys. You went to your sister's house to take a shower and wait for your parents. When you came out of the bathroom, I went in to brush my teeth. The room was practically flooded, and your tennis outfit was lying on the floor. I went over to the small mound of white clothes and knelt down. I picked up every article and held it to my nose. I put your whole body together by inhaling your perfume, like an archaeologist putting a palace together from stone fragments. The fragrance kept me dazed for forty-eight hours. After that, I started biting my hair, gnashing my teeth. And calling you the Muse."

She repaid my honesty with a kiss. A soft, deep kiss, like a sip of cherry brandy. She reached down and rubbed my pubic hair. I was almost ready to go at it again—a little slower, with time to savor what we were doing. That's the way I liked to make love. Furiously at first, then slowly. Talia and I had made love the same way, when we first fell in love. Judo on the first attack. Then an ethereal tai chi ballet. Today, the repertory had been the same. I stared her straight in the eye, rubbed her neck, her shoulders, her breasts. I played it through with the focus of a hockey champion. No bold movements. I moved around in a slow circle. Her soft, slippery vagina was like a slick, waxed court. Languid sensations. We were wrapped up in gentle light. What we lost in intensity, we regained in depth. We were moving along, keeping the same pace. We could have swallowed each other with our eyes. It was like a piano duet. Our passion was in perfect harmony. Spontaneous fine-tuning.

When Julia was resting on the cushion, she reminded me of Talia. One could easily be the other. I hated it. I just wanted Julia to be Julia and nothing more. But wanting couldn't make the likeness go away. So, I closed my eyes.

SEVENTEEN

I was dying to know about Julia's love life. I thought it must be magical and very sexy. It drew me in, like an advertisement for a pornographic movie. What a pity she didn't ever open up and talk about herself. Everything I knew, I'd had to drag out of her.

"You never did tell me about that lover of yours who got electrocuted," I observed.

"Electrocuted?"

"The guy who was trying to get over the fence and got tangled up in the wires."

"Oh. I'd forgotten about him. . . . He wasn't my lover. He was in love with Marina, the maid the mechanic got pregnant."

"I heard a rumor that he was in love with *you*," I said.

"And I never denied it. I even said it was true. It made me mad that the poor kid had died on Marina's account. She was so awful, no one could stand her, not even the mechanic. He said the guy who died had gotten her pregnant. It wasn't true. He just made it up to get rid of her."

"What a crazy mess."

"It worked out all right. It got the maid out of a jam and made Alex jealous, too. He needed a little goading about then."

"Now I remember. That's when you were in love with Alex. How did you ever put up with such a nut?" I asked.

"He was attractive, intelligent, educated, nice, sensitive, understanding, gentle, faithful. He dressed nicely. He was poor enough to respect my family's position, and distinguished enough to know how to act. His future looked promising. I bet you can't think of anyone with so many good qualities."

"Prince Charming?" I asked, looking around the room. "But the feminists had him neutered."

Suddenly, I wasn't curious anymore. I'd heard enough. I preferred her frozen in an eternal present, like a plastic doll. But you know how women are. Ask them the simplest question and they give you a fifty-page answer.

She was eighteen when she went out with Alex. By then, she'd already had a list of boyfriends as long as your arm. Ringo, the *colla*. She was fond of him, but Patroclo, who was a regionalist, wouldn't let him in the house. After him came the friendly Chilean bartender. Out of financial necessity, he took up with a rich villager, who turned out to be a drug addict. Then there was the middle-aged divorcé. A bounder if I ever saw one. Ira was outraged. On the tail end of that affair, Alex appeared. He was the type of suitor that Julia usually turned down. She'd followed the same pattern all along. She'd fall for the aggressive, he-man type, then be afraid to go out with him. Then she'd go out with some nice guy, but never fall in love. Alex was the exception. His intelligence seemed to make up for the milk-toast side of his personality. She felt safe with him. Spent whole afternoons with him. Saturdays, they'd go out to Patroclo's land in the country. They'd walk arm in arm through the cane fields, soaking up the soft rays of the sun. In the evenings, he would read her love poems by Neruda. They were passionate but in a platonic sort of way. Physically, they were just friends. He never touched her except on the hands and face. He treated the rest of her body like some sacred shrine. At first, she interpreted this physical indifference as shyness or respect. But after several months, when she'd learned Neruda's sonnets by heart, she thought it was high time her body inspired something more than poetry. She began to miss the rough caresses. But her fear of aggressive men made it hard to know exactly what she wanted.

That summer Julia got a bad case of malaria with unpredictable bouts of fever. One afternoon Alex was sitting by her bedside when she started having a rigor. She squeezed his hand until the chills and sweats passed. Later on, she felt strong, excited, and curiously healthy. She wanted him to get on top of her. She took off his clothes. Streams of honey-colored light and sweet exhaustion filled the room. He lay down beside her. But when he tried to make love to her, he went limp. "Yesterday I ate three mangoes," he explained. "They've made me weak." He was lying, but his impotence didn't matter to Julia. Just feeling the warmth of his strong body, feeling him touching her, was enough. Alex, trembling and defeated, kissed her again and again. Then he got up, picked a hydrangea from the vase on the night stand, and pressed it between her thighs. She groaned as he rubbed it back and forth. When the petals were off the flower, he with-

136

drew the calyx and discovered the vivid rose of her vulva beneath. He put his lips into the slit and held them there, until her body arched, and she sighed the last sigh. But Alex paid no attention to the pleasure he'd given her. He tried again to penetrate and couldn't. He hung his head and left the room.

After that, their meetings lost their magic. And when Julia broke up with him—to go out with a cadet, who later was killed during some stupid military maneuver—Alex became depressed. Six months later, he went mad. Julia thought it was because he'd heard a rumor about her: that the cadet had forced her to sleep with his sergeant and five buck privates.

"The handsome cadet turned out to be scum," I said.

"Actually, he was a good man. A sergeant who was jealous of him made it all up. Besides, I don't think Alex believed any of it."

I thought for a minute and then asked:

"I don't understand you two. If you wanted to sleep with Alex, and he was impotent, when he got all right, why did he rape you? Couldn't he have just asked? You would have probably said yes."

"Me . . . say yes? I hadn't gone out with him for two years. I wasn't in love with him."

"Lucky for me."

"Don't pretend that you care," she snarled. "If I still loved Alex, it wouldn't affect you in the least. I'm not blind. I saw you sitting there, listening to every detail of our sex life. Enjoying every minute of it. You weren't jealous. And don't deny it."

How could I deny it? I couldn't explain how I felt. Maybe I was a little jealous at first. But not visibly jealous. Not enough to convince Julia, who wouldn't have accepted anything short of a jealous rage.

"You must think I'm being insensitive," I said.

"Insensitive? That's not the half of it. You're cruel. You've hurt me. Talking to you is like confessing to a priest who's doing crossword puzzles while you're pouring your heart out. It's disheartening. Act a little upset, at least."

"You're wrong. I did feel jealous, but I pretended not to." I touched her cheek softly, and she pushed my hand away.

"If it's true, don't be that way. Don't hold back. I need for you to be jealous. Can't you see? We're having an affair. We're depraved. Our only justification is that we're the victims of a mad passion. If people should find out, at least let them think we lost our heads. If we kill ourselves and they perform an autopsy, at least let them find brain tumors the size of oranges."

I knocked on wood three times. Why a brain tumor, for Pete's sake? We could have gotten off for less than that.

"And suppose," I suggested, "we get Alex to show us how to fake insanity."

"He couldn't teach us a thing. He's more normal than we are. . . . I don't feel guilty, not in the least. That's what's bothering me. I've done something wrong. I know it. But I haven't lost any sleep—or my appetite. I'm not even sorry for what I've done."

"I don't feel guilty either," I confessed. "Too bad we can't just go out and buy a little remorse."

"And a baseball bat!" she flashed back, angrily. "Maybe I could coax you into behaving like a human being. You're using me, plain and simple. No love. No commitment. Admit it. The only thing you care about is sex."

How could I make her understand? My life had sprouted wings since I met Julia. Before then I'd been a mere fungus, bored, and without ambition of any kind. Then suddenly, the wind dropped a blank check at my feet. I didn't fill it out for some enormous amount. All I wanted was a little self-confidence and something to care about. And it happened. She changed my life. I wasn't lazy anymore. No one would have believed that I, on my own volition—and behind the General Manager's back—was trying to bring the bank's cases to court. And another thing. My passion for Julia had breathed life into my marriage. I didn't blow up at my wife anymore. I didn't blame her anymore for my shortcomings. I don't know how I loved both of them at once. I didn't want to think about it, either.

Julia never stopped complaining.

"Our relationship is abnormal. This is worse than a priest having sex with a parishioner. Name one couple who never goes to the movies on Sunday. Who never holds hands in public. Who can't even share an ice-cream cone. You and I are weirdoes. A psychiatrist couldn't figure us out if he tried. Homosexuality, incest, infidelity, yes. But not this. The only thing like it is treason. We ought to be shot. I feel like Cain to Talia's Abel. I'm killing my own sister. In cold blood."

"If not going to the movies on Sunday is your problem, the three of us could go together," I ventured.

She slapped me on the face and screamed, "You see? You see? You're depraved!"

"I'm just trying to find a solution," I said, "because I love you. I love you so much, I'd be willing to accept all the blame for what's happened. This isn't a case of fratricide, unless you're planning something you haven't told me about. This is incest-in-law. A new sin. Maybe I could patent it. Make some money off of it. And don't worry about being punished. I'm sure the punishment hasn't been invented yet."

She smiled, beckoning to me with her lips. I kissed her. We might as well make love, I thought, as continue arguing.

EIGHTEEN

The General Manager called me to his office Tuesday and politely fired me.

"It isn't fair," I complained. "I've done my duty."

"I didn't say you hadn't," he said. "That's exactly why I'm firing you. For doing your duty. And if you continue to do your duty, you'll ruin us!" He smiled slyly. He was wearing an old-fashioned, gray suit and a tie as wide as my hand.

"If I went to the Bar Association with this, you might find yourself in hot water," I threatened courteously.

"I doubt it," he said, "not if they realized the good I'd be doing the public by firing an idiot like you. Do you know what would happen to our country if everyone did his duty?"

"Bolivia would become the Switzerland of America," I answered.

"You're wrong. The entire nation would come apart at the seams. It would mean the beginning of the Fourth World. And I'll tell you why. If the police, for example, did their duty, they'd catch all the drug dealers. Then we'd lose our only significant source of income. We'd all starve to death!"

"So, you're justifying crime," I observed.

"I'm not justifying anything. I'm just telling you what would happen if we all did our duty. Suppose the army decided to defend our borders. We'd have an international conflict on our hands. We'd have to force our neighbors to give us back all the land they've stolen from us over the years. The result? War and misery. Keep them camped out in the cities, I say. Playing cat-and-mouse with the politicians."

If only my father could have risen from the grave. And Brother Agustín, my catechism teacher. If they could have heard him—surely an old, liberal politician and a devoted mentor could have protected my unformed spirit, supplied me with weapons to combat the General Manager's vicious arguments.

He went on talking.

"If we did our duty, the black market would cease to exist. Where would you buy your whiskey? And who would change your pesos for dollars, to protect you against inflation?"

"I'd do without the whiskey," I answered, "before I'd give up my own dignity." I could hear Brother Agustín applauding in the distance.

"High-flown sentiments won't put bread on the table. You're a mixed-up idealist, who's just lost his job, because he wouldn't adapt. I, on the other hand, whom you consider immoral, will continue to run this bank. There'll always be a place for me in this country, no matter who's in control. Every government needs adaptable men."

The child whom Brother Agustín prepared for first communion was still alive. He needed to hear his spiritual father applaud again.

"I don't want the job," I replied, "if I have to become an opportunist to keep it."

"Yes. You can say that now. Act like a Quixote. You've got your father-in-law to pay the bills. But, unfortunately, that situation is about to change. Patroclo, I'm sorry to say, is bankrupt."

"I don't believe you."

"Do you think I would have fired you, if it weren't so? But things aren't so bad. Maybe, now that you're on your own, you'll grow up."

That was no consolation. I couldn't see anything good about growing up. Getting rheumatism. Going bald. Living in the same house with a bunch of crazy adolescents.

The General Manager could see I was worried and suddenly became paternalistic. He raised his index finger and pointed to a picture of an armadillo digging a hole.

"Do you want to be successful?" he asked.

"I don't know," I replied.

"Of course, you do. But you're too timid to say so."

"Maybe."

"If you want to be successful, imitate the armadillo. Forget about dignity, pride, and shame. Grow a hard shell, like his. Don't be afraid to get down and grub in the dirt for a living. And if you smell danger, duck into your hole. Don't confront your enemies. Let them be. Eventually, they'll defeat themselves. Be like the armadillo, and you'll be a winner."

The man should have written a treatise on ethics. He really knew what he was talking about.

"By the way," he added, "keep what I told you about your father-in-law to yourself."

"Why?" I asked.

"When a businessman is about to declare bankruptcy, he deposits and withdraws large amounts of cash. That way, he seems to be doing just fine. The bank makes money, and the client may trick a careless creditor or two. Even recover some of his losses. But if the creditor finds out that the bank knew all along . . . Well, the joke falls flat, don't you think?"

I walked out of the bank and jumped for joy. The romantic possibilities of being poor excited me. I imagined myself living with Julia in a little village in the provinces. She would take in sewing; I would raise chickens and grow corn. It would be a pleasant life. Then, suddenly, my fantasy came to a halt. I saw the future from a different angle. I began to panic. We didn't know the first thing about being poor. They didn't teach us that in school. No exercises in poverty. No retreats to a poor country village. We were totally unprepared.

I went into the house. So far, I hadn't met with any signs of economic disaster. I even began to think that the General Manager had lied to me. The cupboard was full. My in-laws had supplied us with the usual fruits, meats, and other items. The flies that buzzed around the house were still fat and lazy.

Talia called me from the bedroom. She was lying on the bed. Her face, pale; her make-up, running down her face. I kissed her on the cheek.

"What's the matter?" I asked.

"Daddy's lost his mind. He sent a man over here today to make a mold of my face for my funeral mask."

"Why," I asked, "does he want to make your funeral mask?"

"He's going to make molds for the whole family, to make a sarcophagus for each one of us. He says we can't be buried in ordinary coffins. . . . Anyway, the man came, and I wouldn't let him in the house. I wasn't about to let him put plaster all over my face. It's like being walled up alive."

How little Patroclo knew his own daughter! Never suspected how frightened she was of her own death. Instead of helping her deal with her anguish, he'd had her measured for a funeral mask! But he wasn't being intentionally cruel. He just didn't know. I was the only one who knew that Talia's greatest ambition was to outlive Methuselah. It didn't matter to her if the face that peered above her thousandth birthday cake looked like a toothless mummy. It was quantity, not quality that counted. Which explained why the slightest allusion to the pyramid sent her into panic. Her own mortality was being rubbed in her face. Deep down, she really believed she was immortal. How absurd, she thought, to reserve her a room in a place she never expected to lodge.

Talia cried and said:

"Papa shouldn't be playing around with anything so serious as this. He's going to bring death down on our heels. I can feel it already. I'm beside myself. I'm afraid to get out of bed at night. I'm afraid to go out on the street. I know I'll be hit by a car or catch some disease and die."

I listened to her lament for a long time. She was really suffering. Lines of deep melancholy were forming on her face. She was beginning to look like one of Dracula's anemic virgins. A zombie—the kind I found so attractive.

"You're a fool," I said, tired of listening. "You're making yourself suffer for no reason. You're not going to die, ever. You couldn't die, even if you wanted to."

"Do you promise?" she whined.

"I'd bet my whole fortune on it."

"I don't believe you."

"I'm not the only one who says so. There's Jesus Christ, Moses, Zarathustra, Mohammed, Plato, the priest who lives around the corner, the chief of police, Ronald Reagan . . . You'd trust them, wouldn't you?"

Talia smiled and blew her nose. She was convinced by my list of authorities.

"Don't worry about the death mask. I'll ask Emilia to pose in your place. No one will ever know, and your father will be satisfied."

"That's all right with me," she said. "One profile is as good as another."

Just then, I heard the doorbell and went to answer it. It was Licurgo, looking especially ugly. He was wearing a lascivious smile that made him look like more of a cad than usual. His expensive, imported suit didn't lessen the effect.

"I won't take up your time," he said. "I just wanted to borrow your car. Were you planning to use it?"

144

"No, I hadn't planned to go out. When do you need it?"

"Later today, but I'd like to take it now. Olga and I are going to a motel, and I'd rather not take mine. You know how my wife is always checking up on me."

It was true. The Gestapo had absolutely nothing over Justina. She was a bloodhound if there ever was one.

"It may not help, but go ahead, take it. By the way, when are you picking her up?"

"I'm not. I'm meeting her there. She's borrowing Julia's car."

I quickly put two and two together. The scenario was a little unsettling.

"Interesting. My car and Julia's car—parked side by side at a motel. What will people think?"

"Nothing. A coincidence. Nobody would think you were making it with your own sister-in-law."

"Maybe, but people do talk," I said, thinking to myself that nothing would actually come of it.

Then Licurgo started bragging. Said he and Olga had plans to make the rounds of every motel in town. I was jealous. I was dying to take the same tour. Of course, half of what he said was a lie, and the rest was an exaggeration. That's what I told myself.

"Do you believe in love at first sight?" he asked.

"No, there's no such thing," I replied.

"You're wrong. Olga fell in love with me the first time we met. She wouldn't go to bed with me right away. But I wouldn't take no for an answer." The idiot. He thought he was Marlon Brando.

"I told her if she didn't go to bed with me, I'd tell her mother about Alex. So, to shut me up, she gave in."

"Excuse me," I interrupted. "If she's so crazy about you, why did you have to blackmail her?"

"I like to take care of business in a hurry," he explained. "I wasn't about to waste time courting her, like some high-school kid."

In time, I thought, Olga would grow tired of Licurgo. Exactly the opposite occurred. She became extremely fond of him, while he grew to hate her. He hated her, because she had qualities that were missing in Justina. She was sweet, sensual, a fantastic lover. He could make love to her and tell her jokes at the same time. Justina was always bored and unfriendly. Love with her was about as mortal as the grave. He was forced to take stock of the situation. He thought and thought, looking for one reason to stay tied to his witch of a wife. There was no reason to stay married, aside from the fact that he was a chauvinistic slob. He hated Olga even more.

"You're looking good these days," Licurgo said. "I suppose the bank is paying you in dollars."

"You're wrong," I said. "As a matter of fact, they fired me."

"It's amazing. No matter where you work, you always end up on the street. You might as well find yourself a job directing traffic." He gave me a friendly slap on the back, and, with a smile that revealed all of his big, yellow teeth, he walked over and opened the door to my car.

What a lot of guff, I thought to myself. In spite of everything he'd said, it was obvious. Licurgo was falling in love with Olga.

NINETEEN

I'd just begun to develop a feel for idleness, when the family put me to work for Pablo del Paso y Troncoso.

My brother-in-law looked older than he was, and people took him for Patroclo's brother instead of his bastard son. He had a face like a bird dog, was nearly bald, and what hair he had left was turning gray, like his mustache. He blamed his premature old age on his father.

"Do you know how old I am?" he asked. "Twenty-nine! I was born the same month and year as Talia. They told me I was older to cover up for my father's infidelity. I grew up thinking I was ten years older than I was. When my hair started falling out, I thought it was normal. If I'd known how young I was, I would have seen a doctor. I'll never forgive my father for doing that to me."

"Why don't you get a hair transplant," I suggested, "and make him pay for it."

"Fags get hair transplants. But never you mind. He'll get what's coming to him. What I don't understand is why he didn't want Ira to know about his little affair. After all, she did the same thing to him."

"Ira, unfaithful? I had no idea," I exclaimed.

"A real bed-hopper," he said. "You remember that guy who got electrocuted?"

"Yes."

"He was Ira's lover. I seriously doubt his death was accidental. . . . Patroclo had the wire electrified."

I wasn't about to get into the love affairs of the electrocuted man. I wanted to talk about Patroclo's finances; I wanted to know whether he was bankrupt or not.

"Someone told me that your father's broke."

"I wouldn't doubt it," he said. "He's been spending money like it was going out of style. Take the pyramid, for example, and that's not the only silly thing he's done lately. A sure sign of financial ruin, I'd say. That's the way losers act. Have you ever seen the way a trapped frog puffs up? It's like that. They get bigger and bigger, till they explode into a thousand pieces."

Patroclo, blowing up, like a human bomb. I had to cover my mouth to keep from laughing. "I hope I'm not around when it happens," I said.

"The well's about to dry up," he warned, "and you're all going to be in big trouble."

"Not I," I said, "but I don't know about Talia and Julia."

"Papa could open a school for the newly rich. There're lots of kingpins who could stand a little polishing."

"No way. He hates their guts," I said. "It frightens me a little. I wonder if Patroclo will be able to handle it."

"Hey, don't get all worked up," he said. "If you're expecting a real washout, forget it. You need experience for that, and Patroclo doesn't have it. I'm the expert. I go through it about every three months."

He wasn't lying. He'd bungled more business deals than anyone I knew. Nothing ever turned out right. Including the Haitian blood deal. The merchandise went bad, and he had to sell it for bull's blood to a sausage factory. I haven't eaten a bite of *morcilla* since.

After that, he tried selling tractors to farmers. He set up his new business—Agri International, he called it—in the most high-class office building in town. He got himself a nearsighted redhead for a secretary, a telex machine that didn't work, posters of fifteen different tractor models, and an expresso machine.

He hired me to look after things. My job was to lie to the customers—tell them their tractors would be ready the following month.

Pablo had sold six hundred tractors dirt cheap. He'd started the business without any capital at all. He asked each customer for a thousand-dollar down payment and promised to deliver the goods in three months. He knew where the cheapest farm machinery was made: Czechoslovakia. So he took the money he'd collected and caught the next plane to Prague. At the factory, he bought the tractors on credit, with the understanding that they'd be delivered in six months. Knowing, of course, that his customers wouldn't mind the delay.

It was my job to deal with anyone who complained. I'd invite them in, make them an expresso, and explain:

"The port at Vladivostok is frozen. The boat won't be able to get out till the ice thaws."

They'd listen to my excuse, then leave the office without so much as batting an eye.

"What about next month?" I asked.

"Tell them the boat broke down off the Japanese coast. Or ran into a hurricane or whatever . . . If they're stupid enough to think that Czechoslovakia has ports, they deserve to be lied to."

"And suppose one of them knows his geography."

"So what. They don't care when the tractors get here. What are they going to do with them anyway? The only crop worth growing is coca. They're just pretending to be farmers so they can get a loan from the government. When the money comes in, they spend it on fancy cars or invest it in the black market. We have absolutely nothing to worry about."

"You're a genius," I said.

"Of course. I inherited my father's knack for business. I don't know how he could ever think I wasn't his son."

He had a merchant's brain, all right. It worked like a slot machine. Except the money always ended up in someone else's pocket. But that didn't discourage him. He licked his lips at the thought of every new adventure.

His MO was always the same. He'd get things started and then pass the work on to someone else. Me, for example, in the case of the tractor business. But I didn't do anything, either. I handed everything over to the secretary.

Pablo, in the meantime, went horse-back riding, played cards at the club, or went to bed with prostitutes. I sat around writing dirty poems to Julia and burning them up with my cigarette lighter.

Agri International had a vacant lot on the edge of town which became my personal firing range. There were six rusted out tractors—how Pablo became their owner was a mystery—and a small house for the overseer. It had a bed with deceptively clean sheets, where Julia and I caught the mange.

I'd never had such a pleasant itch. It was like a continuation of making love. I scratched and thought about Julia. It was *our* itch, and I wanted it to last forever. So I stopped using the lotion the doctor had prescribed.

"How romantic, both of us having the same disease."

"Romantic . . . shit!" she snapped back at me. "How can you say such a thing?"

"A problem can bring a couple closer together. Besides, I like the way it feels. I've even stopped using the medicine."

"You idiot!" Her eyes blazed with fury. "Here I am, boiling my clothes, changing the sheets every day, covering my entire body with that stinking medicine. And you—not so much as taking a bath! Don't touch me!" she yelled, as she started backing away. "I'm leaving. And don't call me till you're completely well."

My spirits fell. She wasn't the same. She didn't care about the little things anymore. The romance was gone. And all that was left were my memories and an album full of bright-colored condoms. It was a grown-up relationship now. She started taking the pill, which put her in a foul mood, gave her headaches, nausea, swollen ankles, and palpitations, and caused her to have to quit smoking. Added to all that, she lost her self-esteem, said she felt like some decadent, long-suffering whore.

"I haven't felt like this in a long time," she said. "I used to feel like this with Roly, the cadet, that time when he made me do it with his sergeant and the other soldiers."

"You swore to me that never happened."

"I'm sorry. I didn't know you well enough then. It doesn't matter. He's dead now."

"Well, I'm not going to die for another eighty years, so forget about using that line on your next lover."

She was beginning to fantasize about my death, just as I had fantasized about Talia's death some months before. I was like the mange to her, and she wanted to wash me away, be free of me. I also knew that I was falling out of love. She told me dirty stories to degrade herself in my eyes. She wanted me to hate her. Then the next day she'd feel better and say it was a lie.

"What I told you yesterday wasn't true. I never did it with the soldiers. I'm an idiot. I made it all up."

I forgave her every time, and I never criticized or pumped her for information. I believed her when she said she'd lied. If she'd said the streets were on fire and the Judgment Day was upon us, I'd have stood by her side and patiently waited for the Apocalypse. It was like I was the mother bear and she was my cub. But it didn't do any good. She was determined to make herself out to be a slut, and nothing I could do was going to stop her.

A few days passed without any dirty stories. Then, at the most inappropriate moment, she dredged up another one. She was resting on my stomach, her hair disheveled. We were wrapped around each other like a couple of octopuses. Julia was playing with my penis. I lifted the head toward her mouth.

"No. Don't ask me to kiss it. I don't like it."

"Relax. You'll like it. You've never done it before."

"Who says?" Her face was flushed.

Then she told me about her Uncle Carlos, called Charles, who got cancer of the penis. He was her godfather, and she was crazy about him. He was a lively, gray-haired gentleman and was always dropping by her house. When Julia was a little girl, she loved to play horsey on his leg. When she was a little older, she sat carefully on his lap and felt the waves of gentle heat. When she was fifteen, she spent many an afternoon at the hospital, sitting by his bed. She waited bitterly for the verdict. They would have to cut off her uncle's penis. It was worse than seeing an innocent prince beheaded. Then suddenly the door to his room began to close. Nurses could be heard walking back and forth in the hall. It wasn't clear if he seduced her or if it was a self-induced act. She held his penis in her hand, hard and real. There was an ugly, round sore at the base. Avoiding the sore, she put her mouth gently around Uncle Charles's penis and licked it, like a nun carefully washing a poor man's wounds. A medieval saint taking care of a leper. The supreme sacrifice. Charles was heaving. Was it pain? Joy? She wasn't paying attention. She was somewhere else. Then she tasted something like soap in her mouth. She went to the lavatory and spit. Blood and pus. Charles died two days later. She didn't cry. The taste of the cadaver lingered in her mouth.

"He was sick, I'm well," I argued.

"Don't you see? It's not disgusting. I'm just afraid I'll bite you."

"You won't bite me. Act like you're licking a stick of candy."

"But I chew candy."

"Julia, come on, don't be afraid."

"Please, don't insist. My stomach's tied in knots."

"You're pale. Calm down. It's O.K."

"Let's wait till tomorrow, Jonah. I can't do it now."

"But this is something women enjoy. It's their favorite sport."

"O.K., if you insist. But don't blame me if I bite you."

I was scared at first. I felt like a circus clown sticking his head into a yawning lion's mouth. Then I began to feel more like a bird being held by a clumsy child. Later I was an ice-cream cone melting in the mouth of some sweet-toothed princess. Julia was relieved to see a stream of warm milk instead of blood.

I reached down and kissed her between the legs. And when we kissed, she discovered the taste of her own body; and I the taste of mine. We smiled, feeling warm and valiant.

Though the sad—and maybe false—memory of Uncle Charles had turned into something pleasant, her stories rarely ended happily. Usually something I said or forgot to say or some unpleasant memory cut her to the quick. She'd throw up a solid, unscalable wall around herself. Other times she would try to hide her pain. I knew she was hurt but pretended not to. I never questioned her. And the silence pushed us further apart.

I looked for ways to make her happy. Schoolboy things. I spent one entire morning picking out a gift for her. I couldn't settle on anything. Jewelry, perfume, candy. Nothing seemed right. Finally I decided to give her one rose. It was a silly gesture, but one I couldn't get away from.

I bought a white rose at the cemetery gate. As white as a baby's tooth. It wasn't a very romantic place to buy a gift, but at least I saved the rose from withering on some grave.

When I got to the warehouse, Julia was waiting for me. She was nervously smoking a cigarette. Since she'd been on the pill, smoking was just one more thing to feel guilty about. Every time she put out a cigarette, she'd swear it was the last. Half an hour later, she'd be emptying out her purse, looking for tobacco.

She looked even sadder without her make-up on. She hadn't been taking very good care of herself. Her lips looked cold and purple. A wind from the south had chilled the morning. But the wind had ceased, and the sun was burning in the distance. She was wearing a sweater she didn't need.

I kissed the corners of her mouth. Her breath was slightly acid. She hadn't slept well the night before.

I gave her the rose. She stared straight ahead. I was playing my role as a clown very well. I kept my mouth shut. The scene was ridiculous enough.

She held the rose in her hand as I began to undress her. She wasn't moved by the gift. It didn't matter. I liked to make love to her when she was sad. Her pleasure wasn't important then. I went right on. It wasn't like I was making love to her. It was like I was caressing her in the sand—even when I pressed inside and moved back and forth, at my own pace. She lay there without saying a word. She wasn't involved in what I was doing to her; it was like she was having some erotic dream. She seemed to be imagining it all: my hands, the white sheets, the filaments of light coming through the window. Suddenly I came; I couldn't help myself.

We'd torn up the rose. Without realizing it, we'd made love on top of it. Julia apologized. I said it didn't matter. I wasn't lying. The flower hadn't meant a thing.

TWENTY

As the days passed, Julia became more and more careless. The things she did could have easily given away our secret. Like arranging to spend a weekend in the country with Olga and Licurgo.

She couldn't see anything wrong with it. When she made the announcement, her cheeks were flushed, and her eyes filled with tears of excitement.

"Sure!" I responded, sarcastically, "and Licurgo can serenade us with his violin."

"It's too late to say we can't go. It's all set. We've already decided where we're going and when."

"Have you lost your mind? Do you want half the country to know we're lovers?" I asked with alarm.

"No one will suspect a thing."

"You think they won't be able to figure it out?" I questioned, completely exasperated with Julia's naiveté.

"No, why should they?"

"Well, didn't we guess what Licurgo and Olga were up to?"

"But they told me. First Olga, then Licurgo. Of course, they don't know I told you."

I didn't care who knew their secret. It was our secret I was worried about.

"And did you tell Olga about us?"

"Well, sort of. I just said, 'Doesn't Jonah have pretty eyes?'"

"'Doesn't Jonah have pretty eyes?'" I mocked. "What's that? Some sort of secret code?"

"It's a woman's way of saying what shouldn't be said," she explained. "She understood intuitively what I meant. Now she knows about it without knowing she knows. Do you understand?"

"Not a word."

"I guess only a woman would understand. See, Olga knows something's going on, and she also knows to keep her mouth shut about it. Don't worry. Trust me. We can have our little trip to the country, and no one will suspect a thing."

I couldn't talk her out of it, and Licurgo and I ended up telling our wives we were going fishing on the Grande. I suppose the girls made up similar excuses. I didn't ask. If the stories didn't match, I didn't want to know about it.

We used Licurgo's old army jeep, which he dragged out of moth balls. A relic of the Libyan sands, it had had three motors and sixteen owners. We loaded up the luggage, fishing tackle, roasted chicken, drinks, bread, coffee, and mosquito nets. I couldn't believe it, but Licurgo brought along a live fish in a barrel of water.

"What are you going to do with that?" I asked. "Let it loose in the river?"

"Of course not. If I don't catch anything, at least I have this to show to my wife. One time I spent the weekend with a cute little Dutch hitchhiker, and I brought back some fish I'd bought at the market. Justina didn't believe a word of it and threatened to do an autopsy to prove they'd been frozen."

"What a wife you're wasting!" Julia said.

"A wild woman," I added.

The girls got attached to the creature. Even determined its sex—a male. And they were right. Every time Licurgo or I stuck our hands in the barrel, we got bit. The girls played with it the entire trip, fed it bread crumbs, and named it Ringo Starr. Olga swore it looked enough like the ex-Beatle to be his brother.

We left at daybreak, thinking it might cloud over soon. But as we went along, the sky cleared. Every now and then, we took a side road. All of them were in incredibly good condition. Which meant they belonged to either smugglers or maybe the big oil companies.

As we made our way through the woods, leaves and brush swiped the jeep. It sounded like a continuous clapping of hands.

The house was located on the edge of a piece of property that belonged to Licurgo's family. We opened all the doors and windows to get some of the humidity out. The river was only fifty meters away. Herons were wading in the dark, foamy waters.

Licurgo swore it was the best spot in the world for fishing. He wasn't exaggerating. There were thousands of fish, but they were smart little creatures and stole the bait every time. But not catching anything was mild compared to the trouble the girls gave us. We had to bait their hooks, put their lines in the water, and then hand them the reel. They sat quietly, eyes glued to the water, waiting for the attack of the giant water monster. At the slightest flutter, they squealed, kicked their feet, and threw down the rod, letting the line get caught on something at the bottom of the river. After they'd lost three sets of hooks and weights, and Licurgo was at his wits' end, I got an idea.

"Why don't you fish without the hook?"

"Without the hook? That's ridiculous."

"No, it isn't. It's something a very wise person might do. I've seen pictures of Chinese philosophers doing it. It was their favorite sport. If you don't kill any fish, you're protecting the environment. Tie the bait on the end of the line, and watch them line up."

They liked the idea, and Licurgo and I could pay attention to our own fishing.

Later, Licurgo whispered to me that he wanted to be alone and was going for a walk in the woods. No one dared follow.

"Watch out for tigers," I warned.

A few minutes later Olga left to pick wild berries. She just had to have some, she said, and promised to bring us some, too.

I decided to get out my camera. The conditions weren't very good for taking pictures. It was too hot; there was too much light. The colors were faded. I looked for some shade under a mango tree. Julia wouldn't cooperate either. She kept letting her hair fall in her face. If I took too long, she'd stick out her tongue. But I insisted. She had a look of veiled resentment I had to capture on film. She posed behind some tall grass, next to some very old trees. There were billowing clouds in the background.

When Olga came back, Julia asked for some berries.

"I looked everywhere, but there weren't any. They must be out of season."

"You were gone long enough."

"I walked a long way."

"Did you fall down?"

"No. Why?"

"You've got leaves in your hair and dirt all over your slacks."

Olga blushed. I came to her rescue by offering to take her picture. Just as she was posing at the edge of the river, Licurgo walked up. He was thirsty. We all sat down in the grass and opened a bottle of wine.

We uncorked the second bottle for lunch. Since the fish in those parts were too smart for us, we opened up a few cans of food and, after an argument, got the girls to warm it up for us. It was hot as hell, especially in the kitchen. If we'd managed to pull something out of the river, we wouldn't have had to even warm it up.

But by mid-afternoon, the day had cooled, and we were ready for another trek down to the river.

The water wasn't foamy anymore, and it had turned from dirty brown to green. We baited our hooks and cast in our lines. The fish were still smarter than we, and Licurgo, after losing his bait four times, gave up.

"I think I'll take a walk in the woods," he said. "Maybe I should carry my gun, in case I see an armadillo."

He didn't ask if anyone else wanted to go. A few minutes later, Olga made a less imaginative exit.

"I'm going to see if I can find any wild berries. Maybe I'll have better luck this time."

Julia didn't like being left alone again. I wasn't exactly thrilled myself. It was too hot to mess around. A breeze was blowing but not enough to do any good. Julia was breathing deeply; her hair was dishevelled. She had sort of a wild look in her eye. I could tell the heat was getting to her.

"Damn it, I can't stand these clothes any longer." She pulled off her blouse, slacks, and underwear. I watched with pleasure as she ran toward the house. She came back wearing a blue bikini. She had a smile of cruel satisfaction on her face.

She dived in and swam toward the shore. She stood up and the water came just above her breasts. She beckoned for me to join her.

"I don't want to," I said. "I can't stand cold water."

"It's warm."

"I forgot to bring my swimming trunks."

"Come in in your underwear."

"My mother never let me swim in my underwear."

"Admit it. You're scared of water," she accused.

"Not really. I drink at least a liter of it every day."

"How brave! I bet you anything you can't even float. I'd have to drag you out by the hair."

"I'd rather swim in a pool, like a civilized person."

"You're scared. Come on, nothing's going to bite you. There aren't any alligators in here."

"Stop insisting! I hate to swim in a river. It's like jumping into a vat of fish soup. It stinks."

"That's O.K. You don't have to make excuses. I guess *chicken* soup is more your style."

She swam off, without waiting to hear my reply. After swimming halfway across the river, she came back and splashed water on me. Just then, Olga and Licurgo came back, saving me from any further humiliation. They were tired, and their shirts were soaked with sweat.

"What happened to your neck?" Julia asked Olga.

Since Olga didn't have a mirror, she couldn't see her neck.

"I don't know," she said. "Do you see something?"

"A bruise the size of an egg."

"A mosquito must have bitten me. There were thousands in the woods."

"A strange one, I'd say. He left lip and teeth marks on your neck."

Olga was embarrassed to tears but tried to laugh it off. Licurgo quickly intervened.

"You're not going to believe this, but the mosquitoes around here are so huge, when they bite you, it's like they were sucking out the blood with a shot needle."

No one laughed, but Licurgo went right on with his story.

"I'm not joking. You'd better put on some repellent, if you

don't want to get eaten alive. You'd think they were having a convention."

"Did you bring any repellent?" I asked.

"No way. I need the evidence—to convince my wife I've been in the country and not in some motel."

"Talk about precautions!" I exclaimed.

Oh, God. I'd given him a chance to brag on himself.

"I've never been bothered by insects," he continued. "A mosquito bite is really a minor thing. Of course, I guess there is a small risk of getting malaria. But I doubt you could catch it around here. There aren't any people . . ."

"You're wrong about that," Julia interrupted. "I've had malaria. If a mosquito bites me and then you, you're a goner."

Licurgo tried to hide his panic. He got up and started walking toward the house. To put on some repellent, I suppose. A little later he came back wearing a bathing suit, jumped in the river, and started splashing around next to Julia.

Olga and I stayed on the bank. I watched a row of ducks paddle by. I was beginning to feel a little woozy from watching the current, and my eyes burned from the sun's reflection on the water. The whole setting was starting to turn my stomach. The giant insects, the bright sunlight, the green water, and those two, rolling over in the water like a couple of pigs.

❧

THE NIGHT was clear and, at the same time, threatening. The house flickered like a light in the desert. Monkeys chattered in the forest. The lightning bugs were giving off little bursts of light. Blind insects persisted in butting their heads against the lighted window panes.

Since there weren't any screens, we couldn't open the windows, and the house had turned into a sauna. Open the windows and get eaten alive. Keep them closed and burn up.

Licurgo was the first to take off his shirt. He didn't seem to mind showing his pot belly. I followed suit. The girls were dying of envy. They wanted to do the same thing but didn't dare.

We played a game of dice—men against the women. One quick game after another. Nobody was keeping score. I was starting to feel drunk; the singani and Coke had gone to my head. The rattle of the dice in the cup was giving me a headache.

We bet a million pesos on each game. Enough to buy a loaf of bread, maybe. But with each round, our heads got a little bigger, as if we'd been betting ranches, herds of cattle, the family honor.

Licurgo suddenly lost his enthusiasm and asked to be excused.

"Sorry. I can't stand this heat. I'm going outside for a while."

Julia slammed the cup down on the table, jumped up from her chair, and lit a cigarette. She wasn't trying in the least to hide her displeasure. To the contrary, she wanted Licurgo to see how pissed off she was.

"Let's stop this charade," she said loudly. "I'm sick of all this pretense. Any minute now, Olga's going to get up and say she's going owl hunting. Do you think we're idiots, or what?"

Olga didn't say a word. Just smiled painfully, like a young girl who'd suddenly had her clothes ripped off her back.

Julia raised her chin haughtily. This was her moment. Her face was beaming. It had soaked up all the light in the room. The rest of us were standing in her shadow.

"Why don't you take your shirt off, Olga?" she said, as she stripped off her own. All eyes were on her white, erect breasts, like two guests who'd come late to a party. She sat down on my lap and attacked me with kisses.

Olga and Licurgo started doing the same thing. I could hear zippers being unzipped, clothes coming off, lips and thighs opening up.

My attention split down the middle. One part made love to Julia, the other spied on Olga and Licurgo. They were looking back. We were cannibals, eating each other alive with our eyes.

We finished, and both women got up at the same time. They stretched and shook their limbs, and then sat down with a drink at the table. They were sitting there in the nude, laughing, their glasses raised, like farm women who'd just slaughtered their hogs. They refilled their glasses and came and went from the bathroom and the bedrooms, their tits bobbing up and down, their bottoms swinging.

Then we went a second round that ended almost as quickly as it began. The odor that lingered from the first time took our appetites, before we even touched our partners.

Licurgo and I sat down in a corner of the room for a private drink. We were thirstier than a team of draft horses. The girls continued their silly game, laughing, running back and forth, proudly displaying their firm breasts and buttocks.

We were too drunk to pay attention. Julia hated it when I didn't notice her and came over to say hello.

"Who wants to go for a swim?" she asked, impersonally, and took a sip from Licurgo's glass.

"I'll go," Licurgo responded in a flash.

Julia held out her hand to help him up. They looked at Olga and me as if to say, "Are you coming, too?" Olga said her stomach hurt. They didn't bother waiting for my answer, but went running off into the clear, warm night.

I could hear the river flowing in the distance, slow, bold, and warm. The soft sound of the wind was hardly audible over the croaking of the frogs.

Olga rested her head in my lap. She could barely keep her eyes open. Her body relaxed like an innocent child. I would have rocked her to sleep if she'd asked. I was too worn out to take interest in her body. I just wanted her to fall asleep, so I could go to bed.

❧

JULIA woke me up at nine o'clock the next morning. What in hell did she want? She was dressed, which surprised me. I thought she'd sworn off clothes for life. Her hair was wet and tied back in a ponytail.

"*Vuelve Ud. mañana.* I'm having my favorite erotic dream. Don't wake me up—the shock could kill me."

"Stop acting silly, Jonah. We have to talk. I feel terrible."

"Take a Valium."

"I don't want to feel good. I want you to see me suffer."

"Can't you put it off till after lunch? How about during dessert? You can show me then," I promised.

"Stop making fun of me. Last night was horrible. Please talk to me."

I raised up in bed. The light hurt my eyes.

"I don't feel like listening to your confession. Go find a priest. I'd rather sleep, if you don't mind."

"I don't need a priest. Nothing happened with Licurgo, if that's what you're thinking. We played around in the water till we were sober."

"Congratulations," I said. "I'm sure you broke the record for the longest skinny-dip."

"Don't be mean. At least I was faithful. I know I behaved badly. But sometimes I get these crazy ideas, and then later I feel awful about it."

"There's nothing to feel awful about. You put on a great show. Your audience loved you. Aren't you pleased?"

"I can't go on like this. I didn't used to be this way. I don't know what's wrong with me." She began to cry, effortlessly and silently, just at the right moment.

164

"It's simple," I explained. "You've been unhappy ever since you started seeing me. It's hurting you; it's ruining your life."

"Don't say that," she begged.

"So what should I say? Had you rather I lied to you?"

"I don't know. . . ."

"There's no way around it. It's been one thing after another, ever since we became lovers. Bluebeard's wives weren't as depressed as you. I can't let you go on suffering like this. I have to forget about myself and think about what's best for you. I have to end it."

"I love you," she said, grabbing me around the neck.

"I love you, too," I repeated, like a trained parrot.

She gently rubbed my hand and whispered, "I want to keep seeing you, but I'll do as you say. Because *you* think it's the only thing to do."

"That's strange!" I exclaimed. "I feel the same way. I don't want to break up, ever. I said that because I thought *you* wanted to break up."

"That's crazy. You said it. It was your idea."

"You're right. But I wanted to please you. I thought you wanted to break up. And I thought you hoped I felt the same. You think people who love each other are supposed to share the same feelings."

"Maybe if you write it down, I can figure out what you're trying to say."

"Figure it out? For what?"

She sighed and held her head. "It's impossible for things to work out for us. Am I right?"

"The word *impossible* doesn't exist. At least my geometry teacher used to say so. He believed that every theorem had a solution."

"But I'm not an isosceles triangle," she said.

"I'm sorry. I should be whipped for all the trouble I've caused you."

"Hey! Don't think it's been so bad for me. In the beginning it was really good."

I held her hand, then ran my fingers through her hair.

"I wonder if we aren't blowing this out of proportion. Is it really as impossible as we think—you and I being together?"

"Yes," she quickly answered.

"I have a friend," I argued, "whose stepmother is his mother's sister."

"What happened to his real mother?"

"She died of arteriosclerosis."

"If we have to wait for something like that to happen to Talia, we might as well reserve a double room at a retirement home."

"Not a bad idea. We could just put everything off till we get old. I'll still love you. There may not be much passion left in me. But I'll wait for you till I'm a hundred and twenty-four."

"And I," she vowed, looking into my eyes, "will never stop loving you. I'll be a hundred and eleven then. The perfect age to start my life with you."

"How will I recognize you?" I asked.

"I'll have a beak like a parrot. My left knee will be stiff, and I'll be using a cane. Rheumatism, as you might have guessed."

"That's O.K. I'll set you down on my lap, and we can go for a stroll in my wheelchair," I promised, with a knot in my throat.

TWENTY-ONE

Olga, Julia, and I saw Ringo Starr get killed. Before our very eyes, he was put to death by Licurgo, the smiling butcher. No one uttered a word in his defense.

Twenty years from now, I will have forgotten that weekend, Julia's threat to end our relationship, Licurgo and Olga's affair. Time will erase names, faces, my own identity, Julia's daring charm, but nothing can erase the memory of Licurgo slaying the fish.

As if the nonsense of the night before hadn't been enough, our trip had to end in an act of pure cruelty. There I was, getting ready for the trip home, struggling with the burden of a broken romance. Then came the additional weight of Ringo Starr's demise.

Every now and again, that scene flashed through my mind. Licurgo and me lifting the barrel off the jeep. Him dragging it away, kicking it over, and the water rushing out. The fish jumping up like a silver sword, vainly slashing at the air. A demented sword, without an arm to wield it or an adversary to attack. He kept beating himself angrily against the ground until he died. I couldn't find anything to cut off his head. I wasn't about to crush it under my heel. Didn't have the nerve. What nerve I had, I'd used it up that morning, breaking up with Julia.

At least the fish didn't know we were killing him. He thought he was taking his own life. If Licurgo had only waited for him to suffocate. But no! He walked over to the fish, held him down, and ripped open his stomach with a knife. His dead pupils dilated. His gills opened and closed uselessly. Then Licurgo reached inside and pulled out the intestines. He turned the fish over, and with the same knife, scraped off the scales. Tiny bits of nacre sparkled on the ground. The body was still throbbing. Wasn't he ever going to die? Was he going to live forever?

I heard Julia sniff. A muffled sob? The first sign of a cold? I didn't know. Volumes of unspoken words separated me from her. Painful and very present anger. She might have been crying for me and not Ringo. I hoped she was crying for the fish. He deserved it more than I. Ringo was a serious, stately fish. A big phallus that had risen up out of the water. Without an owner or a soul. As short-lived as an erection. He deserved to be mourned by a willful, young widow.

The following Tuesday, I dropped by Licurgo's office. While I was there, I let him know what I thought about the way he'd killed Ringo. Two clients were waiting in the outer office. He was taking his time, hoping they'd think he was busy. If your clients got callouses on their backsides, it was the sign of a good professional. He didn't want to attend them too eagerly.

"How can you come in here and accuse me of mistreating a fish?" he asked. "You've been spending too much time at your mother-in-law's charity teas. You'd better watch it. She'll have you tending the soup line before you know it."

"There are more humane ways of killing an animal," I said.

"What was I supposed to do, call an anesthetist? But maybe you're right. Ringo deserved better than he got. After all, he was our alibi for the weekend. Justina didn't suspect a thing. . . . I suppose Talia didn't either. Of course, your trip didn't turn out so well. I know you and Julia had a fight. You wouldn't be in such a bad mood, if it weren't for that. I doubt you'd be thinking about the fish."

He offered me a cigarette. I took one without noticing the brand: a third-rate domestic variety. I smoked it and managed to stifle the urge to cough.

"You seem a little depressed," he said sympathetically. "You look like you've been crying. I guess Julia won the first round."

"Don't be ridiculous. Julia's no match for me, not even with one hand tied behind my back. I got sunburned. That's all."

"You don't have to lie to me. You and I were cut from the same cloth. No need to hide anything from me. So . . . Julia was the Muse. Congratulations! Your taste in women is excellent."

I laughed out loud.

"Ha, ha, ha. You think Julia's the Muse! She doesn't hold a candle to the Muse. What happened between me and that silly sister-in-law of mine wasn't because we love each other. We were drunk! Otherwise, nothing would have happened. And believe me, it'll never happen again. I'd like to forget about it, and I'd like you to forget about it, too. Can you imagine what would happen if my father-in-law ever found out? He'd have me castrated."

"Sorry, pal, but you don't look like a guy who's recovering from an innocent flirtation."

"Well, if you don't believe me . . ."

"O.K. I believe you. But what I don't get is why you don't find her attractive. Put your glasses on, man. Julia's a fox if I ever saw one."

"Julia, a fox? You need to take another look. I, on the other hand, having been around her quite a lot, would say she was average. Did you notice the stretch marks on her thighs? And she's beginning to get cellulitis, at twenty-one, mind you. Besides, I don't like possessive women."

Licurgo chuckled. My list of Julia's shortcomings amused him.

"You know what?" he broke in. "I'm beginning to figure this thing out. You like Julia, but you're afraid of getting mixed up with your own sister-in-law. It could make things rather complicated. . . . By the way, the other night on the river, I didn't try anything with Julia. I thought you and she were an item. I was sure she was the Muse. But now, I guess I'm free to call her up. If you're sure you're not interested, of course."

"Me . . . interested? Of course, . . . not," I stuttered. I took a deep breath and relaxed my jaw. "It doesn't matter to me. But, if you want my opinion, I don't think it's a very good idea. You wouldn't be able to trust her. I wouldn't put it past her to call up Justina and tell her the whole thing. Not to be mean, just for laughs."

"I like a girl who's naughty, rebellious . . . A guy with the right stuff could tame her. Don't worry. I'll look after her like a father," he said, patting me on the back.

Then he looked at my face and exclaimed, "Shit, man. You're as pale as a ghost. Are you sure you haven't been crying. Your eyes are puffy. . . . Maybe you *are* sunburned. You'd better get some drops for your eyes and drink plenty of fluids. The same thing happened to me last year."

I went home and ran straight for the mirror. My eyes were bloodshot. I crawled into bed and fell asleep. The next morning, I couldn't even open my eyes. The lids were glued shut. I had pinkeye.

Blindness was a gentle prelude to what would happen to me that week. A mangy dog bit me on the calf at the corner of my street. The doctor gave me a rabies shot that left me half dead. I started foaming at the mouth and had to be carried to the emergency room. At the door of the hospital, a truck backed into my car. Two nights later, a bolt of lightning struck my patio and burned up my tamarind tree, just a few meters from where I was standing. And every time I fell asleep, I'd wake up in the middle of either a wet dream or a nightmare. I looked up at the dark void and cried: "Jehovah, I'm not the Pharaoh. So why the seven plagues?"

I got my answer the next day at Pablo's office. As sick as I was, I kept going to work.

"Bad news," said Pablo, as he took a sip of hot coffee that burned his tongue.

"I've stopped believing in good news," I said, adjusting my dark glasses. "I can't remember the last time I had any good news."

"The boat with the tractors sank in the Atlantic."

"Oh, really? I wonder if our clients will believe it? Last month I told them the boat was in the Sea of Japan."

"For God's sake, man. Don't tell anyone. This time it's the truth. And I don't know what the hell to do about it."

"Shit, man, this is bad news. I feel sorry for your insurance company. I suppose they'll have to pay for the entire cargo," I said, trying to calm him down.

"Insurance company! What insurance company? I didn't get any insurance. I was trying to cut costs."

"Well, I'm sure the factory will cover it. After all, the product never reached you."

"I didn't buy them at the factory. I bought them from a dealer in Paris, and now he's disappeared. He hasn't paid his phone bill in three months," he explained. This time, Pablo had really wiped out.

"So you have to reimburse the customers out of your own pocket."

"I'm flat broke. I spent what I had left gambling."

"Six hundred thousand dollars?"

"Five hundred and ninety-nine thousand, to be exact, bribes included. There is one thing that may save me. The Bank of Commerce cosigned the contract."

"Don't count on it," I said. "I used to work there, and I know they're bankrupt. The General Manager's kids play cops-and-robbers in the safe."

"That's no big deal. The Bank of Commerce is insured by the National Bank. The government will end up paying for it. Or rather the taxpayers."

"So, with things as they are, . . . when might I expect to be paid?"

"You might as well turn in your request along with the requests of my secretary and customers—all six hundred of them. The government will decide how much each one gets. I'll give you an IOU right now," he said, trying to be nice about it.

"Is it worth anything?"

"Not monetarily. I'm bankrupt."

Two hours later, limping and nearly blind, I managed to reach home. When I went in, I saw through my matted lids that my wife and the young medium were having tea. The table was piled high with food: four kinds of bread, cookies, *empanadas*, chocolate and cream tarts, raspberry jam, salami, baloney, caviar, pâté, fruit, and steaming pots of tea.

"What are you celebrating? Allen Kardec's birthday?"

"I've invited Lucio for tea," she replied.

I limped over to where they were sitting.

"You're dirtier than a pig," she exclaimed. "You've tracked dirt all over my carpet. What is this? Red clay?"

"They call it blood. A dog just sunk his teeth into my left leg."

"But that happened yesterday," she corrected, looking at me as if I were some ghost out of her past, come to crash her tea party.

"Yesterday he bit me on the right leg, today it was the left. I suppose he forgot."

"Don't tell me it was the same dog."

"The same mangy dog, unless he's got a twin."

The young medium came to my rescue. He helped me into the kitchen, and together, he and Talia washed my wound. They said the teeth hadn't gone very deep. In other words, he hadn't bitten my leg off. I refused to look at it myself, but Talia, who didn't seem to mind, said I ought to see a doctor.

"For Pete's sake, don't call anyone. I know what he's going to say, and one more shot would put me in my grave."

Though I'd made it home on my own two feet, after they'd finished with my leg, I couldn't walk a step. They helped me into the bedroom, and on the way, Talia ran through the entire list of afflictions that had befallen me that week. She was sure I was cursed and ought to seek the help of the supernatural.

"Take him with you to the séance tonight," the young medium suggested.

"I'm not going anywhere," I said. "I'm not moving from this bed, ever again. I don't care if I go blind, get rabies, or if the ceiling caves in on my head. I'm not going to any séance. With my luck, I'd probably be possessed by Rasputin's ghost."

❧

GETTING SICK was the best thing I ever did for my wife. She had me trapped between the sheets, and now she was going to look after me.

At first, I thought we ought to hire a nurse. But I didn't insist. If she wanted to be the one to clean my wounds, I wasn't going to stop her. Her bandages usually fell off half an hour later, but that was all right. She never once forgot to put the drops in my eyes or give me my pills. She didn't think the doctor had prescribed enough of the antibiotic. So she doubled it, and I got a terrible case of the runs. Too much medicine had destroyed the intestinal flora, the pharmacist said. In her determination to drive off the enemy, Talia had wiped out the good with the bad.

Looking after my health wasn't enough. She also wanted to make sure I wasn't struck by lightning. But no sooner had the lightning rod been installed on the roof than she learned from the young medium that such an apparatus might attract every bolt in the entire neighborhood. The next day she had it taken down, along with the television antenna. The eight o'clock movie looked like a pointillistic painting, which my infected eyes could not appreciate. Patroclo called a stop to the nonsense, when he marched over, gave his harangue against irresponsible fanatics, and had the antenna and lightning rod put back on the roof.

Then Julia popped in. I'd convinced myself I'd be better off staying away from her. I even dreaded running into her again. Of course, I was lying to myself. No matter what, I couldn't get her off my mind. My imagination allowed her to do as she pleased, though my jealousy kept a constant watch. I didn't have her locked up in a convent by any means. I could see her making dates with despicable types, coming home drunk at five o'clock in the morning. Still, it wasn't as bad fantasizing about it as seeing her in real life. What she did was her own business, and I couldn't do anything about it.

One afternoon, she came by to see me. My eyes cleared up the instant she walked into my bedroom. My heart started to pound. I thought she'd come by for old-times' sake. But actually she'd come on family business. My eyes became inflamed again, and my heart shriveled up like a prune.

Talia was already late for work, but she didn't care what time it was. She was carrying on over me, like an idiot. What difference did it make to her if she caught my eye infection or if I suddenly reached up and bit her ear off. Which could have happened, since I'd quit taking the rabies shots.

After covering me with kisses, both ears still intact, Talia left for work, leaving me with Julia. I could feel the Muse's rump pressing against the mattress, leaving its lusty imprint on my bed.

"How do you feel?" she asked.

"Fine. I put my ad in the paper today for a Seeing Eye dog."

"Blind men can be very attractive. Think of José Feliciano or . . ."

"I know a blind beggar over at the Cathedral who's just your type. I'll introduce you."

"Some people whose eyes are fine constantly fall on their faces," she replied, with irony. "But you don't have to worry about going blind. You'll get over it. The doctor told Talia you would. And I was glad to hear it."

Her consoling manner made me even more uneasy. I didn't like being talked to as if I were a child with mumps. Get-well cards, flowers, and demonstrations of affection put me in a dismal mood. I didn't want people doing things for me. I knew exactly what I didn't want. But if someone had asked me what I wanted, I wouldn't have known what to say. Julia was the only one who could give me what I really wanted. She was my fairy godmother. If I could have seen a little more clearly, I might have seen she wasn't magic at all. Just a wet-haired girl who was sitting on my bed, chomping steadily on a piece of Dentyne gum. Turning me on—and turning me off with her triple dose of cologne.

"Do you think I ought to see other guys?" she asked, not suspecting I already had my answer ready. I'd decided to act indifferent.

"I think you'll get over it sooner if you do," I said.

"I don't know . . ." she replied. Her eyes widened into an almost frightened stare.

"Licurgo called me."

"What did he want?"

"He asked me to go out for a drink."

"Did you say you would?"

"I haven't decided yet. I thought it was too soon to start seeing other men. But since you don't seem to care, I guess I could force myself."

"I do care," I said, with alarm. "I was talking about guys your own age. Licurgo is married."

"So are you."

"And you see what happened."

"Are you jealous? I've never seen you jealous before."

"My dear girl," I explained, "my feelings aren't what matter here. But if I'm willing to give you up, I don't want to see you repeat the same mistake." I went around and around in circles and ended up convincing her to go out with some decent fellow, which hadn't been my intention at all. I tried to back up a little.

"Don't misunderstand me. I'm not suggesting you get involved with the first guy you meet. There aren't many decent guys out there. About one in ten thousand. When you meet the right one, I'll be the first to congratulate you."

"One in ten thousand? I'm more likely to win the lottery."

"A lot more likely. Your chance of meeting the right guy is more like one in a million. I just said ten thousand not to discourage you. But don't give up. Sooner or later, you'll meet the right guy. It's inevitable. But please, stay away from Licurgo. I'd rather see you in a convent than with that pig."

"Don't worry. I'd never go out with him. He's not my type."

Suddenly I saw what she was doing. She'd told me about Licurgo just to torment me.

But before I could say a word, she hurled back an accusation that really caught me off guard. "If you wanted to hurt me," she said, "you've succeeded."

"Hurt *you*? Isn't it the other way around? You're destroying me. Carrying on about other men. You can't wait to start seeing someone else."

"I'm just trying to get through this. I wanted your advice. But I see you're ready to put me off on the first guy who comes along. I didn't realize I was such a bother."

I didn't reply. Maybe she was right. I wanted to see her suffer, just as she wanted to see me suffer. I wanted her to be depressed. I wanted her to lock herself up in her house and sob for weeks and weeks. But she wasn't about to fall apart. She went right on smacking on her gum and swinging her hips all over town. While I—unlucky sap that I was—lay in my sickbed, out of work, nearly blind, dog bit, and pursued by a bolt of lightning.

She said she was miserable, trying to even things up, but I wasn't convinced. Proof—that was what I wanted. But there wasn't any. Her wounds were philosophical, she said. I might have felt a little better if she'd threatened to kill herself. But she just sat there, asking me a bunch of silly questions: "Does love exist? Am I unlucky in love? How many men do I have to sleep with before I find Mr. Right? Half a dozen? A hundred?" If I could just give her a number, she'd start to work right away. It didn't matter who the men were—criminals, alcoholics, perverts. She'd hold her breath and close her eyes, and it'd be over before she knew it. She had often fantasized about a hard, promiscuous life, sleeping with dozens of men and never feeling the slightest flicker of emotion. But now that the fantasy was coming true, she was frightened, like a weak, trembling child.

Her next move would be to lock herself up in her house and bug the hell out of her parents. Actually, she'd been bugging the hell out of them since she was thirteen. And I was her strongest supporter. Maybe she'd decide to take it up full time and forget about filling her quota. I kept my fingers crossed.

TWENTY-TWO

Talia decided to fatten me up and started stuffing me with foreign dishes whose languages were unknown to my stomach. Every meal ended with a sticky sweet dessert. I brushed my teeth till my gums bled. It would all stop, I thought, as soon as I was well. No such luck. She went right on fussing over me. She'd go to work, give me a call to see how I was, pin notes up all over the house: "Here's the kiss I wasn't able to give you when I left. You were sleeping. I didn't want to disturb you." Or: "If you get depressed, send me an SOS. Your dedicated nurse will come running."

The dishes she was feeding me came out of a French cookbook. Talia would translate them for Emilia who would whip them up into the culinary delights which then became the bane of my stomach. A plain piece of steak would have tasted wonderful!

As soon as Talia left the house, I'd sneak into the pantry and treat myself to something ordinary. One morning I was about to eat an orange but couldn't find a knife to peel it.

"Emilia," I said, "where are the knives?"

"They're locked in the cabinet."

"Would you get one for me, please?"

"I can't. The missus told me not to."

"Why the hell did she tell you not to?"

"I don't know, but she told me to peel it, if you wanted any fruit."

I went next door to my in-laws' house and borrowed a knife. I walked right back into the kitchen with the knife in plain view. Not knowing what else to do, Emilia called Talia.

Talia came running. Her face was pale as a sheet. It looked rather nice above her pretty yellow dress.

"Give me the knife," she said.

"What's the matter? Have the spirits said to stay away from oranges?"

"It's not going to work, Jonah. Put down the knife."

I handed her the knife. She locked it in the cabinet and started to cry.

"How could you do it?" she sobbed. "How could you leave me alone? Don't you care about me anymore?"

"Do what?" I asked. I didn't know what the hell she was talking about.

"Take your own life. What else? I've seen this coming . . . and I know why. You lost your job."

"So what? You think I'd commit suicide over a thing like that?"

"Don't forget—I'm a social worker. And statistics say that the unemployed have the highest rate of suicide."

"And if I swear, scout's honor, would you believe me?"

"Jonah, I caught you red-handed. If I'd gotten here a minute later, I would have lost you."

"You're crazy."

"That's all right. You don't have to admit it. You're embarrassed because I caught you. I know all about suicide. I was in Dr. Enríquez's class at Córdoba. I sat through it twice. I didn't study hard enough the first time and had to take it again."

"Talia, you're letting your imagination run away with you. I lose my job, and you think I'm going through some sort of existential crisis. . . . With all due respect to the bank, I don't give a hoot about that job. I'm glad they fired me."

"You're lying. According to Dr. Enríquez, people who are suicidal sometimes act very cool and indifferent. Sometimes they act like they're really happy. A few days later, you find them hanging in a closet."

She sat down next to me. Her perfume reminded me of something . . . something that happened years before. When we first dated. When we first fell in love.

She put her arm around me. "Please talk to me if you ever get a crazy idea like that again. I don't want to read about it in a note, when it's too late to do anything. I'm your wife. I wouldn't do anything important without talking to you first. I expect you to do the same. Understand?"

Nothing I could say would convince her. And the solution, in Talia's estimation, was to find me a job.

With the whole Third World teetering on the brink of economic collapse, it was hard to believe that anyone could enjoy being out of work. It was downright subversive to act like you didn't care. The Government, Society, the Family, the Heavenly Choirs of Angels demanded that I act depressed. And whether I was depressed or not, my friends assumed I was depressed and took it upon themselves to help me out. They had to find me a job. It wasn't so easy as before, with Patroclo's solvency hanging by a thread. Many who would have gladly offered me work in the past suddenly found that their hands were tied.

Four weeks passed. The Del Paso y Troncoso clan got tired of waiting. So Ira put me on the payroll at her agency: the Center for Aid to the Needy. She put me down as a legal advisor, just like at the bank. Which meant that either I wouldn't have to do anything at all or that I might have to perform some pretty tricky managerial tasks. The legal advisor who'd been working there for years was none too pleased with the competition. As soon as he set eyes on me, he bristled and started to growl under his breath.

"This place is a paradise," Ira told me. "I don't know why Talita never wanted to work here. She'd be a lot better off."

That was the day I signed the contract. And Ira seemed happy. So it must have been before Julia left for the States.

Ira's curiosity was actually the cause of Julia's leaving the country. One day she was digging around in Julia's closet and found the album with the condoms. She couldn't believe her own daughter was a pervert. When *she* was a young girl, *she'd* collected rose petals and Spanish dolls. Why couldn't *Julia* collect something ordinary? If she didn't like flowers or dolls, why not stamps—Cousin Clo's son collected stamps. She was going to handle this like an adult. She was going to consult a professional, a sexologist. The sexologist had a big nose and a nasal voice. "Your daughter isn't a pervert at all," he said. "She is simply trying to overcome her fear of penises." Many young women were frightened of penises, he told her, and she—Ira—ought to give her daughter a plastic penis and tell her to play with it . . . until she was ready to deal with the real thing. Ira left without paying the bill.

At home, she asked Julia, "Why do you collect condoms?"

"They're cheaper and smaller than dolls, and besides, I can fit them into an album." Ira could accept that answer. It made sense.

She thought the whole thing over and decided to raise her allowance and send her to the States to study English.

"What do I need to learn English for?" Julia asked.

"Well, nobody studies French anymore. And Russian is out of the question. If you stay here, what can you study? Quechua? Guaraní?"

My mother-in-law was a distinguished woman. She thought it was her social charm, not her good looks, that got her noticed. But she was wrong. Good looks didn't mean much to her. She couldn't depend on good looks—she might be beautiful one day and look like an old hag the next. At a distance, Ira was sexier than a nude statue. Up close, her attraction acquired warmth. Ira was something you could sink your teeth into. You wanted to pinch her, but her cold, clear eyes said, "Keep off." Her skin made her look ten years younger. Everybody told her that, but, actually, nobody knew what "ten years younger" meant. They suspected she'd reached the age when women start to fall for younger men. But not Ira. She didn't give a damn about younger men.

Flores, the other legal advisor, was infatuated with Ira. He was in and out of Ira's office fifty times a day. Until one day, Ira said to him, "Flores, if you're so crazy about this office, I'll give it to you. I'll trade my office for yours." Ira couldn't stand him. Criticized his work every chance she got. Flores would just stand there grinning, like an idiot. Anything Ira said was music to his ears.

Ira worked for over a dozen charitable organizations. She was a veteran philanthropist, but nobody knew how much of a veteran she was. She didn't like it if anyone suggested she'd been at it for more than thirty years. It made her sound like an old woman. She couldn't remember when she'd gotten involved in charity work, she said, and she wasn't about to figure it out. She hated it when reporters asked for exact dates. Rehashing the past was a waste of time, she thought. Refined people, like the gods on Mt. Olympus, lived in a timeless dimension. A person's importance ought to be judged by the number of appointments he or she had each day. Hers wouldn't fit on her calendar; she couldn't remember them all, either. She'd gotten a reputation for not showing up at meetings, even when she was the principal speaker.

It wasn't because she was just sitting around. More likely, she was off working on some other futile project of hers. The only thing she never overlooked was the Center for Aid to the Needy. Since she held the title of Perpetual Director, her clients thought she owned the place. No one seemed to know if it was public or private. It got some funds from the government, but it didn't have to answer to anyone.

"What do you do, mostly?" I asked.

"Organize charity drives," she said.

"That's a joke," said Flores, laughing. "First you sign your contract, and then you ask what your duties are. What if she'd said we sold babies?"

"Be quiet, Flores, and mind your manners. This is a business conversation. If there's a flood," she continued, "we might sponsor a benefit ball."

"That sounds like fun. They suffer, we go dancing."

"It's the way we get money to help people," she said, coldly. Ira hadn't appreciated my joke.

"I suppose there's always a worthy cause?"

"Yes, thank goodness, we never run out of things to do. There's always an emergency somewhere."

The C.A.N. (abbreviation for the Center) outdid the UN in cases reviewed each day. Poor women—with a wealth of children—trying to get a handout for their brood. Sick people looking for free medicine—it never did them any good. Babies apparently delivered by the stork and abandoned on some street corner.

They warned me about the rip-off artists who came in pretending to be poor. That's why we had to have proof from our clients that they *were* poor.

The interviews took place in a long, narrow room.

"I'm here to help you—that's my job," I explained to a white-haired man with a beard. "But before I can do anything, I have to have a certificate . . . from a judge."

"I don't have one. I could probably get one, if I could afford it."

"What do you suggest I do?"

"Couldn't you just put down what you thought, more or less?"

"Sounds reasonable to me," I said. "Let's see. What can I say?"

"Put down I'm wearing rags."

"That's not good enough. You could have borrowed them from someone."

"I did borrow them. I can't even afford rags."

"Do you have lice or any skin diseases?"

"No."

"You just lost five points. You bathe too often. Poor people aren't supposed to bathe. Are you an alcoholic?"

"No, I don't drink, it makes me sick."

"Good God, man. You aren't helping me at all. You don't seem to have any symptoms of poverty."

"Like what?"

"Alcoholism. Tuberculosis. Do you live on the street? Beat your wife? Abuse your children? Rape your daughter?"

"I have prostate trouble. Does that count?"

"No, that's too middle-class."

"My pockets are empty. That's the best proof I've got. I haven't seen a peso in so long, I can't remember what color they are."

"Me either. Well, don't worry about it. I'll give you a certificate, so you won't have to go through this again with the social worker."

When Flores found out I'd helped a client out, he went straight to Ira. She asked us both to step into her office. She listened impatiently to Flores's accusations.

"O.K., Flores. I need proof that Mr. Larriva has done the things you said—ignored the rules, falsified documents, aided an impostor . . ."

"I can't actually prove it," said Flores.

"So what do you expect me to do about it?"

"It's his word against mine," he argued. "But surely you'd trust a loyal employee over somebody who'd falsify a certificate. I have faith in your judgment, and I'm sure you wouldn't let the fact that he's your son-in-law get in your way."

"I wouldn't trust anyone who denounced a fellow worker without proof," Ira said, dryly.

"Stop arguing," I pleaded. "What he said is true. I fudged a little on the rules. I couldn't stand sending people away who really needed help."

"If that's the case, I *should* fire you," Ira said.

"Good for you," said Flores. "I'm glad to see you defend the standards."

"But you, Flores, are the one I'm going to fire. You're an old fuddy-duddy. Anything the least bit imaginative upsets you."

Ira made short work of Flores's complaint. We had to get to the airport to say good-bye to Julia. We got there thirty minutes before the plane left.

Julia looked festive in her parrot-green dress—like she was on her way to a party. Her sunglasses helped to hide the way she really felt. Patroclo was making her check her papers again. Ira was off talking to some friends. Talia was going over her list of things to do—it got longer and dirtier but never ended up in the wastebasket.

The flight to Miami was announced, and we hurriedly said good-bye. Julia handed out a dozen or more kisses. I only managed to get one of them. It lasted about as long as a whiff of ether, and I turned away disappointed.

When she was going through customs, the agent asked if she'd had her yellow-fever vaccination.

"No," she said.

"You can't leave the country without it," he said.

Patroclo turned red in the face. "Are you suggesting that my daughter might have yellow fever?"

"Not at all," said the agent.

"Well, let her pass then. Don't cause problems, man."

"It's an international requirement."

"This is unbelievable. I've raised my daughter according to the strictest health standards, and now you're barring her from an international flight. Because she might be infectious. Why don't you worry about all these filthy Indians and leave decent people alone."

Then Ira put in a good word for the agent. It wasn't his fault, she told her husband. If he let her on the plane, what would she do when she got to Miami? Besides, there was time to get the certificate—the plane wasn't leaving for half an hour. Then Julia got an attack of needle-phobia. Said they'd have to tie her down to give her a shot. So they ended up bribing a travel agent to fake a certificate.

❧

WHEN IRA fired Flores, he said he'd complain to the Bar. The Bar would probably call a national strike, and with the C.O.B. on their side, the whole country would have been shut down indefinitely. The entire nation would be up in arms.

And since Ira wasn't about to see her agency turned into a three-ring circus, she gave Flores his job back. Just as well. There was no one else as mediocre as he to be her errand boy.

From his first day back, Flores worked like a dog to regain the respect he'd never had. Right off, he called an emergency meeting.

We all gathered around the conference table—Ira, a painted-up social worker named Raquel Linares, Lourdes, the psychologist, two haughty women, Flores, and me.

Flores read us an article he'd just read in a journal. It accused charitable organizations of being "oligarchical teats that made infants out of the poor and diverted them from their real struggle—the people's struggle against the ruling class." Welfare foundations, in general, were interested in perpetuating misery and guaranteeing a steady supply of exploitable men and women.

"I read it," the sociologist said. "It says in times of systematic aid, the number of indigents actually increases."

"Of all the nerve," said one of the haughty women, "saying we create misery."

"Ignore it," Ira advised. "It's absurd, like blaming doctors for disease."

"However," Flores interrupted, "it's true that one of us did fabricate some new cases of poverty."

"If you're referring to me," I said, "I don't deny it. I issued fourteen certificates of poverty."

"Let's not go through that again," said Ira. "I thought that had been taken care of."

Flores apologized and added, "The author of the article is wrong about everything but one point: poverty has increased. We get more applications every day. When you leave a restaurant, you have to fight your way through a crowd of beggars. If you park your car, you've got ten kids fighting over who's going to watch it. The charity wards at the hospitals are booked up six months in advance."

No one disagreed with anything he said. Carried away by his own words, he looked at us as if we were schoolchildren and asked: "What do you think is the cause of this wave of poverty?"

"The recession," we responded in chorus.

"You're wrong," he said, triumphantly. "The recession is nothing more than a scapegoat. If you look a little more closely, you'll see the real reason. They're importing poor people," he whispered. "The *collas*, in the mountains, are sending them here every day. Two years from now, they'll all be here. Only rich people will be living there, and we'll all be trying to emigrate to the Andes."

A reverent murmur went around the room, canonizing Flores's thesis. They all began to make suggestions.

"Let's round them up and send them back to the altiplano," someone said.

"Send them to Argentina. That's where they came from in the first place."

"Forget about them. All we have to do is take care of our own—the ones from around here."

Then the sociologist put in her two-cents' worth. "Poverty is just a mental complex. It doesn't exist, here or anywhere. It's a figment of our imaginations, like a ghost, a projection of hidden fears."

"So," Ira said, sarcastically, "I might as well turn the C.A.N. into a travel agency or private club. Or worse, hire an exorcist to expel the evil spirits. But, if you don't mind, we'll go on, as before, doing what we can for our clients."

Her determination didn't go beyond her words. She was full of doubt—systematic, obstinate, obsessive doubt. She couldn't help herself. For good or bad, she was always in doubt. As sure as Patroclo had lost his shirt, Ira had lost her self-confidence. Her interior strength was in hock, right along with her husband's real estate. It was slipping away, bit by bit, and soon there'd be nothing left.

Ira was worried about money, but that wasn't all. Her younger daughter worried her more. She'd brought her up to be a princess, but from the looks of things, she'd been taking lessons from Shere Hite. She didn't know if Julia was just an innocent playing with things she didn't understand, or if she'd lost it completely. That afternoon, sitting at her desk with a picture of Sister Teresa on the wall behind her, she asked me:

"Do you think it's normal for a girl to collect condoms? One of my friend's daughter has an album full of them. How should I advise the mother?"

"What kind are they—cloth or rubber?"

"Rubber, I guess."

"Then it's all right. She's probably just a normal, curious girl."

"I didn't know they made them out of cloth."

"I didn't either."

Her doubt didn't confine itself to the family. It was creeping into her philanthropic work. She'd always thought of the poor as God's creation. God was like a jeweler who made good pieces and others that weren't so good. But He liked all his handiwork, especially the people that nobody else liked. The same way a father loves a crippled child. So the easiest way to please God was to be poor. Ira didn't want to please God the easy way; that's why she had chosen to be rich. She wanted to enter heaven through the needle's eye, like the camel in the Bible. She thought she could do it by helping the poor. And in spite of recent disappointments, she wasn't about to give up. It was getting harder to help people. She knew that. There were a lot more of them than before. And some of them didn't want her help. They were stingy trouble-makers. Said the land belonged to them. Huh! If they didn't like the system, why didn't they just go live in some commu-nist country? She'd be glad to help raise the money to send them there. If there really was such a place. She didn't think there was. It was just like all the other silly things her parents made up to make her act right when she was a child.

As if all that wasn't enough to worry about, there was still room for more. The psychologist's theory had raised another doubt. If what the woman had said was true, then she'd spent her whole life washing wounds that didn't really exist. If it was all a product of her imagination, she ought to be able to clap her hands and make it disappear. There'd be a nice, clean world in its place—a world where there wasn't any poverty. She called an emergency meeting and, in front of the entire C.A.N. staff, told the psychologist to snap them out of it.

Lourdes, the psychologist, was wearing dark glasses. She was short, her hair was short, and she loved to read Mexican wrestling magazines.

"You didn't understand what I said," Lourdes began. "We aren't the ones who are hypnotized. To the contrary, we are quite lucid. It's the poor who are hypnotized. And they pass it on to their children. It's just as if they were carrying a tape recorder around in their brains, saying over and over, 'You're poor, you're worthless, things are never going to get any bet-ter for you.'"

"That is the most inane statement I've ever heard," the social worker muttered.

"That's interesting," Flores said. "You've combined Freud and Marx."

"I want practical solutions," Ira insisted. "What can we do to wake up the poor?"

"Stop giving them charity. What they need is therapy, to change their way of thinking."

"How long would it take?"

"It might take awhile. Longer than if they were rich. Let's say it takes your average person three to five years. It'd take a poor person ten."

"So, if we've got a hundred thousand poor, in our area alone, it'd take a million years of treatment to cure them," said Ira, figuring aloud. "It won't work. It'd take us till doomsday."

Flores wasn't quite so ready to drop the subject.

"How much would it cost per patient?"

"Figure fifteen dollars a session, four times a week; that makes two hundred and forty dollars a month."

The price was figured in dollars, since the national currency was completely unreliable.

Flores was bending over backward to make a good impression. Every time he said something, he'd look at Ira, to see how she reacted.

"Imagine," he said. "At forty dollars a month—that's our per capita income—it would take half a year's salary to pay for one month of therapy. And that's how much it would cost every month for ten years. Doesn't it make more sense just to give the needy person two hundred and forty dollars and forget about the psychiatrist?"

The psychologist stood up, though her head remained at the same level, sitting or standing.

"You're missing the point. What good is the money going to do him, if he continues to think of himself as poor?"

"If you ask me," said Flores, "it's better to think you're poor on a full stomach than the other way around."

190

"You can't appreciate having a sound mind, because you've never had one!" the psychologist said sharply. An approving murmur traveled around the room.

Right in the middle of the most serious part of the discussion, I stopped paying attention. I was daydreaming about Julia. Then, all of a sudden, I couldn't see her face. It vanished, leaving an oval-shaped gap. I looked at Ira and tried to recreate her daughter's face. Nothing happened. There wasn't a trace. The neurons that contained Julia's image were gone, wiped out by premature senility. I needed to see a picture. I needed that face. I had to have it, for my erotic fantasies. I couldn't picture her with a hood over her face. What was happening to me? One of two things—either I was mad or I didn't love her anymore.

TWENTY-THREE

Once Julia was gone, I didn't have to try to forget her. I could have tried to put her out of my mind. Chased girls on the street. Called up my favorite ex-student. But I didn't. I turned up my nose at women and settled into a quiet, comfortable home life.

If I'd had any fire left in me, her first letter would have put it out. I read it, put on my monk's robe, and sat down at my desk. From that moment on, I was a scribe, constantly bent over a writing tablet. It's a wonder I didn't become hump-backed.

"I want to know every word," I wrote, "—what you're doing, thinking, and dreaming. Think of the letters you write to me as a private diary."

I read every letter as if it contained her very essence. They weren't just words scrawled on a page. They were a material-ization of Julia, a living force. And dumber than that, I truly believed that writing would be enough to keep our love alive.

Now I look at them and laugh.

If I asked her if she still remembered me, she'd write:

"Forget you? How could I forget you, when all I see is your face, day and night. If it weren't for you, my brain would blow out, like a burned-out light bulb. It's like a jukebox with just one record—"Jonah"—and I play it over and over and over. Jonah . . . Jonah . . . Jonah. I'm crazy about you. I want you. My body wants you. I know in my mind that it's over between you and me. I know I can't do anything about it. But my body doesn't know that. If I didn't stop myself, my body would run out the door, and it wouldn't stop till it found you. Last night, I tried to pretend that my hands were your hands. I ran my fingers all over my body. It felt like a lot of tiny little lobsters. My fingers started to smell like your fingers. I put them inside of me. I wanted something desperately . . . something I can't have. I'm suffering. Please help me."

Her letters were like a trap—and I fell in every time. The first time I read them, it was O.K. But the second time, I'd start to read between the lines. I'd start to see things that weren't there. If she said she was full of blind, raging passion, I'd take it to mean she wanted a lover. I knew it would hap-pen, sooner or later, and there wasn't a thing I could do about it. How was I going to keep her satisfied—in Miami, of all places? By mental telepathy? I was desperate, so desperate I prayed for a national disaster, a cold wave that would sweep down from the North Pole and bury the whole country under a foot of snow, Julia included.

As bad as things were, I went on pretending she was

there—sitting across the table from me. I could talk to her anytime I liked. I read every letter half a dozen times. Till another one came and took its place. That way, when our words finally met, they were still warm and alive, even if it took days for them to reach each other.

JULIA: Today I think I realized for the first time that we really don't have a future together. It makes me so sad to think about that. Sometimes I pretend like we haven't broken up at all. Actually, we haven't broken up completely. Because if I can't have you physically, at least I can still carry an ideal of you, and I'll carry it with me always. If I fall in love again, he will have to measure up to that ideal.

JONAH: I read your letter and was glad to hear you weren't suffering anymore. I couldn't believe you'd made me into a platonic ideal. Then I read it again, and I started getting angry. I will *not* be your stuffed peacock. I will not sit quietly on your shelf, like some kind of decoration. Neither will I allow you to make me into a sexless dummy. I'd rather be remembered as a callous jerk, thank you very much!

JULIA: No matter what I say, I always end up hurting you. I didn't mean to. Please forgive me. With things the way they are, it's hard for us *not* to hurt each other. I know that we can't go on this way. I'm not happy, and neither are you. I've tried to put you out of my mind, but that doesn't seem to work either. It's not fair. Love shouldn't be this way. I remember when we first started seeing each other, I was happy, I felt alive! Then I started getting depressed. I started taking tranquilizers. I don't really understand what happened. I was very confused.

JONAH: I thought you loved me, but I was wrong. You *never* loved me—the whole thing was just one big horror show to you. How do you think it makes me feel, knowing you were taking tranquilizers? You were so unhappy with me, you had to dope yourself up. That's not what love is like. Can you imagine Juliet taking tranquilizers? Passion and tranquilizers do not mix. And believe me, if I'd known about it then, I'd have put an end to your misery on the spot.

JULIA: You asked me to tell you about the city. I really can't say what it's like. I haven't been able to take it all in myself yet. At first I didn't go out very much. Those first few weeks, I hardly left the apartment. I didn't want to see anything, if I couldn't see it with you. Finally I started feeling more like myself, but I'm still not crazy about the place. It's like a huge cemetery with lots of lights. That's the way I see it, because I don't have you anymore. There is one thing I'm glad about. Everything here is new to me. The bars and places don't remind me of anything. They don't remind me of *you*. That's the only good thing about Miami.

JONAH: You're lucky. Every place I go reminds me of you.

JULIA: Aren't you sick of letters? I can see it now: "Lover Smothers to Death under Mountain of Letters."

JONAH: I love your letters. If I had to choose between a letter from you and a good bottle of whiskey, I'd take the letter any day. Keep them coming. The guys down at the post office have pitched me a tent.

JULIA: Don't worry. I'll never stop writing to you. It's the only thing I care about. I was the one who suggested we write each other every day. Remember?

The minute I get out of bed, I start thinking about what I'm going to say to you. I pick up a pen as soon as I sit down for coffee. I write a sentence, scratch it out, and write something else. But no matter what, I always mail the letter at lunch. Otherwise, I'd go on writing all day. By the time I'm finished, I'm worn out. But at least I feel better. It helps to get it out of my system. I feel relaxed for the rest of the day.

JONAH: If you keep writing, I'm afraid you're going to run out of passion. But never mind. I'm not suggesting that you slow down—as long as it makes you feel better, that is. Maybe I'm being selfish. Maybe you should slow down a little bit.

JULIA: This Cuban guy I met asked me to go out with him. We went to this bar—the place I told you about. He wasn't very cute; he wasn't very friendly, either. But after I had a couple of Brandy Alexanders, I decided I kind of liked him. He was fun to talk to.

JONAH: Maybe one day we'll be able to talk about other people without getting jealous. I don't know when that will be. Maybe tomorrow. Maybe the next day. I hope it doesn't happen soon.

❧

ALL DAY at work I was in a daze. My right hand had become addicted to letter-writing and refused to do any other kind of work. I looked around me. Nobody at work affected me one way or the other, except Flores, who got on my nerves. I wanted to swat him like a bug. Julia was the only thing I cared about. I didn't have any energy left for anything else, for other people or things. Every now and then I felt a twinge of emotion, when Ira said something to remind me . . .

"I couldn't believe my ears," she said. "Somebody just told me that Alex Tambas has been committed, and there wasn't anything wrong with him. Have you ever heard of such a thing?"

"The last time I talked to him, he told me he was dating Caroline of Monaco."

"Lots of young men fall for Caroline or Brooke Shields," Ira argued.

"But Alex said he'd already bought a tux for the wedding."

"You're talking like an eighty-year-old. You used to have some pretty wild fantasies yourself. When I was a girl, I used to dream about marrying Rock Hudson."

When Ira made up her mind about something, it was a waste of time trying to talk her out of it. Especially if it had to do with Alex; she was fond of Alex. Ever since he started dating Julia, she'd treated him like a member of the family. Even paid his doctor bills. She got fed up with all the psychological bullshit and decided there really wasn't anything wrong with him. She was convinced that Alex was fine, it had all been a mistake, and she was going to have him released. She called up the hospital, told them that, and sent Alex a ticket home.

I told Julia about it in a letter but then tore it up. I wrote her another letter and tore it up, too. It didn't seem important. Julia wasn't at home. Alex could have moved in with Ira, and it wouldn't have mattered.

We weren't writing so often anymore, so I left out a lot of details. But our passion didn't diminish. If anything, the letters got more passionate. Julia was hornier than ever. I could tell—she was starting to talk dirty. It was obvious to me just from reading her letters; it had to be obvious to her friends in Miami, too. That was the bad part. I knew there were plenty of guys around. She told me she went to a discotheque with a Brazilian guy. They spent the whole evening making out in a corner; but, when he took her home, she wouldn't let him in the apartment.

"He called me a teaser," she wrote. "That's what they call mares they use to get the stallions excited. But the stallions don't get to do anything to them. He was right. I'm like that. I turn them on, and then I tell them to get lost. I'd rather save myself for you."

In another letter, she wrote, "I'm sending you this curly, black hair from you-know-where. Plant it, and it'll grow a velvety, black rose."

A week later, she wrote, "I'm tired of empty words. I took a piece of paper and rubbed it between my legs. I came. See this spot? It'll be dry by the time it reaches you. I'm sorry. This spot is the only thing my pussy can say to you. If she had a tongue, she'd say she missed you."

And in another letter, she said, "My letters are getting obscene. I've forgotten how to be innocent. I want you so much, I'm going crazy. I want to run up and down the street with a torch in my hand, looking for the biggest dick in Miami. I want to fuck a queer, the devil, anybody . . ."

I wrote back, "I love it when you talk dirty. You're back on track. I was getting tired of all the love talk."

"I love your thing," she wrote. "I want it to get as big as the

Washington Monument, and then I'll crawl on top of it. I want it to live inside of me, like a baby. And stay there forever, making me think I'm pregnant, not with a baby—with a hard cock that won't ever leave me."

After that, the letters started to thin out:

JONAH: Congratulations, Julia. You aren't writing as often as you used to. You don't need me as much as you thought you did.

JULIA: I hadn't realized that I was writing less. I've been a little out of it lately. I don't always notice things. And sometimes I do stupid things, like, today, I painted my mouth bright purple. I was feeling sort of sassy. I was thinking about writing you this letter with lipstick. Then I decided not to. But I am going to sign it with a big kiss.

JONAH: I've discovered that getting over you isn't going to be as hard as I thought. You haven't *been* here. I just dreamed you. All I have to do is put you out of my mind and start over.

JULIA: There's one man from Bolivia that I like better than anyone else. He's very friendly—people like him right off. The first time I ever talked to him, he said to me, "Julia, you can't be in two places at once. Either you have to settle down and make the best of your stay here or go back home." I was amazed he could figure me out—without me saying anything.

We practically stopped writing one another, and I didn't die. Actually, I was relieved. We'd been fooling ourselves. And the letters were largely responsible for our false hope.

The passionate words scrawled upon those pages faded quickly—as such things do. Actually, the relationship had ended months before. It was time to bury it. I practically stopped writing.

❦

ON SUNDAY, Talia and I went to her folks' house for lunch. I sat down with a drink in my hand. The glass was cold against my fingertips. Talia sat down beside me and started thumbing through a women's magazine.

"Look at this dining-room suite," she said. "Isn't that pretty? I think I'll have one made just like it."

"Not now," I said. "That would be stupid."

"Stupid—why?"

"We have a perfectly good table and chairs. Besides, this isn't a good time to be buying furniture."

"Why not?" she snipped. "I suppose you're going to start talking about the economic crisis!"

"No. Actually, I was thinking of your father. He's having financial problems right now."

"That's just a rumor."

"Ask the servants. They didn't get paid last month."

"He probably forgot. He has a lot on his mind."

"Open your eyes, Talia!" I said, lowering my voice. "If you want a cup of coffee around here, you have to tip the cook."

"You're exaggerating."

"He even stopped construction on the pyramid," I argued.

"Well, that's a blessing. It's the dumbest looking thing I've ever seen."

"But if he doesn't finish it, he's going to lose everything he put into it—a million dollars down the drain."

"But it's not worth anything, even if he did finish it."

"That's beside the point. The point is your father is broke."

"I see what you're doing. You're trying to frighten me. And if you keep on, I'm going to get sick. Of course, the doctor will say that it's psychosomatic, that there's nothing wrong with me. And everybody will think I'm stupid and make fun of me. That's what you want, isn't it? I'm getting a headache already. If it doesn't go away, I'm calling the doctor."

"Why call the doctor, if you know it's psychosomatic?"

"Because I want to look stupid. I don't care what everybody thinks."

"Fine, think whatever you please. Your father's in great shape. Everything is just fine."

During lunch, Patroclo picked at his food. He cut up his steak and then let it sit there getting cold. Nobody was hungry. Which spoiled my usual healthy appetite.

I'd never been comfortable with so many servants buzzing around. And once Patroclo stopped paying them, they became insufferable. One snatched my plate right out from in front of me, before I could finish my meal. The rice was too salty; the drinks, too warm. But Patroclo never said a word. Or even noticed, for that matter. He wouldn't have noticed if Talia had levitated the table up to chin-level.

I asked him how the pyramid was going. Talia glared at me.

"I've stopped construction," he said. "We can't get the materials . . . with things the way they are. There's a cement shortage. Fortunately, there's no rush to get it finished. None of us is going to die tomorrow. Unless you, Jonah, are keeping something from us."

"Not I. Take your time."

"As far as I'm concerned," Talia added, "you can put it off indefinitely."

"I think I'd better spend my time taking care of the living," he said, filling my wine glass. "Which may be harder than finishing the project, since someone I know is making me old before my time."

"I suppose you're referring to Julia," Talia said.

"You're right," he said, with a sigh.

"What sort of problem could Julia be causing?" I asked innocently.

"The worst kind—she's ruining the family name."

"She's practically caused her father to have a heart attack," Ira said, wrinkling her brow.

"What has she done now?" Talia asked.

"I'd rather not say."

"For God's sake, Daddy," Talia insisted. "Stop being so mysterious. What did she do?"

"Of course, you could keep it a secret forever," I said jokingly.

"The little idiot," he began, gulping down some wine, "has fallen in love with the son of a *pichicatero*. I sent her to the States, hoping she'd get straightened out. So what does she do? She goes and falls in love with the son of a *pichicatero*."

I had a sudden fit of coughing, and Talia came to my rescue.

"Damn wine!" I said. "It got stuck in my throat. There was a seed in it. Damn! Where do you buy your wine, anyway?"

TWENTY-FOUR

Julia was coming home! Things began to pick up.

She'd been home for a week when I ran into her one day downtown. Her arms were full of packages—gifts she'd got for her friends back in Miami. We went into a bar for a Bitter Kas.

"It's funny, but you don't look the same to me," she said.

"I'm just the same."

"No, you aren't. Your nose is bigger, you look paler, and your hair is falling out."

"I look just the same!" I said emphatically. "I know. I look at myself every day in the mirror."

"Well, maybe so. When you're away from someone, you develop sort of a touched-up image of them."

"So, I looked better to you when you were in Miami, and now you're back, and I look awful. Thanks a lot!"

"You don't look awful—just a little worse than before. You're all right."

Strangely enough, I felt the same way about her. The Julia sitting in front of me, sipping a Bitter Kas, didn't hold a candle to the Julia I'd been thinking about. It was strange that I'd never really checked her out, up close. I'd never really paid much attention to her defects before. She had a low forehead. Her hands were too big for a woman. Her movements weren't very graceful. I felt the way men must have felt seeing their mail-order brides arrive, looking very little like their pictures. It didn't matter, though. The way I felt about Julia, it wouldn't have mattered if she'd grown hooves and a curly tail. Looks weren't important.

I didn't want to hear about her trip to the States. I'd already heard her telling her family about it. She'd gone on for hours—with occasional interjections from Talia, who'd spent a year in the States, too. I already knew enough to draw you a map of Orlando and could explain in great detail the human-like habits of the porpoise. I knew more about marine life than your average zoologist and more about urban violence than the Miami police force.

I learned more from her pictures than her stories. Who the hell took all those pictures of her, I wondered. The same turkeys who're always hanging around, looking for foreign girls, I said to myself. It's the same, everywhere you go. Fortunately, she didn't learn English. That must have slowed down the local skirt-chasers.

Of course, her parents would have loved it if she'd come home babbling a few phrases in English. But, from the looks of it, she hadn't learned a thing. Of course, she hadn't. She never went to class, and she hung around with Latin Americans the whole time. She said she got a sudden attack of chauvinism and didn't want to muddy up her pure, Latin heritage with Yankee habits. That really pissed off Patroclo, who'd paid—in advance—for a whole year of schooling at the best language academy in Miami.

We were a little surprised to see she'd picked up a Cuban accent. She sounded like she'd just stepped off the boat from Havana. She was still talking like that when we were sitting in the bar. I couldn't concentrate on what she was saying because of the singsong in her voice.

She hadn't come back because her parents wanted her back—I was sure of that. If she'd wanted to stay, nothing Patroclo could have said would have changed her mind. Even if he'd threatened to cut her money off, I'm sure she could have found some guy to support her. And she probably would have thought it was the thing to do. She came back because she didn't like the United States. She hated frozen food, vending machines, cops you couldn't bribe and who weren't impressed by the fact that she was Patroclo del Paso y Troncoso's daughter. She was glad to be home and sitting in a noisy bar where you had to wait for half an hour and then they ripped you off, to boot.

Her boyfriend's name? Grigotá. That was Chico Lindo's son's name—Chico Lindo, the drug lord. And damned if it wasn't the same guy. He was a student at the University of Miami. And he'd dropped out of school to follow her back home. He was so crazy about her, he would have followed her to Katmandu.

"Is he better than me in bed?" I asked.

"How should I know? I've never gone to bed with him."

"Why? Are you afraid to?"

"He thinks I'm a virgin. He respects me."

"Did you lie to him?"

"No, he just thinks it. He says he can tell if a girl is good or bad."

"That's a shame. It sounded to me like you really needed a man. I guess you never got satisfied."

"Hey, don't worry about me. I'm as happy as a lark. I needed someone to look up to me, to treat me like a queen. Women like being put on a pedestal. We like to make our man suffer a little every now and then, like the day I made Grigotá wait for me for three hours in the rain. And he got sick and had to go to the hospital. And he made one of the nurses bring me a note that said, 'I love you.'"

"Are you still taking Valium?" I asked. I knew she wasn't.

"I haven't taken any in months."

Grigotá was totally enamored with Julia. He trusted her completely. Told her his life's story from start to finish. Which she passed on to me, while we were drinking our drinks.

Grigotá was about twenty, of medium build, muscular, with high cheekbones and piercing eyes. He had so little to say that, in school, his teachers thought he might be retarded. They advised his parents to put him in a special school, but Chico knew his son better than they did. He found another school, where the teachers recognized his talent, even said he was smarter than average. The problem was that the boy *thought* he was dumb. But later he changed his mind, after he'd seen his first spaghetti western and learned what it really meant to be dumb. Ringo and Django never opened their mouths except to belt down a glass of whiskey. He wasn't like that. He was quiet in an attractive sort of way, and that wasn't bad.

If the boy could have chosen his own father, it wouldn't have been Chico Lindo. He would have preferred a retired general with medals on his chest or a rich businessman. It wasn't easy having Chico Lindo for a father. Though he had to admit, it did have its advantages. No one dared get in his way. But Grigotá wanted more than that. Too bad his father wasn't a preacher or something—anything legal. People would have respected him then. In Florida, Grigotá had made a big hit with the American girls: he was a male chauvinist. They liked it when he got jealous and picked fights with other guys. They even flirted with other guys on purpose, just to make him mad. And just to please them, he cultivated a Rudolf Valentino style. A certain type of woman loved it: the type that worked out every day, ate health food, and carried a vibrator in her purse.

Two years of playing the stud was enough. He needed a rest, the kind of rest he could get with Julia. She couldn't stand it when he acted jealous, even if the sentiment was real. "I'm not a gringa, so cut the Don Juan act. Besides, you're lousy at it," she'd say. The poor guy was confused. He really was jealous, but he didn't know what it meant, being jealous. Maybe it meant he loved her.

From the first time they'd met, Grigotá had followed Julia around like a little kid. That wasn't his style, though, and eventually he realized that he needed to get away for a while. If he could only go back to being a student in Miami, where his friends had taken him for the son of some rich politician and expected Grigotá to follow in his footsteps someday. Then he wouldn't have to put up with the sort of thing that had happened at Julia's house a few days before.

He was sitting in Julia's living room, when a man with bushy eyebrows walked in. The man took one look at Grigotá and turned bright red. They said hello, and then the man with the red face asked, "Would you mind telling me what you're doing in my living room, sitting on my sofa, drinking my whiskey, and dropping ashes all over my rug?"

"Waiting for Julia," he answered. "She's getting dressed. We're going out."

"And who gave you permission to go out with my daughter?"

"I'm sorry, I didn't know I needed permission."

"Well, you do. You need permission to do a lot of things, including going out with my daughter! She doesn't date just anyone."

"Very well. Would you mind if I dated your daughter?"

"Yes, I certainly would."

"May I ask why?"

"I don't know you. And coming in here, raiding my icebox won't make you family."

"Grigotá Rodríguez's my name. So . . . now you know me."

"Grigotá? What kind of a name is that?"

"It's my name. Sorry if you don't like it."

"Grigotá . . . now I remember. You're the one who kept my daughter from learning English. Chico Lindo's son . . . I hear the cocaine business is really booming," he said sarcastically. "You must be proud of your father!"

"I hope you won't blame me for what my father does."

"I'm an old-fashioned man," Patroclo said. "A fascist, a racist, and prejudiced against many things. I don't want you here, even if you and your father have nothing to do with one another. I don't want my daughter associating with people like you."

Later Grigotá regretted having held his tongue, but he'd promised Julia he wouldn't get into an argument with her father.

"But I love Julia," he said, "and she loves me. We belong together."

"Nonsense. There's no such thing as love."

"There is, and we love each other."

"Prove it then," Patroclo insisted, picking up the ice bucket. "Take this and bring me some."

"That's impossible. Love isn't something you can put in a bucket. It's something you feel inside."

"You can cut the poetic bullshit. I'm not some naïve schoolkid. This is Julia's father you're talking to."

So Patroclo wouldn't let Grigotá take Julia out, and I was glad. I watched the whole thing at a distance and leapt for joy every time the relationship hit a snag. Of course, it didn't help me out any. Julia and I were through.

In spite of evidence to the contrary, Julia swore she wasn't interested in Grigotá. And to prove it, she gave me the gifts he gave her. I took some of them, just to go along with the gag. I guess I'd scored a point, but what good was it going to do me in the end? If it'd been a real competition, any joker could have whipped me before the first whistle. I'd been kicked out of the game at the start and left to watch from the sidelines, like some cripple.

Grigotá had given her enough presents to fill a junk shop. A chiming table clock, a jewelry box shaped like a pagoda, a small Pandora's box, little coffin-shaped boxes, a gold chain with a sexy Egyptian symbol, a whole collection of record albums, all kinds of stuffed animals—dogs, cats, bears—and a Spanish doll.

Talia should have the gold chain, I decided. She deserved something. In the last few weeks, she'd become a different person. Either something strange had come over her or something strange had come over me. To me, she'd become the heroine of a pastoral romance, and I loved her purely and passionately.

It was wonderful to wake up one morning and find her there, shimmering like a clear liquid in a crystal vial. Was this maturity? A biologist would have said she had reached a perfect hormonal balance. She woke up like some winged creature, free and facing the light. She wasn't dependent on me anymore. And I decided she deserved a gift.

That afternoon, I walked home with the chain in my pocket. The street lights came on automatically. I still couldn't see a thing and stumbled along in the dark.

The house lights were off. I went in and felt my way along the corridor, anxious to see my wife. I heard voices in the living room but couldn't tell who was there. Whoever it was, was sitting in the dark—there wasn't any light coming from beneath the door.

I pressed my ear against the door—something I'd never done before—and listened. I could hear glasses clinking, and I could smell alcohol. Talia was talking to the young medium.

She was offering him another drink.

"I can't," he said, refusing her offer. "I won't be able to make it home."

"Spend the night here, if you'd like. There's plenty of room."

"In your bed?"

"Sure, it's king size," Talia said, slurring her words. "You wouldn't be embarrassed, would you? It wouldn't be the first time. Three hundred years ago you begged me to sleep with you."

"And you refused," the medium replied. "Not only that, you burned me to a crisp."

"But now you're as good as new, so don't complain. Of course, you might want to look up the number of the fire department before you turn in."

"You wouldn't . . ."

"What do you think? I've been asleep for three hundred years!"

He got up from his chair and fell flat on the floor. Talia ran to help him up, and they walked together into the kitchen—too far away for me to hear what they were saying. I left the house.

I hated my barrio—the cement sidewalks, streets, and facades of buildings, the carefully pruned trees, the perfectly molded passers-by. The moon, like a ripe plum ready to drop, was the only sign of life.

I got into my car and drove off. I passed a line of cars moving along like a slow procession of insects. At the intersection, brakes screeched. Angry drivers honked their horns. By the time I reached downtown, my shirt was dripping wet. I stopped the car in front of the bar where Julia and I had stopped for a drink.

I was desperate and looked for relief in a glass of Campari. I finished the first drink and ordered a second. It was eight o'clock—dinner time—and the bar had emptied out. Except for three German tourists—two men and a woman, blond, unkempt, unattractive—several half-lit teenagers, and a poker-faced couple who sat in a corner, looking like two post-coital peacocks. In that crowd, I felt like a buzzard choking down his own insides, which divine providence had forced him to eat.

"Drinking alone. That's a bad sign. I didn't see you, so I sat down over there, laid my gun on the table, and proceeded to drink myself into a coma."

"I imagine service was pretty poor."

"I was thinking about killing myself," Licurgo said.

I didn't believe him. Licurgo was stuck to life like a leech. He was exaggerating—to get my attention. I hadn't seen him for a long time, but he hadn't changed. Still the same good-time Charlie, the same babbling parrot he'd always been. I knew his line so well, I could have recited it by heart, if I could have gotten a word in edgewise.

"I'm glad you're here. Otherwise, I would have called you. I have to talk to somebody."

"Why? Justina kick you out?"

"I wish the hell she would. But that's not it. I've fallen in love with Olga."

"So?"

"I asked her to marry me. I said I'd ask Justina for a divorce, and if she wouldn't give me one, I said I'd drown her in the bathtub. She turned me down flat! And then she broke up with me!"

"That's strange. Did she say why?"

"She said I was ugly. She hadn't noticed in the beginning, but now she did. Can you believe it?"

"Love is blind, but sometimes sight returns. Looks like you're out of luck, my friend."

"That wasn't it," he insisted. "I'm more handsome than a lot of guys, even movie stars, Belmondo, to name one. That wasn't the reason. She just didn't want to say why. She said it over and over, that I was ugly, and she'd hate to have my kid. I've never been so humiliated in my whole life! I threatened to kill myself. So what does she do? Goes straight to a hardware store and buys some rope. She told me to go ahead, hang myself, I wouldn't be such a bad sight dangling from a rope. Then I said I didn't want to do it that day. She got mad.

210

Said I'd gone back on my word, a real man would have gone through with it. I said I was sorry I'd disappointed her, but I'd never committed suicide before. I was sorry I'd wasted her rope. If she wanted to, I said, she could tie it around my neck and drag me down the street, like a dog. I'd even crawl on my hands and knees and piss on fire hydrants, if it'd please her. She said she wouldn't have an ugly mongrel like me."

"What do you want me to do about it?" I burst in. "I can't make Olga love you. I can't make you handsome."

"Did I say I wanted you to?" Licurgo replied. "All I want is for you to tell me how to convince Olga that I love her."

"No. What you want to know is how to convince her that she loves *you.*"

"You're right," he admitted. "How can I?"

"Forget about her," I suggested. "You can get a hundred girls as good as Olga."

"I can't forget about her."

"Then get used to being dumped on. There's nothing meaner than a woman who used to love you but doesn't anymore."

"Then you think she did love me?"

It seemed that Licurgo had forgotten how much Olga loved him in the beginning, and how little attention he'd paid her.

"I've got to go," I said, fed up with listening to him.

"Stay a little longer," he begged. "I promise not to bore you with my love life. We can just sit here and drink, till one of us falls out of his chair."

"Sorry, I can't keep you company. But I can give you something to make up for it. Give it to Olga. Women like this sort of thing."

"Is it solid gold?" he asked, running the chain through his fingers.

"Solid gold. It belonged to a French prostitute. She gave it to me as a keepsake."

Licurgo was impressed. Any reference to Europe

impressed him. I managed to slip away and, on my way out, gave the waitress a couple of dollars to buy him a drink. "Take care of him," I told her.

His theatrics hadn't convinced me. Licurgo wasn't capable of loving anyone deeply. He probably had gotten indigestion and took it for love pangs. He was attracted to her. I knew that. But he didn't love her. He wanted her to treat him like a dog, and that's why he put up with it. He was a dog. It was in his genes.

I passed by a theater where they were showing an old Italian movie. I bought a ticket and went in. I'd already seen the film, but I didn't care. I just needed some place to hide.

Later that night, I was lying in bed and flipping through a magazine. Talia was lying next to me, removing her fingernail polish. A boring musical comedy was playing on TV.

"I've been keeping something from you," she said, her speech still a little slurred. "But first you have to promise to forgive me."

"That depends on the sin," I said.

"It's not a sin. It's something that's been bothering me."

"I'll forgive you," I said, ready to hear about her flirtation with the medium.

"Do you remember that boy who got electrocuted on Daddy's fence?"

"How could I forget him?" I exclaimed.

"Well, it was my fault. He was in love with me. He started following me around. I was flattered to have such a persistent admirer. One day he stopped me on the street and asked me my name. I lied to him. I told him I was single. He must have thought I was still living at my parents' house. The night he died, he was trying to get in to see *me*. I felt like it was my fault. I still feel that way."

"Who the hell was he, anyway—Don Juan's great-grandson?"

"I don't know. We never really talked. He never told me his name."

"Probably some fiend. Don't worry about it. It wasn't your fault he fell in love with you."

I got up and went to the bathroom, and, while I was brushing my teeth, I thought about the electrocuted boy. Poor guy, he'd been dead for years! But every now and again, some female member of the family would dredge up his memory and claim him for her lover. If he'd been a rag doll, he'd have been torn to shreds.

TWENTY-FIVE

Patroclo told Grigotá to get the hell out and never show his ugly face around there again. Or around the barrio, either. Or Julia's favorite places—clubs, restaurants, churches, and hospitals, as well as her friends' houses and her friends' servants' houses. If Patroclo had thought of it, he'd have hung a bell around Grigotá's neck, just as they did to lepers in the Middle Ages.

My joy from that victory was brief. It ended that same afternoon, when a Mercedes Benz with tinted-glass windows parked in front of Patroclo's mansion. You couldn't see anyone on the other side of the glass; the car looked self-propelled. Then the door opened, and Chico Lindo and three of his hit men stepped out.

Patroclo and Chico talked for a long time. Neither one of them was in a hurry to end the conversation. Chico's men surveyed the front of the house carefully. The street, brightly lit by the sun, didn't pose a threat. It was a hot, sultry afternoon, and the tar between the blocks of cement had begun to soften. Butterflies fluttered from puddle to puddle and eventually lost their lives on the radiators of passing cars. A garland of yellow and white wings trailed across the pavement.

The heat made short work of Chico's gunmen. One fell asleep on the front seat with the radio at full volume. One sprawled on the grass near the sunflowers and cleaned his gun. The third flirted through the window with the cook, a large-breasted woman, who, after a few minutes, appeared in the garden carrying a tray of drinks.

Chico Lindo's visit marked the beginning of a new era at the Del Paso y Troncoso mansion. In nothing flat, he brought the entire household around to his way of thinking. Patroclo was soon convinced that unscrupulous behaviour wasn't catching. You could associate with criminals, even marry them, without losing your respectability. Their money wasn't contaminated, either. Decent people could use it, even invest it, with total immunity. He breathed a sigh of relief. Before he knew it, he'd be back on his feet financially, and, in no time, he'd be able to finish the pyramid. He decided to let Grigotá come and go as he pleased.

"Your father has sold out to the *pichicateros*," I told Talia.

"Nothing of the kind," she replied. "Julia's in love with Grigotá, and Daddy's accepted it. That's all."

No one I knew would listen to my version of what was happening. Licurgo thought I was speaking out of jealousy. Patroclo couldn't be bribed, he said. Esteban wondered if I'd been drinking. Not even Arminda, my ex-secretary, would believe me. When I told her I was wild about her, she believed that, but when it came to Patroclo's honor, she refused to be taken in.

What a girl, Arminda! I'd completely forgotten about her, till one day, out of the blue, I saw her standing at a bus stop. I pulled over to the curb and opened the door. She got in without even looking to see who the driver was, as if fate had ordered her to take the first ride that came along. I drove her to her place in Villa Mercedes, a small house she shared with her cousin Betsy, a nurse who worked days—and many nights—at the hospital.

A few weeks before our meeting, Arminda's baby had been born dead—the umbilical cord wrapped around his neck. Losing the child was bad, but what upset her more was not knowing—in advance—that things would turn out that way. If she had known, she could have saved herself all that worrying. After the stillbirth, she was more determined than ever to love the child and to moan and groan whenever anyone mentioned it. She asked me not to talk about it, so I didn't. But *she* talked about it all the time—even in bed. She would describe its pale, little body and its blank face. I could almost see it. Then she'd lay her head on my shoulder and sob shamelessly.

Arminda's heart wasn't eager to forget me. She fell in love with me for the second time and made a place for me in her life—not a very big one. A serious, young notary—a guy who'd probably marry her—was already taking up most of her time. Every now and then, Arminda would find a night when her suitor was busy and Betsy was on duty at the hospital. Then, I'd enjoy rubbing my hands over her firm thighs, her belly still soft from the pregnancy. She wouldn't look at it—she was afraid she might see a stretch mark. Begrudgingly, she'd offer me her firm breasts, deprived of their motherly function, and I'd touch them, carefully, like touching a wounded bird.

I wanted Arminda to be my confidante. I wanted to tell

her about my father-in-law's sordid business deals and have her comfort me. But she wouldn't go along. Wasn't it enough she'd given me her body? I wasn't interested in sex, but she didn't understand that. It wouldn't have mattered to me, if we'd spent our afternoons on a seesaw in the park.

What I needed was someone to listen to me. One day I walked into Ira's office at the center. I told her what I suspected. I didn't know if she was listening or not. Her face was a blank, but a slight batting of the eyes suggested that something had made an impression. She remained calm and thanked me for confiding in her. She promised to look into it.

The next day, she stopped talking to Patroclo, Julia, and Grigotá. She still sat down at the table with them and went out with them at night, but she never said a word. She was like a nun, trying to keep her vows and work in a bar at the same time. She was mad at them, but she was worried about them, too. Every now and then, I'd catch her mumbling a prayer.

Sometimes Julia and Grigotá would be listening to records in the living room. Ira would sit with her back to them or behind a column, her nose at a forty-five degree angle, like she'd smelled a rat. She found the entire situation distasteful and baffling. What could her daughter see in a common, tight-lipped creature like Grigotá? And how could he venerate Julia, like some Spanish virgin, and, at the same time, probe every inch of her body, as if he'd been searching for a crack in the plaster. I couldn't figure out why Ira would want to watch them all day long. She wasn't jealous. She wasn't nosy. Maybe she thought a constant vigil would drive them into doing something outrageous. They might make love right in front of her. And if they did, what would she say? Would she pretend she hadn't noticed or send them a pack of condoms by the maid?

Ira woke up one morning to find a diamond necklace glittering on the night stand by her bed. She hoped her husband hadn't left it. She didn't want anything from that hypocrite.

Maybe the tooth fairy had brought it. The following week, she found the keys to a new car in the same spot. Gifts were popping up all over the place, and everyone was thrilled except Ira. The servants were thrilled to receive their paychecks, Julia to have a new stereo—which she immediately lent to a friend who returned it broken—Patroclo to get back his land and his credit rating. Only Ira, the implacable inquisitor, stood apart, like an exotic flower whose unpleasant odor filtered into every corner of the house.

At lunch, one Sunday, she finally broke her silence. She didn't say she was sorry. She didn't even raise her eyes from the wine glass she was holding in her hand. She simply joined in the conversation, as if she'd never left it, and asked if anyone liked the dessert.

"Delicious," Julia said.

"Yes, delicious," Grigotá said.

"Excellent," Patroclo said.

"Can you guess who made it?" she asked.

They looked at her admiringly, assuming she'd made it herself. Smiles and words of praise rose from each side of the table. Harmony returned to the Del Paso y Troncoso household.

Julia was least affected by the new calm, since the change in her mother's behavior hadn't bothered her in the first place. What affected her a great deal, on the other hand, was Alex's return to the city. She ran into him downtown, sunning himself in front of the National Bank. He was wearing a white shirt and faded jeans, clothes he'd been wearing for years and donned with the air of an old soldier putting on his army uniform. Clothes that, nonetheless, failed to disguise his obvious insanity.

He was bumming cigarettes off the passers-by. He'd smoke half of one, throw it down, and bum another. He stopped all the people he knew, most of whom were successful businessmen—or pretending to be. They would listen to him for a few minutes, bribe him with a cigarette, and with a clear conscience (they'd contributed to the happiness of a crazy man),

hurry on down the street. Julia was distraught and came looking for me the next morning. An unexpected wind had
blown in from the south and was rattling the window panes.
A winter coolness was settling over the city. The cold
reflected in her sad face and firm nipples, which stuck out
under her T-shirt. Her skin was rough and chapped.

"Alex is back," she said.

"I know. I don't suppose you're planning a welcome-home
party. But if you are, your mother ought to pay for it. She
brought him here."

"She doesn't know what Alex did to me."

"Julia, why are you here? What do you want me to do?"

"Nothing," she replied, her face pale. "I've taken care of it
myself."

I wasn't going to press it—I could tell she didn't want to
talk about it. But gradually she began to loosen up. Staring at
the wall in front of her and pretending she wasn't hearing
her own painful words, she told me the whole, pathetic story.

Her heart had practically leaped out of her body when she
saw Alex. That night she'd taken three Anacin to get to sleep.
I told her Anacin wasn't a sleeping remedy, but she wouldn't
believe me. She had great confidence in its tranquilizing
potential. Probably the warm, damp air had put her to
sleep—the smell of rotting plants that infected the barrio at
that time of year. But what Julia wanted was to go to sleep
artificially and wake up artificially. The only thing that
seemed real to her—that mattered in the least—was the
thumping of her own heart.

She didn't care what she put on that morning. A short
dress—too short to wear to church—and a white teddy had
been laid out for her. Her black leather boots had been
placed next to the bed. She dabbed cologne behind her ears,
on her wrists, and on the inside of her thighs. She applied
more make-up than usual. She sat down in front of the mirror and painted her lips and eyes to look like a young hooker.
She gave herself a tragic face, the kind of face you might see
on a wall calendar or the cover of some scandal sheet. Then

she left for Alex's house, knowing full well that her dazzling sensuality—her only weapon—might get her into serious trouble.

Alex's room looked the way she thought it would look. Books on the chairs. Clean clothes on the bed. Dirty clothes all over the floor. The door to the closet, which contained only empty hangers, was standing open. She didn't know why she had come there, but she went in, thinking she might see some sort of sign. Alex, as soon as he saw her, knew exactly why she'd come and what she was going to do. Julia thought she had come there out of fear; and, standing under the heavy light of the ceiling lamp, she decided to grab her own life by the tail—like a scorpion—and ordered Alex to take off his clothes. He docilely removed his shirt and pants, without a word. He could have said he was cold; he could have thrown her out. His insane mind could have invented many reasons not to do what she'd asked. And she would have accepted any excuse he'd invented. But Julia's sudden entrance unnerved him, disabled his only weapon—his insanity. There was something remarkably sane about Alex, standing there in his boxer shorts, and Alex knew it. His sanity became even more obvious when he stepped out of his shorts, stood there for a moment, naked and ridiculous, and then quickly covered his genitals with his hands, like a child.

When he looked up, Julia was naked, too, though he hadn't heard her taking off her clothes. But somehow he'd known she would take them off, even before she did. He'd imagined her lying in his bed, legs spread apart, a toothy grin on her face—an expression that frightened him a little. Then, suddenly, his vision collided with reality, and Julia was screaming, "Rape me, you bastard! If you want to rape me, get it over with." He wasn't sure if she'd actually said it or if he'd read it in her smile. She hadn't exactly invited him. But somehow, for some unknown reason, he was supposed to hurt her, the way mean boys hurt trapped animals.

He smiled an idiotic smile, walked over to her, kissed her on the foot, and laid his head on the bed. Then Julia kicked him, and he rolled to the floor, holding his bleeding mouth with one hand, his genitals, with the other.

"Don't ever come near me!" she screamed. "Leave me alone." Later, when she thought about that scene, she nearly got hysterical, remembering that Alex had bummed a cigarette off her as she walked out the door.

"Did you give him one?" I asked.

"No," she snapped, and jutted out her chin. She was proud of putting him down.

"What if he'd raped you?"

"I knew he wouldn't."

"You might have been wrong. What if he'd tried to hurt you?"

"I don't know," she said, impatiently.

"Just tell me what you *think* you would have done," I prodded.

"No!"

"Tell me how you knew he wasn't going to rape you."

"I knew what I was doing, that's all."

Her involvement with Alex made me jealous. I wanted to say something mean to her, ask her why she was so goddam sure of herself all of a sudden. Was it her victory over poor, dumb Alex, or was it seeing she was worth a nice sum on the open market? But I held my tongue. She didn't know what was going on—that much was clear. She thought she was free, could run her own life at last. Julia was about as free as a trapped pawn. But she didn't know that.

I decided not to ask her anything else, and not to tell her anything either. If I'd told her about my latest scheme—which was to become a drug runner—then I would have to tell her what Patroclo was up to. It would have tickled me pink to grab a couple of frying pans and go banging them down the street yelling, "Patroclo's a hypocrite!" But it wouldn't have done any good. I'd already told my friends. I might as well have told them I'd seen a flying saucer.

My words had become meaningless. No one listened to anything I said. I felt like I'd been swallowed by an enormous, dark silence, and the city was that silence. The streets and buildings overwhelmed me. Sometimes I had to drive down to the river to get away for a while. I'd lie down with my face in the sand and let the water rush over me. Thoughts would come rushing through my brain. Silly ideas. I thought about running away with Arminda, or marrying Julia in some bizarre, native rite. Dressing up in a tuxedo and drinking a lethal dose of rose oil. Taking up the cause of the working class, becoming a union leader, maybe running for office. I wore myself out thinking of all the possibilities. My brain felt like it was about to explode, but it didn't. The ideas just burned themselves out.

All but one, the one about becoming a drug runner. Everybody was doing it, even the upper class. Young executives. Youths with brilliant futures. Pregnant women, or women who pretended to be pregnant. Frustrated lovers. Weekend Don Juans. The terminally ill—in a last ditch effort to maximize their estates. If I were going to join their ranks, first I would have to find a rationale. A reason to justify such an action. I couldn't think of a single motive, except for the total lack of motives in my life. Maybe the act itself would fill the void. My old world was crumbling around me. My friends were turning into zombies. Patroclo, Ira, Julia, Talia—zombies who refused to stay in their tombs. My entire universe, learned line by line since childhood—from catechism to the law codes—all of it was sifting into obscurity. Corpses and darkness were the staves of my existence. And if one of them began to come to life, I'd blink my eyes and see it for what it really was—a termite-infested structure that looked solid enough, but, when touched, would collapse into a heap of dust. I wasn't entirely convinced of that, though. Maybe I was being too hard. Maybe it was wrong to judge. The last flicker of light was snuffed out by my own disbelief. At that point, I became indifferent. Boarding a plane with a bag of cocaine or a box of violets—it was all the same to me.

But first, I had to find someone to hire me. I thought of Antonio Extremadura. A strange duck! We'd been in school together. He was the most responsible kid in my class. A straight-A student. After high school, he'd gone to the States to study economics. Years later, he reappeared, already mixed up in the drug trade. It didn't surprise me, after I'd thought about it and realized that he was doing the same thing now that he'd done in school. Licking somebody's boots. In school, he'd licked his teachers' boots. Now he was licking Chico Lindo's boots. If Antonio had been raised in a monastery, he would have become a monk. If he'd grown up in Treblinka, he'd have become a world-renowned torturer. The standard didn't matter. He could conform to any set of guidelines. He was destined to live in the shadow of a powerful man. To bend his morals to fit the situation. Of course, his most important asset was not having any morals. He was a nice, neutral sort of guy—the sort of guy who doesn't clash with anyone. He was mediocre, and he knew it. To make up for his mediocrity, he ordered his clothes from the best tailor's shop in New York. But clothes couldn't solve the problem. If anything, they called attention to his worst features: his small stature and large nose. Without the flashy clothes, he would have faded into the woodwork. With them, he looked like a court jester. Sooner or later he'd have to face it: he was just an ordinary remora, and no matter how big the shark he attached himself to, he wasn't going to amount to much.

I went to see him at his hotel. He always chose the swankiest place in town, even if he planned to stay for six months. I walked into his suite, and he immediately filled two glasses with whiskey. The whole room was done in whiskey. It smelled like whiskey. The walls were papered in a heavy, whiskey-colored brocade. The drapes, carpets, even the music coming from the intercom—the entire ambience was expensive and decadent, like whiskey. Since he couldn't think of anything to talk about, he bitched about not having a telex in his room. One of the inconveniences of living in South America. He hadn't been able to find a poly-lingual secretary either. Any girl who spoke English, French, German, Dutch, and Japanese would have done. He'd put an ad in every paper in South America. It was a shame. South American women didn't prepare themselves to do anything. And he wasn't about to hire just a pretty face.

Antonio was beginning to look old for his age. He wasn't gray or wrinkled. But the years were beginning to show. His nose seemed larger than before and twitched avariciously, like a rat. His eyes looked squirrelish. His shoulders were stooped. He resembled a butler waiting to receive orders.

He was surprised when I told him what I'd come for.

"You must be joking," he said. "I never expected to hear from *you*. And don't think I haven't had offers from all kinds. Old girlfriends, relatives of friends. None of them ever surprised me . . . but *you* . . . I can't believe it."

According to Antonio, I wasn't cut out to be a drug runner, and he had a good eye for hiring, he claimed. The best drug runners were the fresh, go-getter types. The highly motivated kind, who dreamed about sports cars, classy prostitutes, and lots of money. The kind of guy who'd sell his own mother to get what he wanted. He liked to send them off, fearful but optimistic, like recruits leaving for the mission field. He never stopped to think that many of them would end up in jail. He had men in Mexican jails, American jails, European jails. They might never show up again. Or if they did—if they lived that long—they'd be senile, old men. The ones who managed to slip past the law would be ringing his doorbell and smiling—with fewer teeth than before, sickly, and skinny—but ready for another trip. He'd get them some false teeth, fatten them up, and send them off again, knowing full well that they'd keep on going, till they landed in jail permanently or disappeared into some back alley in the Bronx.

"Jonah, I know you're an artist—a photographer. Dope smuggling isn't your thing, and making one run isn't going to do you or us any good."

"I need the money."

"You can borrow more from your father-in-law than I can pay you."

"I *want* to go," I insisted. He was in too much of a hurry to haggle. He gave in and sealed the agreement with a gaping yawn. Three days later, he showed up at my doorstep carrying a large leather case.

"This suitcase contains ten kilos of cocaine. Take it to San Pablo, by land, and deliver it to the address I'm going to give you."

"Couldn't I fly?"

"It's too dangerous."

To my dismay, the suitcase was empty. Playing games with me, eh? Antonio read my thoughts.

"There's a secret compartment between the leather and the lining. But don't go poking around."

He bought me a ticket, gave me some money, and promised to pay me a nice sum—in dollars—when I returned. I watched him drive away and counted the hours until I would board the train for San Pablo.

TWENTY-SIX

The night before I left, Talia dreamed that my train derailed. She could see my mangled body twisted around the smoking steel of the passenger car. She could hear the moans and groans of the dying in the background. She begged me to delay the trip, but I brushed her aside. Though I must admit, her dream made me a little uneasy, and, if it hadn't seemed like a sissy thing to do, I probably would have stayed at home. I halfway hoped she'd drug me and make me miss the train. No such luck. Talia had already resigned herself to imminent widowhood.

She granted me the privileges of a condemned man. But instead of cooking me a special meal, she offered me herself as hors d'oeuvre, main dish, and dessert. She straddled me and rode me bareback, digging her nails into my flanks. She wanted me to remember her with the wild face of a Valkyrie. My approaching death excited her, and suddenly my passive wife had turned into a bedroom Wyatt Earp.

When she finished her ride, she laid her head on my shoulder and said, "I don't understand why you want to make this trip. You never cared about business before. What do you need factory samples for? Surely you wouldn't want to become a salesman. You'd be wasting your talent, your whole life! You're an artist, a photographer. If you aren't doing what you do best, you won't be happy."

"I think someone else told me the same thing."

"How could that be? No one else knows you the way I do . . . not even your own mother."

"Did you really mean what you just said . . . about me being an artist?"

"You . . . an artist?"

"Yes."

"Well, don't you consider yourself an artist?"

"No, not at all."

"Then how should I know?"

When I got to San Pablo, I thought I would buy something for Talia—a diamond, gold earrings, or some less expensive personal item. But I never got to buy anything, because I never reached San Pablo. They arrested me at Puerto Suárez on the Bolivian side of the border.

Bad luck was never far away. It was always crouching behind a bush or hiding around the next corner, ready to wrestle me to the ground and get me into a leg-hold. The entire trip was that way. My train, which was scheduled to leave at six that evening, didn't pull out until the next morning. The delay foiled my plans to cross the border as soon as I got there, without having to spend the night on this side. There wasn't a decent hotel within a fifty-kilometer radius, and I was forced to rent a room at the worst pigsty in town— easily the worst hotel in the whole Third World. Spiders, fleas, and bedbugs were crawling all over the place and propagating at record speed. They had created a veritable paradise off the blood of unfortunate guests.

The narcs arrived at the crack of dawn, but not before the regular pensioners had begun to stir. They had gotten up before sunrise to wash themselves in the patio and to arouse the sleepyheads of the neighborhood—the roosters, the chickens, and me. The agents burst into my room on the heels of a tremendous crack that ripped the door right off its hinges. They were wearing civilian clothes and, except for their guns, could have easily passed for smugglers. Two of them waved revolvers in my face; the other two were carrying machine guns. A pudgy, dark-skinned man with a mustache—who later identified himself as Inspector Juárez—was shouting orders to the rest.

"You're under arrest," he told me, "and if you value your teeth, hand over the money and the cocaine."

"I'm just a . . . tourist," I stammered.

"Don't try to lie your way out of it. We know who you are. You're an Argentine, and you're carrying a shipment of cocaine to San Pablo."

"I'm not Argentine," I said, taking out my passport.

One of the men took it from me, read it upside down, and stuck it into his pocket. Meanwhile, the others were emptying my suitcase onto the floor, ripping open the mattress, and tracking straw all around the room. Looking for secret pockets, they tore my suit and sports jacket to shreds.

"There's nothing here," said Felipe, a skinny, snaggle-toothed agent.

"Take him in," the inspector replied. "He'll talk, when we get him to the station."

"You can't arrest me. You haven't got any evidence. I'm a lawyer. I know my rights."

"Shut up! You're under arrest for using a false passport. An Argentine carrying a Bolivian passport! Huh! The nerve of some people. I saw a guy get a life sentence for less than that."

The runt of the group tried to straighten the inspector out. He told him that the Argentine smuggler, arrested the week before, had been set free and allowed to go on to Brazil. The police hadn't been working that day, since it was Juárez's birthday. The information they'd just received that morning concerned a snobbish Bolivian lawyer.

"So what's the problem, meathead?" shouted the inspector. "Isn't he Bolivian? Isn't he a lawyer?"

They restrained me with a pair of rusty, broken handcuffs and pushed me in the direction of a brand-new Land Rover. I was instructed to hold my hands still, so that the handcuffs wouldn't fall off. The sun was shining scandalously bright as we walked through the patio. The noisy, bare-chested pensioners were amused by my arrest and stopped their bathing to observe our exit.

Inside the jeep, the pint-sized agent, who was sitting on my left, whispered to me, "You've got yourself into a hell of a mess. These assholes are going to torture you until you tell them everything. But . . . if you give me twenty grand, I'll help you get out of here."

"Twenty thousand cruzeiros?" I asked, thinking he meant Brazilian currency. Bolivian money was worthless.

"No, you fool. Dollars!"

"Would you accept a check?"

He answered me in body language—a swift, left hook to the stomach. I crumpled over.

I woke up tied to a chair. A bright light was shining in my face. My face was scorched, and I couldn't see a thing—except for a pitcher of water and two glasses on the table next to me. Felipe and the inspector were acting like they felt sorry for me.

Obviously they didn't.

"I demand a writ of *habeas corpus!*" I cried.

"What's that?" Juárez asked Felipe.

"Some sort of medicine," he said. "He may be on medication. Remember the Colombian diabetic who didn't get his insolence and . . ."

"Insulin, you fool." Juárez was proud of his high-school education.

He walked over to me and told me authoritatively, "You may *think* you're in a hospital, but you're at the Narcotics Bureau—under arrest for a serious crime."

"I'm not sick," I told him.

"Then stop asking for medicine!"

"You can't hold me here," I protested. "You haven't got any proof."

"No proof, eh? Well, let me tell you a thing or two. Your own men informed on you. They called us up, told us you were about to cross the border with a cargo and ten thousand in cash. We want the coke. You can keep the cash. After all, we aren't thieves."

"I'm innocent!"

"Felipe," he said, turning to his colleague, "where do you think he hid it?"

"He probably swallowed it. It's common practice nowadays to put it in plastic bags and swallow it."

At that moment, the light went out. No one had turned it off—it just blew out. Their dark, greasy faces jumped up at me.

"Hey, wise guy, did you hear what Felipe just said? He's an expert. No one can fool him." He turned to his assistant and asked, "How can we prove it?"

"X-ray his stomach. If it's in there, it'll show up."

"Very good. I see you listened when the man from the DEA was here. But, I'm sorry to say, we don't have the right equipment."

"Well . . . I suppose we could improvise," Felipe said, placing a butcher knife on the table. "Besides, this way is faster. These guys don't seem to care how they treat people. Why should we care how we treat them? Last month one of them

230

stuffed the body of a dead child with cocaine. Remember that?"

I started to squirm in my chair but couldn't get loose from the rope. I felt like an animal about to be slaughtered.

"Not so fast," I said. "There're other ways. You could make me drink castor oil. Or better still, take me to a clinic. I'll pay for the X-ray, gladly. My insurance will cover it. It won't cost you a thing. I'll make you a print—a color print with a frame. You could hang it on the wall."

They weren't listening to my suggestions. Technology didn't interest them. They preferred old-fashioned methods. They untied me, unbuttoned my shirt, and made me lie down on the table. Then Felipe began to poke at my stomach.

"Stop!" I shouted. "I'll tell you everything. The drugs are hidden in my suitcase, between the leather and the lining."

With the same knife he would have used to cut me open, Felipe ripped into the leather of the case. He ripped the whole thing to shreds but didn't come up with a single gram of white powder. They were standing there, scowling at me, wondering what to do next, when the telephone rang. The inspector picked up the receiver, listened briefly, and turned to me. "You're free to go. This has been somebody's idea of a joke."

"A joke?" I couldn't believe my ears.

"Yeah, a real funny joke! Funny enough to make a parrot laugh," he said, angrily. "I guess you think they pay us to sit around here talking to jokers like you. Why didn't you tell us you were innocent? Or did you enjoy wasting our time?"

They were obviously frustrated. I put on my clothes and signed some papers swearing they hadn't hurt me in any way. The inspector explained that some cocky journalist had been making false accusations against the police force. I got out of there as fast as I could before they decided to slap me behind bars again.

The inspector yelled, as I walked out the door, "I don't want to see you around here again. Go back to Argentina.

We've got enough bandits of our own. That's all we need—a bunch of outsiders coming in here."

"I'm Bolivian," I yelled back at him.

"Yeah, the worst kind. I ought to have you shot for treason—talking with that phony Argentine accent. What's the matter? Bolivia not good enough for you?"

❧

BY THE TIME I got back home, I'd started to miss Talia. It was a strange feeling. I was really anxious to see her. Could I be falling in love with my wife? I wasn't sure. Maybe I was just homesick.

As I walked into my house, suddenly it really seemed like my house and not some stopping-off place that, sooner or later, I'd be leaving.

I took Talia in my arms and hugged her tenderly. We held hands off and on for the rest of the day and, from that time on, were never apart for more than a few hours. We started going places together—movies, exhibitions, parades, clubs. And it wasn't boring. We didn't stand around yawning or gaping at other people. We started double-dating with Esteban and his wife, and that wasn't half bad either. I wondered if I was going crazy. If the four of us went to a club, we'd spend the entire evening dancing—me with Talia, Esteban with his wife—like couples who'd just completed a course on marriage and the family.

I began to notice that Talia was no dog. I wasn't the only one who noticed. Esteban drooled every time he looked at her. I knew he liked her, but I never knew how much. She returned the compliment by hanging on his every word. They chatted back and forth, completely ignoring their mates. I pouted. Esteban's wife didn't seem to notice.

I told Talia I didn't much like feeling like a spare wheel. She immediately changed her attitude, glad to see the passion she'd once aroused in me surfacing again. To me, it was a lot of sentimental hogwash. I was just starting to feel like my own man—thanks to the money Antonio had given me. Though I had never reached San Pablo with so much as a rusty nail, Antonio forked over the whole ten grand he'd promised me. He didn't care about the suitcase. He knew it was empty. In fact, he'd called the police himself. He'd used me as a decoy—to distract the narcs while a huge shipment was crossing the border.

I hid the cash in an empty box of Danish bonbons and placed it in the chest of drawers, between my shirts. I didn't touch a single bill; I didn't even count them. It was enough just knowing they were there, stacked up like dead tobacco leaves, like the coins your grandfather gave you and you never dared touch for fear they'd fall apart in your hand.

Since Talia and I got married, I'd always dreamed of having a reasonable sum of money all my own—that hadn't come from my wife's family. Money that would symbolize my freedom and allow me to bum around for a while—after my inevitable divorce. Money that would allow me to forget the Gregorian calendar and live by my own visceral time chart. I had friends with similar schemes. Some managed to carry them out; others were still waiting for a magic carpet. As soon as I got my money, I realized I couldn't do it. I could see the hurt look on Talia's face—her emotions turned on full force—doctors bending over her bed, friends dropping by to ask how she was holding up. According to my fantasy, she would dress in mourning for the rest of her life, never find anyone to replace me, and wither away into a sad, stubborn old woman.

But now that I had the money, instead of saying "So long, baby," I wanted her by my side all the time. I know it sounds dumb, and, to be perfectly honest, I'd rather not try to explain it. If I had to, I suppose I'd say I was like green wood, and a stack of bills wasn't enough to get me started. A nice pile of sticks might have done the trick. But until someone set a real fire under me, I was going to stay married to Talia.

Of course, what I've just said is pure horse feathers. Any man who really wanted to leave home would do it, if it meant leaving with the shirt on his back.

Want to hear something even stranger? Well, the truth was, I didn't want to leave her anymore. My life was so thoroughly tangled up in Talia's that extricating myself would have required considerable pruning. I would remain by her side for the rest of my life and, like a rational Prometheus, learn to sympathize with my chains.

Resignation spread into other parts of my life, too. I realized that it was over between Julia and me. I wasn't ready to wish her good luck with Grigotá. It still hurt when I saw them wrapped around each other. But I didn't fall apart.

I continued to watch her at a distance and suspected that she and Grigotá were now lovers. I deduced this from small signs: she'd come home from dates with her hair messed up and her sweater on inside out. Grigotá would put his arms around her whenever he felt like it. If Julia hadn't already given him a bite of the forbidden fruit, she didn't lack much. I knew her so well, I could guess how far they'd gone. She would soon begin to tarnish her own image by telling him details from her sordid past. He would have to swim the rough waters of her erotic imagination. Nothing could save him, for example, from hearing about the time the soldiers raped her. There'd be more stories than before—ones about us. I could see her giggling and telling him about the nasty things we'd done together.

I also knew that Julia would never finish veterinary medicine. Six months before graduation, she would tell her family she'd chosen the wrong career. Her father would open a small business for her, and it would go bankrupt before the year was out. At that point, he'd find her a job as an assistant administrator in one of his offices or one of his friends' offices.

She would be among the last of her friends to marry. After lagging behind as long as she could—but through no fault of her own—she would marry a serious type, a mature, dependable man. She wouldn't be in love with him—not passionately in love—which would keep the marriage stable. She wouldn't marry Grigotá, but, before she dumped him, poor fellow, he'd have had his share of headaches.

As careless as she was about birth control, she would probably end up having several abortions. I hoped she'd find a decent doctor and not some butcher who might ruin her for life. I couldn't see anything wonderful happening to Julia, but at least she would never realize the extent of her misery, just as she had never known how happy she'd been with me.

The love I'd once felt for her was turning into pity. I knew that. Of course, I pitied all the women I'd ever loved. When Arminda mentioned her dead child, I felt awful. I couldn't stand a sad ending, even at the movies. If Talia pricked her finger, my stomach would turn over. Just yesterday, I got depressed seeing her walking home from the market loaded down with grocery bags and balancing a plastic carton of eggs between them. She couldn't manage with the groceries, her handbag, and seven or eight books. Every few steps, she'd stop to shift the parcels from one hand to the other, and the books, tucked under her arms, finally fell to the ground. A prime target for some juvenile delinquent, I thought, who'd as soon stick a knife into her as look at her. I wanted to lock her up, protect her from all violence. She was too fragile a flower to be out on the street, ready to be knocked down by any thug who came along.

When Talia was feeling unsure of herself, she usually got the idea that I didn't love her, that I'd married her for her money. At those times she loved me more than ever and could see new virtues in me she'd never seen before.

"Daddy wants us to sell him the house," she said one day, out of the blue.

"What for?"

"So he can give it to us again, but this time, he wants to register it in my name. He also said he would open an account for me—in Panama—if I promised not to tell you."

"So . . . pretend like I don't know. If you want to make secret pacts with your father, go right ahead."

"Would you still love me, if everything was in my name?"

"Yes, but it would be different."

"How?"

"The way you love a woman who has everything in her name. See the difference?"

"I suppose so. But understand . . . if I really wanted to go along with him, I wouldn't have told you anything. . . . I can't help but wonder if you would have married me, if I'd been terribly poor."

I thought to myself, if Talia had been terribly poor, she wouldn't have been Talia. She wouldn't have owned a medical encyclopedia, so she wouldn't have been able to come up with a whole inventory of exotic diseases. She would have had to stick to common illnesses, like tuberculosis. Panamanian bank accounts wouldn't have been a problem either. Instead, we might have had eight hungry kids to feed, a pack of dogs, and a broken-down house with a forty-year mortgage. Most likely, we'd be living under a constant cloud of poverty, drunkenness, and ill humor. If Talia had been terribly poor, we would have felt terrible and poor, not just poor, as we'd been feeling lately.

"Have you ever been unfaithful?" she asked, to my amazement.

"Technically, no."

"What do you mean by 'technically'?"

"Just what I said. Technically, I've never been unfaithful. Understand?"

"Sort of. And suppose I'd been unfaithful to *you*—would you forgive me?"

"I think so, if I never found out. Why do you ask?"

"No reason. Actually, I came close."

"With whom?"

"Ildefonso."

"The medium?"

"No, his name is Lucio now. He was called Ildefonso before I slept with him."

"Where did it happen, you little hussy? Here in my own house?"

"No, it was at the cabin, in Portugal. You act like you didn't

236

know it. I already told you about all of this. It's what made me the way I am now, with this passion that wells up inside of me and makes me do things that aren't right, like flirt with Lucio. But he's even worse than I am. He loses his head completely, like when he threw me against the wall, and kissed me, and fondled my left breast."

"Three hundred years ago?"

"No, last week. But nothing happened. We both knew it was wrong."

"Did you stop because of me?"

"Partially. But mainly I knew I couldn't handle it. I'm a simple person. I didn't want to complicate my life. It would have been Talia and María Antonieta versus Lucio and Ildefonso. María Antonieta loved them both. Talia didn't love either of them. Then I found out that the situation was even more complicated than I'd thought, since, according to what came out at our last séance, we each lived three incarnations in the last three hundred years. There were five personalities who wanted to play a part in the affair. It would have been like going to bed with a basketball team. I want a man, not a tribe. We decided to forget it. Besides, Lucio realized that he was in love with the guy who teaches him economics. And I love you."

"You mean Lucio is gay?"

"No, he isn't gay, but recently, a feminine principle has emerged—one that remained silent for centuries."

"You ought to know if he's gay or not. After all, he kissed you and fondled your left breast."

"He kissed María Antonieta."

"Yeah, but on your lips!"

"The body doesn't matter, if you're a spiritualist."

"It matters to me. I'm not a ghost."

"You're jealous. But you needn't worry. Nothing is going to happen. I love you."

Then she went over to the bar and poured two martinis, which, for Talia, was like playing the first slow notes to a hot, spicy tango.

TWENTY-SEVEN

Unfortunately, none of my predictions about Julia came true. Reality treated her much more harshly than I had in my imagination. I had overlooked death completely—that uncommon adversary which only seemed to threaten old people and undernourished children. Death belonged back in the Middle Ages; you read about it in books. How was I to know that Julia, my Julia, might actually die?

But she did. It was just like her to do something shocking. Something no one might have foreseen. They found her in a little German-style chalet on Circunvalación Avenue. She was lying in bed, lifeless, with her arms wrapped around Grigotá. They looked like two frozen angels; their bodies were slightly blue. According to the doctor who performed the autopsy, Julia was carrying a fetus of three months.

I couldn't believe it when they told me she was dead. I wanted to scream at them, "No! Don't say that. You're lying." I stood staring through the rain-streaked window panes. It was a day ripe for tragedy. But I still couldn't believe it. The rain was falling in torrents. For three days, the only light I'd seen was the will-o'-the-wisp in the cemetery, which flared up at dusk but was quickly doused by the rain.

The sullen sky confirmed it. Julia was dead. Somehow I wasn't convinced.

No one understood what a difficult time I was having. I needed to be shaken, to be forced to see what was going on around me. But no one had time to bother with that. Julia's untimely exit called for decisive action. The family had to keep their heads on their shoulders. Somebody had to straighten out the mess Julia had left behind.

As soon as they entered the chalet, they dressed Julia. Ira couldn't believe that no one had thought to put something over the bodies. Chico had arrived ahead of them. The caretaker had notified him first. But he hadn't stopped to do anything for modesty's sake. He and four armed men had immediately begun searching the area around the chalet. It wasn't clear what he was looking for—a killer or his dead son's soul, which could have been lingering on the premises.

Dressing the bodies was easy. The hard part was patching up the couple's reputation. No one was going to believe they died of a heart attack—even supposing that passionate love might have weakened their hearts. Ira knew the kind of gossip that such a scene might create, and she hurried to find a reasonable explanation. She would have to get the jump on the scandalmongers. What might they say if Talia, Julia's own sister, was already suspecting suicide? A very romantic notion. Two ill-starred lovers, suffering under the weight of an unknown frustration. Ending it all, rather than accepting a less-than-perfect solution.

"Have you lost your mind? What kind of bullshit is that?" Ira retorted, smashing Talia's supposition to bits. Who could possibly believe that Julia—who wouldn't even take cough medicine—could have managed a dose of poison? Ira recalled that, on the day before she died, Julia had talked about going on a diet. What woman thinks of dieting when she's about to kill herself?

But Talia wasn't the only one who suspected suicide. The doctor who examined the bodies raised the same suspicion. After discovering the fetus, he began to concoct a scenario. Two young people, faced with an unwanted pregnancy, had chosen death over parenthood. "Hog wash," Ira thought. Her daughter wouldn't have reacted that way. Besides, Julia probably didn't even know she was pregnant. She never remembered when her period was supposed to start. She might have skipped a few without noticing. The doctor was obviously off his rocker. At any rate, what he said didn't matter—the findings weren't official.

Then, when someone noticed their clothes were missing, we began to suspect an act of violence. Had the clothes been stolen, hidden, or perhaps burned? A few pieces of coal were still burning in the stove, but not a scrap of cloth could be found. It was unusual that the chalet was equipped with a coal-burning stove. Few city homes used that type of heat.

Other strange clues began to surface. Julia's left earring was missing. Her back was scratched and muddy, as if someone had dragged her across the patio. Had she been raped? The doctor took a sample of seminal fluid from her vagina, but he couldn't tell under what circumstances it had been left there. The sperm of rapists was no different from the sperm of a normal man, he lamented. Ira asked him to leave speculation to the experts.

The situation would have shocked anyone, and more so, a

lady of Ira's social standing. She had known of young people who had been killed in car wrecks or who had died of leukemia, but she hadn't known anyone who'd died such a scandalous death. Of course, Julia had been the youngest, and sometimes youngest children felt driven to rebel. Ira was able to forgive her though. She hadn't been old enough to understand the social aspects of death. She hadn't realized that death was the final act, the act that crowned and synthesized all of the other significant rites in one's life—baptism, first communion, confirmation, debut, graduation, and marriage. If Julia had known that, she wouldn't have exposed herself to such an irksome finale. She wouldn't have left such a mess for her parents to set straight.

Ira felt a little better after she'd read the newspaper. "Police Investigate Mysterious Death of Youths." She read the article several times. She was afraid there might be some reference to Chico Lindo; if there was, people would suspect her daughter's death had been drug-related. But nothing of the kind was implied.

One of Julia's friends couldn't believe how unfeeling the family seemed. I tried to explain things to him. They all would have given their eye teeth to bring Julia back. But instead of sitting around, moaning and groaning, they had chosen a different approach. I suppose you could have called it "martial." They were acting like a platoon of soldiers that's lost the nicest guy of the lot. The stronger ones were exaggerating their composure in order to buck up the weaker ones. Instead of sitting around moping, they were busying themselves with all the necessary preparations. They were preparing for the guests who would soon be arriving, clearing a room for the caskets, and setting up chairs around the walls. Later—when the river overflowed its banks—that line of chairs would float out of the house, through the patio, and across the lawn, flattening geraniums, sunflowers, and other obstacles in its path.

Olga was the only one of Julia's friends whom I recognized. I couldn't tell the others apart. Marthita, Marcia, Iris.

Their names sounded like exotic flowers, and none of them looked like their names. It was even more confusing, seeing them in identical outfits. They were all wearing their school uniforms—blue skirts and white, silk blouses. They sat down in the casket room and shed genuine tears until some member of the family took notice. They figured that, at a wake, you were supposed to offer your tears to the most bereaved. Ira fortunately arrived in time to receive this sincere expression of grief. Most of the other guests would be crying out of self-pity or social necessity.

Olga said it was romantic—burying them together. Ira was pleased. She had vacillated considerably before settling on a double funeral. She hoped to dissipate the ill will of bad-mouthers by presenting the couple as enamored mystics. The only disadvantage was the presence of Chico Lindo. Ira suggested to him that the sight of armed guards at a wake might be disconcerting. He assured her that only the immediate family would attend. And though it was hard to believe that the dozen or so dark-suited types with suspicious-looking bulges in their pockets were Grigotá's relatives, you could forgive Chico. At least he'd taken the trouble to disguise them as 'people.'

The first guests were arriving, and there was still plenty to be done. Sending the invitations, receiving wreaths, opening cards and telegrams, getting rid of reporters, listening to condolences, and giving instructions to the kitchen crew. I helped a little. Patroclo didn't stop for a second. With a flick of his wrist, he produced a casket for Julia. As soon as we saw it, we knew that similar ones had been prepared for each member of the family. It wasn't bad for a coffin. The lid was engraved with a perfect profile of the deceased.

Patroclo also arranged the display—a large, blazing cross and two spotlights, which cast a golden aura around the body. In addition, he found time to console his other daughter, who was either overcome with grief or—more likely—terrified, imagining herself the owner of a bright, new coffin. I wasn't there when the fit occurred. I probably couldn't have helped anyway. When I returned, she was asleep on the couch, with a childlike expression on her face. The room smelled of alcohol from the shot the doctor had given her.

Patroclo had managed to take care of everything except the weather. He became furious when rain started to wet down the chairs on the patio. Just as he was getting over that upset, he noticed an ambulance parked in the middle of the street, blocking traffic. Actually, there was no other place to park. There wasn't space for a toy truck within walking distance of the house.

"I won't allow it!" Patroclo exclaimed. "I won't let them touch her." The attendants had just told him that they'd come to pick up the bodies. Autopsies had to be performed.

"We have to take them," the man insisted. "In these cases, an autopsy must be performed. The law requires it."

"Don't tell me what the law requires!"

"We have a court order."

"You can stuff it down your throat for all I care," Patroclo told him. "And get off my property, before I have you thrown off."

"We have our orders from the chief inspector."

"Tell him I want to see him."

About dusk, I got up the nerve to go over to Julia's coffin. The loud blast of the siren was fading away in the distance. The rain, which had darkened the living room for most of the day, had stopped, and the room was suddenly light again. For a moment, time seemed to be moving backwards. Then the light falling on the tiles changed to blood red. The sun was going down.

Julia's face had lost its bluish tone, thanks to the work of the embalmer. Her face had been given a permanent adolescent glow. I was startled. Had her lips moved? I looked closely. If something had stirred inside of her, it wasn't a life force. It was more like the automatic blinking of a porcelain doll. Every living cell had been annihilated. She was a zombie, a mannequin. I didn't want to remember her like that. If she had to be dead, she might as well look dead, too. A rotten apple was better than a plastic one any day.

I left the room feeling as though I'd been thrown out.

Maybe my thoughts had been inappropriate. Licurgo and Justina were sitting in the next room. Their knees were touching, and they were looking solemnly into one another's eyes. I said hello and sat down next to them. They gave me their condolences. Licurgo seemed nervous. He wanted to talk to me about something. He hesitated and then spoke. He told me he'd bought a new car, a wine-colored Santana. He described it to me, as if he'd been telling me about a new lover. He spoke more passionately than I'd ever heard him speak. Nothing that was whirling around us affected him in the least—not Julia's body, not even Olga's splendid thighs. Olga, who'd sat down on the other side of the room, in plain view, was trying to give him a peek from time to time, but he wasn't interested—she'd left him for good.

"Would you like something to eat?" I asked them. They didn't care for anything.

I got up. The house was getting dark. Guests were gradually coming in. By night the house would be full. I decided to get some rest, since I'd planned to stay up all night. I wanted to spend some time by the casket. I wanted to be the last one to say good-bye.

I went upstairs to Patroclo's study. He, Pablo, and Druout were having a discussion. We didn't exchange greetings. I dropped down unceremoniously on the sofa, and, gradually, the constant drumming of their voices put me to sleep.

Druout was telling them that the river was dangerously high. The thawed snows from the mountains, added to the continuous rain, had brought the river to flood stage. It had already toppled a house, killing thirteen people, some hundred kilometers upstream. According to the radio, the current already posed a threat to the outskirts of the city. Druout believed the threat was real. We were about to have the worst flood of the century. And our barrio was going to be hard-hit.

"Ten years ago, you said it was safe here," Patroclo reminded him.

"The only reason I said that was because you told me to. We were building houses on the old riverbed. You said our clients needed reassuring."

244

"I didn't tell you to lie to them."

"I didn't lie. I just gave them a little pep talk."

"They won't see it that way. But I'm not really worried," Patroclo said, rearing back in his chair. "It's never flooded around here. And it's not going to flood now. I don't know why you're getting so excited."

Druout could see that no one was going to take him seriously. They never had. No one really believed that he was Belgian or that he had a degree in engineering. Rumor had it that the pyramid had been Patroclo's invention. That Druout hadn't done anything except sign the papers. He was a bluff, they thought, and nothing was going to make them change their minds.

I fell asleep on the sofa and probably wouldn't have waked up till the next morning. I might have missed the entire wake, which wouldn't have bothered me. If the decision had been mine, I would have wrapped Julia in a silk sheet and buried her in the garden. Her body would have decomposed and blossomed forth as lilies, amaranths, orchids, darnel, and mallow. Its reintegration into the life cycle wouldn't have been blocked by embalming fluid.

I woke up with Pablo shaking me. I'd only been asleep for about five minutes. The inspector had arrived, and his large gut was blocking my entire field of vision. I recognized the mustached face of Inspector Juárez.

Patroclo introduced me as his son-in-law.

"I think we've met before," he said, "but I can't remember where."

"Would you know me, if I were sitting in a chair with my hands tied behind my back and a light shining in my face?"

"That's funny. I see you like to joke."

"I'm not joking. You arrested me—near the Brazilian border."

"That's impossible. I never forget anyone I've arrested. I trust my own memory more than the police files."

They all seemed to believe him, and that was the end of that.

Juárez had put on weight. His mountainous belly looked

like it was about to cave in. I wished he wasn't there. He was always popping up at the scene of the crime, like some television detective. I was amazed to see that my life was being subjected to the artifices and licenses of a script writer.

"I hear you don't want an autopsy," he said to Patroclo.

"I won't have it, and that's my final word on the subject. In my day, detectives didn't have to cut up the bodies of innocent victims to find a killer. They went out on the street and looked for him, asked questions, and, most of the time, they'd get their man."

"I'm of the old school myself," he replied. "I work fast, and I solve my case. My only problem is a tight budget. Sometimes I can't even fill up my gas tank. Of course, if the families were prepared to cover some of the expenses . . ."

"We've already discussed it," Patroclo interrupted, "and both families are willing to pay a reward. You can talk to my son about it tomorrow. Pablo," he said, turning to his son, "write the inspector a check in the morning." Then, looking back at Juárez, he asked him what he'd come up with so far.

"Well, I think I could safely say that the deaths occurred between eight P.M. and six A.M. The bodies were found in a bed, which doesn't necessarily mean they died there. They were unable to call or leave any message explaining what had happened. I don't know yet if your daughter arrived nude and wearing only one earring or if her clothes and earring were stolen. The cause of death is still unknown."

"How very insightful!" Patroclo said, glaring at the inspector. "You must have used a computer to arrive at all those brilliant deductions."

"I know that what I've said is obvious, but that's the way I operate—from the obvious to the obscure. I've got my theories about what happened, but I'll keep them to myself for the time being."

"Well . . . I hope your theories aren't based on rumor. If you think my daughter died from an overdose, you can just forget it. She was a good girl, and you remember that. I won't

246

allow the pathologist to touch her, because she was never touched by a man when she was alive."

"I'm sure you know your daughter better than I. My theories don't have anything to do with that sort of thing. I believe this was the work of an international crime syndicate that's been operating in the city."

"I'm really not interested in hearing the details. I'd just as soon stay out of it. I wouldn't want to influence your thinking. I want you to work with absolute freedom."

❧

WHEN IT came right down to it, the flood was Druout's fault. He had known about it ten years before, but he'd kept his mouth shut. It was as much his fault, as if he'd dumped the water on the city himself. In ten years he could have warned everyone in the barrio individually. In ten years he could have built a dike with his own hands. But Druout hadn't lifted a finger. Hadn't said a word. Which, paradoxically, absolved him. Instead of taking him for the scoundrel he was, people just thought he was a lousy engineer.

When the water began to creep into the house, the guests rushed out in a stampede. We didn't have time to save anything. We were lucky to get out with our own hides. Justina was the only one left behind. She had left the wake and gone upstairs to sleep for a while. The room she picked was practically soundproof. She hadn't heard the rushing water or the screams of the escaping crowd.

Licurgo was snoozing in a chair on the same floor. Probably dreaming about his new car, caressing it passionately, more passionately than he'd ever caressed Olga. The rising water caught him off guard. He ran to a window and saw a foamy, coffee-colored liquid running down the street. He panicked—the current might carry off his new car; it might drown Justina. The water was getting higher. "Justina," he screamed. "Hurry! Get out, before it's too late!" He knew there wasn't time to save his wife and his car. The car or Justina? Justina or the car? He decided not to decide. Something told him that Justina was probably already out. She was a light sleeper. She was also very athletic and could take care of herself. He thanked providence in advance for saving Justina and shot out in search of his car. He found it, jumped in, and raced away from the house, as if he'd been chased by a monster. He didn't look back. He didn't even stop to pick up hitchhikers along the road. They might get his new seatcovers dirty. Besides, there would be other cars to pick them up.

Justina told us she'd woken up groggy and disoriented. She thought she was sailing through a storm in a small boat. Crests of gigantic waves were crashing against the windows. The room seemed to be rocking back and forth. It was incredible. She was in the largest house in the whole barrio, and it was swaying back and forth like a straw hut.

She went to the window and looked out. Of the one-story houses nearby, only the roofs were showing. The houses looked like they were sinking into chocolate sauce. Chairs, tables, even mattresses, bobbed up-and-down in the current. In the dense light that managed to penetrate the rain, she could make out Julia's coffin. Flanked by wreaths and flowers, it sailed along in a straight line, as if the river were directing it toward an underwater cemetery.

After the flood, a team of volunteers rescued Justina. She came out, squeezing water out of her hair and clothes and looking a little strange. One of the paramedics thought she was crazy and tried to give her a shot to calm her down. She shoved the man out of the way, walked up to Licurgo, and hit him right square in the mouth. They walked off together, embracing.

There was a sleepy farming village called Quebrada Mansa, some seventy kilometers down river from the city. The villagers were mostly Indians from the altiplano, farmers who made their living from corn, tobacco, tapioca, and—why not say it?—coca. Half of them had never learned Spanish, and the ones who'd learned it, spoke very poorly. Their language was Quechua, which had survived along with a number of pre-Columbian traditions.

Julia's coffin berthed on the shore near the village. The flowers and wreaths washed up around it. The people thought they'd been given a gift by the river and never doubted for a minute that Julia was a saint. It was obvious. Julia had made a pilgrimage from the mountains down to Quebrada Mansa. Her arrival marked the completion of a sacred mission. She could have come to rest at a hundred villages, but she had chosen theirs. At first they thought she was a statue. Then they realized that their dark, sensual maiden was made of flesh and bones. What an extraordinary being! The body remained incorrupt during the three days of celebration. She looked as if she might open her eyes at any moment, and, for that reason, they never left her alone. Someone ought to be there to help her up, if she should come to. They sang, prayed, and drank chicha in the shack they'd changed into a temple. Fifty meters farther down the shore, they built a crypt where the maiden would be placed permanently.

Inspector Juárez couldn't get Julia off his mind. She haunted him day and night. Day and night, he ran up and down the river throwing dynamite into the water, hoping to bring the cadaver to the surface. He waded in mud up to his Adam's apple, until, at last, he found the body as clean as a pen in the Indians' hut, which he'd approached in search of food. But even harder than finding her was getting her body back from the Indians. In three days' time they had hammered her so deeply into their tradition that Juárez—or anyone else, for that matter—would never be able to pull her out. Of course, a round of fire from a shotgun might have convinced them otherwise. But Juárez, only recently transferred from the Narcotics Bureau, wasn't about to endanger his position for a dead woman. Diplomacy was the best path, he decided. After a lengthy discussion, he and the village leaders reached a compromise. The Indians would return the body provided they could deliver it themselves to Julia's parents.

If I could have waked Julia up, I would have asked her where she preferred to be buried. Without a doubt, she would have chosen Quebrada Mansa. Being buried in a crypt on the beach would have suited her to a T. And the Indians wouldn't have demanded much. Just the occasional small miracle, like restoring sight to a phony blind man or giving the farmers a good harvest. In exchange, she would receive the constant adoration of those simple people.

She would have never allowed herself to be put away in Patroclo's pyramid. But she couldn't voice an opinion, or throw dishes, or stomp her feet, the way she did when she was alive. Rather than thinking of her lying there, powerless and unhappy, I imagined her going on strike in the spiritual realm. "Either put me in a warmer place, or don't ever expect to hear from me, in any form or fashion, ever again!"

I was sad to see her buried alone. Grigotá hadn't waited for her. After the flood, they found his body stuck in a heap of mud and slime. It had already begun to putrefy and had to be buried at once. It was placed in a blue mausoleum, guarded by two marble angels, on the extreme east corner of the public cemetery.

The family was truly flattered by the Indians' veneration of the dead girl. Too, it added local color to the burial service. Their chants were more effective than a Latin mass would have ever been. They dignified the mystery of Julia's death and, at the same time, goaded the curiosity of the crowd to find out immediately how the youths had died. Inspector Juárez wasn't pleased. Everywhere he went, people were talking about the case. "Anything new, Inspector?" they asked him again and again. But worse, he'd started getting calls from his higher-ups, demanding a quick solution.

I remember the thoughtful expression on the inspector's face at the burial. Also his dirty glasses, twisted tie, and muddy shoes. He didn't have a clue, and his failure was making him the talk of the town.

At the burial, people were making comments, out loud, so he could hear them. They must have gotten his dander up. He walked away determined to solve the case as soon as possible.

To begin with, he was convinced that the couple had been murdered. He reached that conclusion the same way a doctor suspects that anyone who comes into his office must be sick. If someone had come knocking on *his* door, it had to mean that a crime had been committed.

Next, he considered the killer's MO. No traditional weapon had been used—no firearms, knives, ropes, wrenches, or candlesticks. The killer must have used poison, which he'd administered with a blowgun or a spray.

Third, only foreigners used such sophisticated methods. His compatriots preferred beating each other over the head with blunt instruments.

Armed with such logical arguments as these, he sent his men out in search of suspicious-looking foreigners. Aliens, he liked to call them. That was one of his favorite words. In no time, they brought in two Chileans who lived near the chalet and had already been booked for robbery. As soon as he laid eyes on them, Juárez's instinct started to beep, like a Geiger counter. He told his men to make them talk, by whatever means necessary. After a good roughing up, the Chileans confessed. Granted, what they said wasn't very coherent, but bad men were often contradictory, the inspector explained. At any rate, they'd said enough to convict them and to convince the press to write them up as the authentic killers.

Inspector Juárez didn't completely trust the system of justice. He knew from experience that when confessed criminals get to trial, they often take back much of what they've said. They manage to confuse the judge and lawyers and end up receiving immunity. For that reason, he hoped that the fruit of his investigation would never reach the courts. On the other hand, he wasn't an executioner, and he wouldn't have killed anyone without provocation. This is what he would do. He'd see to it that the criminals were left unattended. If they were innocent, they wouldn't budge. But if they were guilty, they'd try to escape. As soon as they stuck their snouts out the door, they'd be greeted by a round of gunfire. That was the practical way to solve the problem, and Juárez liked to think of himself as a practical man.

TWENTY-EIGHT

As it turns out, the last chapter in this book is numbered twenty-eight. You've probably never heard of "hacer veintiocho," but, in the slang of my youth, it was when a whole gang of guys did it with one girl. A gangbang. It makes me think of one pitiful, stray bitch and a pack of hot dogs. Sometimes, when guys would go out together in a big group, they'd find a girl, and, with or without her consent, they'd line up and bang her, one after the other.

The reason I'm explaining this is because I feel like a bastard, after telling you Julia's secrets. I feel like I've handed the girl I loved over to a mob. Only a scoundrel would do a thing like that, expose her right in front of you, open her legs, and let you gaze at the pretty, pink spot between them. And poor thing, now that she's dead, she can't even cover herself with a towel. I'm sorry I did it, but, at the same time, I think I had to—it was the only way to keep her alive. If I had my way, Julia would be made a saint. But you, the readers, will have to decide that. So I'm turning her over to you, to undress, examine the pustules, the insensitive areas, the sacred stigmata.

Right now, I wish the keys on my typewriter would play some melancholy adagio, like the music at Julia's funeral. I ought to describe all the masses that were said, at the end of the first month, the second, and so on. But I'm not up to it. I've had enough of funerals.

I suppose I ought to say that my life hit rock bottom when Julia died. Except it'd be a lie. In a way, I was glad. I could sleep at night. Which doesn't mean I hadn't been in love with her. It just means that her death hit me like a hard winter, froze my juices, turned them an icy blue color, the color of maturity—or resignation. That's the way my life is now. Sometimes I like things to be dark and wet, like rain falling on a grave. Because, sometimes, sorrow is what keeps the ghosts inside us shifting around. When the pain ends, the dead disappear.

I never did stop loving her, and, though the passion soon went away, I could still feel her presence. It wasn't anything you could see or hear. When I spoke to her, she didn't answer. But sometimes I'd get this strange impulse—to do something I wouldn't ordinarily do. It was one of those impulses that led me to solve the mystery of her and Grigotá's deaths. Sometimes I would follow the impulse; sometimes I wouldn't. When I did, it usually turned out all right for me. In fact, I managed to do some things I wouldn't have thought possible.

I even had my first one-man show. The Cultural Center agreed to exhibit a collection of my photographs. Ira helped me get the mayor's permission, and Patroclo financed it for me. He paid for the whole thing—enlarging, framing, advertising, programs, and invitations.

I let out a hoot when I saw my name in the newspaper: "Jonah Larriva. Portraits. Expression and Humanism." I must have read it ten times. I couldn't believe it was me they were talking about. After all those years of lugging a camera around, spending entire days in a darkroom, and shuffling through mountains of photographs, finally I'd come up with something. A whole gallery full of portraits. Every picture had a human theme. There wasn't a single abstract, still life, or landscape. I put together an entire collection of faces— pleasant faces, mystical faces, stingy faces, sensual faces, stupid faces. I didn't want them to just hang there and allow themselves to be raped by the viewers. I wanted them to jeer back, to mock them, snap at them with their teeth.

I was disappointed when I saw them hanging in the gallery. They'd looked meaner in the studio. I guess, in preparing them for the public, I'd tamed them down. The whole process of framing, polishing, and classifying had taken the bite out of them. The same thing happened to my name! As soon as it got printed on the billboard, it wasn't a real name anymore. It was like Coca-Cola, Kotex, or Hershey's Chocolate. Just another crummy product, ready to be stamped and shipped out.

The exhibition was a success. We went through forty guest registers. They'd been pouring in for two weeks. Standing around looking at my pictures with their mouths hanging open.

The boldest ones came over to congratulate me. I heard all sorts of comments—some stupid, some fairly accurate. Somebody said that my next show should be of female nudes. He told me nothing attracted the public like a great ass. I wouldn't forget.

As I said, the exhibition was a success, but I didn't sell a single photograph. I wasn't upset. It would have been hard to part with any of them. The only problem was Talia. She was beside herself trying to figure out what to do with so many framed photographs. She would have gladly burned them, before cluttering up the house. But she wouldn't have been doing it out of meanness. Deep inside, my dedication to photography made her terribly happy.

"At last," she said, "you've found your calling." Her tone was definitive. There wasn't any point in arguing. She was starting to get a little bossy. Even her clothes were different. Instead of a silky, feminine dress, she was wearing a black jacket and pants, a white blouse, and black tie. I hadn't seen her in a skirt in weeks.

"You haven't answered me. Have you found your calling or not?"

"I don't know. It took me forever to put that shit together!"

"Don't talk that way about your work. One show can be the beginning of a whole career."

"That's not what the experts say. They say I'm a promising amateur."

"That's ridiculous. You're a professional."

"Don't say that word in front of your parents. They think a professional photographer is someone who takes snapshots at a party. They wouldn't want a professional photographer for a son-in-law. It's all right as long as it's just a hobby."

"It doesn't matter what they think. I say you're a professional."

"I wish I were, but I don't have the experience."

"Someday you will," she insisted. Her words felt like spurs digging into my sides. That wasn't the first time that week that I'd felt like Talia was riding me, like a horse.

Julia's death had changed us both. Talia suffered more than I did at first. She took tranquilizers for a while. Then she stopped and started feeling livelier. And before I knew it, she was acting like a completely different person. She wasn't about to be controlled by anyone—not her parents, her husband, not even the Holy See. She was becoming an absolute tyrant. Nobody was going to get the best of Talia!

My reaction to Julia's death was different. For the first couple of weeks, I felt like she was following me around all the time. It was like having a cloud hanging over your head. Like being followed around by a giant manta ray threatening to eat you alive at any moment. The first thing I heard in the morning was Julia's voice, which made me feel like she'd been sitting on my bed all night, waiting for me to wake up. Every schoolgirl I met on the street looked like Julia. Once, when I was combing my hair, I looked in the mirror and there was Julia staring back at me. It nearly scared me out of my wits. Which, I'm sure, wasn't the reaction she'd hoped for. But that's the fate of mortals. To die and come back as bogeymen.

After I got over the shock, I tried to find an explanation. I told myself it was all in my head. My imagination was working overtime. I tried to get hold of myself. It didn't do any good. That same night, I heard the wind blowing. I looked outside and there was Julia running around in her nightgown. I was becoming more and more convinced that she'd come back from the grave. The real proof came one evening when Talia and I were having dinner with Esteban and his wife. It was typical of the evenings we spent together after Julia's death. No music, lots of cigarettes, not too much drinking, erratic conversation. After our guests had gone, I walked out on the patio to put away the chairs. Then I noticed a wet spot on the lawn and a faint smell of urine. It had to have been Julia.

I carried on the following dialogue with myself:

"Julia, dammit, what are you doing pissing on my grass?"

"If I'd done it on the concrete, it would have splashed on my ankles."

I wanted to believe it had been Julia who had lifted up her skirt and squatted in the middle of my roses, but the fantasy didn't last for long. I found out what had really happened when Talia, her parents, and I were traveling in the interior. We stopped to visit a monastery surrounded by beautiful olive trees and filled with paintings from the Santa Cruz school. We were the only tourists, and a friar was giving us a private tour. I noticed that Talia had left the group, and I went to look for her. I figured she'd stayed behind in the church. As soon as I entered the nave, I saw her squatting on the floor behind the confessional. She didn't see me. I tip-toed out and rejoined the group. I was tickled to death. Talia had taken on her sister's eccentricities. That was her way of expressing her grief.

Before I completely got out from under Julia's spell, I read quite a few books on spiritualism. All of them concurred on one point: it was Julia's duty to abandon the earth and to reintegrate herself into the cycle of reincarnations. Hanging around wasn't considered proper.

Before taking off, she gave me one more scare—actually the worst one of all. I was passing by the Cathedral one day and saw Julia sitting on the steps, her back turned to me, and wearing the same gray skirt and navy blue blazer she was wearing the night she died. I was terrified. Then, when she turned around, she had a face like a guaraya. Her clothes were dirty and tattered. The books were right—my own panic confirmed it. The dead shouldn't return. When they did, they made havoc with the living.

After getting hold of myself, I walked over to the woman. I was certain that those were Julia's clothes. They'd been bought in the States. I could tell by the gold, embroidered fishhook on the pocket.

I tried to talk to her, but we had a hard time understanding each other. I finally managed to find out that the clothes had been given to her; but she didn't know the person's name, and furthermore, didn't want to know. What difference did it make? All the puebleros looked the same to her. They were all pale and smelled like perfume. I asked her if she could take me to the house. I said I would pay her for her trouble. She agreed and got into the car.

My face was dripping with sweat; my hands gripped the steering wheel. There was an unpleasant smell inside the car.

The guaraya wasn't partial to bathing, and I guess I smelled, too. I didn't care about that. I just wanted to get to where we were going. The guaraya pointed the way with her index finger. She pointed down one-way streets and across medians. We drove around and around in circles, until we came to the West Zone of the city. She looked around in confusion and then tried to get out of the car. Finding the door locked, she thought I'd tricked her. I convinced her to continue. She blamed me for the difficulty she was having. My demand for exactness was flubbing her instinct. I agreed to keep my mouth shut.

We wandered from one street to the next, passing the same spot several times. She looked at the trees, the sun. She was enjoying it. Maybe she was making fun of me. I didn't mind. I would have driven into the river, if she'd told me to.

Just as I was beginning to lose hope, we turned down a street I'd seen before. The guaraya pointed at a green, frame house with a split door and fruit trees in the yard. The top half of the door was open. Shit! It was Alex's house. Why hadn't I suspected him before? How could I have been so dumb? I imagined myself handing him over to Inspector Juárez, like dropping a fish into a pan of hot grease.

I was shocked to see him looking so sane. He was smiling. His hair was slicked back; his face recently shaved. His clarity was disarming. I nearly apologized for dropping by without an invitation. He led me into his room. I could still hear the rustling of Julia's clothes, her foot smacking him in the mouth. There was a damp smell of old clothes. The room was in order. The bed was made, and the books—mostly religious titles—were neatly placed on the shelves.

The only trace of the old, insane Alex was his voracious appetite for tobacco. His fingers were stained with nicotine. The room was full of smoke. He lit one cigarette after another. He didn't deny having given Julia's clothes to the guaraya. He shouldn't have done it. He knew that. He'd kept the earring for himself, as a keepsake.

"You think I killed her," he said. He didn't blame me for

thinking that. He'd thought it himself for several weeks. He'd run every time he'd seen a policeman, cringed every time he'd heard a knock at the door. He wondered if he'd left fingerprints at the chalet. Even if he hadn't, the police would know he was the one from the smell of blood on his hands. He'd washed them fifty times a day.

Eventually, he calmed down and remembered what had happened. He'd gotten into the habit of following Julia. He adored her. He knew her routine by heart: her waking and sleeping hours, her outings with Grigotá, her habits, like pissing in strange places. He knew everything there was to know about Julia.

He knew that she and her fiancé made love at the chalet on Circunvalación Avenue. They didn't bother to close the curtains all the way, which afforded an excellent peephole for Alex. He was so crazy about her that seeing her having intercourse with another man was enough to satisfy him. It was like watching your favorite actress; all you had to do was pretend you were the actor performing opposite her.

The couple always went to the chalet on Fridays. That last time, they lit a fire, to be romantic. It hadn't been cold enough for a heater—it never dropped below freezing in the city. It was a crazy, gringo custom they'd picked up in the States. Alex had stayed out of it. It wasn't the voyeur's place to offer an opinion. He simply watched for a few minutes and then went for a walk. During that time, Alex had taken more walks than he'd taken in his whole life. He'd worn out three pairs of heels. He never headed in any particular direction. He'd just walk around in circles, fantasizing about Julia, and eventually end up back in front of the chalet. When he returned that night, about dawn, he was surprised to see the lights still burning outside the chalet. Usually, by that time, the couple would have already left for their respective homes. He walked over to the window and looked in. His eyes met with a beautiful but frightening sight. Julia and her lover were lying naked and motionless on top of the sheets. Their bodies were a marble blue. They looked like two Greek statues toppled by an earthquake. The fire from the coals cast a blood-red glow around the room.

At first, Alex couldn't imagine what had happened. Then he remembered a similar, tragic scene. Two friends in Boston who had died of carbon monoxide poisoning—also from a wood fire. The door wasn't locked. He went in and tried in vain to revive Julia. He carried her out onto the patio, but the fresh night air didn't help. He tried artificial respiration. Nothing was going to work. He even tried something he'd done as a kid. When the kids in the barrio would find a dead bird, they'd try to revive it by blowing on its tail. He admitted blowing on Julia's behind that night, but she didn't blink an eye. She was dead. She'd been dead for some time, long before he'd gotten back to the chalet. He might as well put her back where he'd found her. What a job! When he'd carried her out there, she'd been light. Now she was as cumbersome as a sack of cement. Since he couldn't lift her, he had to drag her back through the patio and into the bedroom. Right before he left, he picked up her clothes and one earring. The next day, he imagined himself the killer.

As I was leaving, he gave me the earring. He couldn't think of anyone who deserved it more than I. He knew I had special feelings for my sister-in-law. "I'm sure she liked you, too," he said. "I wish she hadn't hated me so much."

❧

THAT NIGHT I told Talia about my trek around town with the guaraya and my talk with Alex. She was wearing a short, see-through gown. She listened with a perplexed expression on her face and rubbed her foot against mine. Her legs were firm and pink, like Julia's. Family genes. Strange I hadn't noticed it before. I was starting to pay more attention to the family resemblance. Their heads were shaped alike. They had the same profile, the same coquettish way of bobbing their chins up and down, instead of saying yes. I felt like I'd bought a box of candy and been given two for the price of one.

I couldn't resist adding a little to the story as I went along. I spiced up the part about Alex. I told her that when Alex had seen Julia lying on the bed, looking like a statue, he'd wished for a stone penis to penetrate her stone body and be joined to her forever, like Siamese twins. I made up lie after lie. She didn't believe half of what I said. That was all right. I caressed the nape of her neck. It looked just like Ira's, like Julia's. Her breasts, her waist, her pelvis—she looked just like her mother and sister. I was making love to the whole clan.

I put our favorite Tchaikovsky waltz on the record player. We loved the rhythm of that piece, its delicate sensuality. Our spirits rose and fell with the music. Our bodies swayed back and forth, in perfect rhythm, till we fell back, exhausted.

"I really miss Julia," I said.

"I miss her, too," said Talia. "People have changed since she died."

"Yes. I've noticed that, too."

"It would be good for us to leave here for a while—get out of the country. The other day I was looking at a pamphlet on photography courses in New York. I thought you might like to take a few courses, and I could do some post-graduate work."

"How? We don't have the money."

She reminded me about the money I'd gotten from Antonio Extremadura. I didn't have it anymore. It had been carried off by the flood. I hadn't missed it; in fact, it was a relief to be rid of it.

"Then I'll ask Daddy for the money. I'll do anything to keep you from becoming apathetic again. I want you to work on your photography."

I agreed with everything she said. I could see myself walking down the streets of New York—the New York of George Gershwin, Portnoy, Woody Allen—walking along to "Rhapsody in Blue." Gangs of black and Puerto Rican teenagers fighting on street corners. Lesbians holding hands in Central Park. That was the place for me. My whole life stretched out before me. Yesterday I'd never planned more than one or two days ahead. Today I was looking at an entire year, a decade, the next century.

A weight was lifted. I felt so light, I could have floated up in the air, waved good-bye to absurd jobs and silly preoccupations. To the time when my only luminous act had been to create a love for Julia. When all of my organs had atrophied except my genitals.

My mind was doubt-free. I was meant to go to New York. We would leave as soon as possible. We would prepare ourselves for another culture. A culture that probably wouldn't accept us—Licurgo said so. "You're an idiot, leaving a city where people know you, respect you. Wasps treat Latin Americans the same way they treat blacks and dogs. You're crazy to go there." I said it didn't matter, as long as I could study photography. That was my dream.

Then Patroclo said he wasn't going to give us the money. But Talia wouldn't take no for an answer. She kicked and screamed, even foamed at the mouth. A sensible father would have given her a rabies shot. Patroclo gave in. Said he'd pay our way, under one condition—that I'd enroll in law school. He thought international law would be a practical choice. He told Talia to forget about social work and have a child. If she did, he'd support the three of us. Talia said she'd think about it.

Once again, I'd hung my head and allowed myself to be muzzled. It was my destiny to live the life of a dog, even if the doghouse was New York.

Talia consoled me. It didn't matter how we left, just so long as we left. She would have ten children, if it would help us get away from there. Anything to get us out of the rut we'd been in. As soon as she was pregnant, her father would soften. We'd be able to lead him around by the nose, like a babbling idiot.

I dreamed about the future but with some foreboding. I

was pessimistic. The "buts" and "ifs" of my indecision were snapping shut on my dreams like traps on rats. What if Talia changed her mind and refused to get pregnant? What if we weren't fertile anymore? Or Patroclo changed his mind? I might have to take the damn course in international law after all.

My own shortcomings infuriated me. I hated myself for depending on other people. I should have told Patroclo to go to hell. I could pay my own way. Wash dishes if I had to. I was beginning to get a glimpse of myself as a free man. That's the way I wanted to live my life—as a free man.

I closed my eyes and imagined myself getting on the plane. Then suddenly I was afraid. I wouldn't be able to leave. My chains had buried into my flesh. No! That wasn't going to happen. When the time came, I'd be ready to leave.

But would I, or wouldn't I? Anyone have a crystal ball?